WHEN IN ROME

WHEN IN ROME

*

NGAIO MARSH

THE
COMPANION BOOK CLUB
LONDON AND SYDNEY

This edition, published in 1972 by
The Hamlyn Publishing Group Ltd,
is issued by arrangement with
William Collins, Sons & Co. Ltd.

Made and printed in Great Britain
for the Companion Book Club
by Odhams (Watford) Ltd.
Standard 600771423
Deluxe 600871428
1.72

For
H.E. The Ambassador and Mrs McIntosh
and the Staff of the Residence,
New Zealand Embassy in Rome,
who made it possible.

CAST OF CHARACTERS

Patrons of Mr Sebastian Mailer's conducted tour:
        Mr Barnaby Grant, *author of 'Simon in Latium'*
        The Baron and Baroness Van der Veghel
        Miss Sophy Jason, *writer of children's stories*
        Lady Braceley
        The Hon. Kenneth Dorne, *her nephew*
        Major Hamilton Sweet
        Superintendent Roderick Alleyn, *CID London*

Officers of the Roman Police Department:
        Il Questore Valdarno
        Il Vice-Questore Bergarmi
        Sundry members of the Questura

Dominicans in charge at S. Tommaso in Pallaria:
        Father Denys
        Brother Dominic

        Mr Sebastian Mailer, *Il Cicerone Conducted Tours*
        Giovanni Vecchi, *his assistant*
        Violetta, *a postcard vendor*
        Marco, *a restaurateur*
        A British Consul
        Signor Pace, *a travel agent*
        A porter and sundry waiters

1. Barnaby in Rome

ONE

BARNABY GRANT looked at the Etruscan Bride and Bride-
groom who reclined so easily on their sarcophagal couch, and
wondered why they had died young and whether, as in
Verona, they had died together. Their gentle lips, he thought,
brushed with amusement, might easily tilt into the arrowhead smile of Apollo and Hermes. How fulfilled they were
and how enigmatically alike. What signal did she give with
her largish hands? How touchingly *his* hand hovered above
her shoulder.

'——from Cerveteri,' said a guide rapidly. 'Five hundred
and thirty years before Christ.'

'Christ!' said a tourist on a note of exhaustion.

The party moved on. Grant stayed behind for a time and
then, certain that he desired to see no more that morning,
left the Villa Giulia and took a taxi to the Piazza Colonna for
a glass of beer.

TWO

As he sat at a kerbside table in the Piazza Colonna, Barnaby
thought of the Etruscan smile and listened to thunder.

The heavens boomed largely above the noon traffic but
whatever lightning there might be was not evident, being
masked by a black canopy of low and swollen cloud. At any

9

moment, thought Barnaby, Marcus Aurelius's Column will prick it and like 'a foul bumbard' it will shed its liquor! And then what a scene!

Before him on the table stood a glass and a bottle of beer. His mackintosh was folded over the back of his chair, and on the ground, leaning against his leg, was a locked attaché case. Every so often his left hand dropped to the case and fingered it. Refreshed by this contact his mouth would take on an easier look and he would blink slowly and push away the lock of black hair that overhung his forehead.

A bit of a swine, this one, he thought. It's been a bit of a swine.

A heavy rumbling again broke out overhead. Thunder on the left, Barnaby thought. The gods are cross with us.

He refilled his glass and looked about him.

The kerbside *caffè* had been crowded but now, under threat of a downpour, many customers had left and the waiters had tipped over their chairs.

The tables on either side of his own, however, were still occupied: that on his right by three lowering young men whose calloused hands jealously enclosed their glasses and whose slow eyes looked sideways at their surroundings. Countrymen, Grant thought, who would have been easier in a less consequential setting and would be shocked by the amount of their bill.

On his left sat a Roman couple in love. Forbidden by law to kiss in public, they gazed, clung hand-to-hand, and exchanged trembling smiles. The young man extended his forefinger and traced the unmarred excellences of his girl's lips. They responded, quivering. Barnaby could not help watching the lovers. They were unaware of him and indeed of everything else around them, but on the first visible and vivid flash of lightning, they were taken out of themselves and turned their faces towards him.

It was at this moment, appropriately as he was later to consider, that he saw, framed by their separated heads, the distant figure of an Englishman.

He knew at once that the man was English. Perhaps it was his clothes. Or, more specifically, his jacket. It was shabby and out-of-date but it had been made from West Country tweed though not, perhaps, for its present wearer. And then —the tie. Frayed and faded, grease-spotted and lumpish: there it was, scarcely recognizable, but if you were so minded, august. For the rest, his garments were dingy and nondescript. His hat, a rusty black felt, was obviously Italian. It was pulled forward and cast a shadow down to the bridge of the nose, over a face of which the most noticeable feature was its extreme pallor. The mouth, however, was red and rather full-lipped. So dark had the noonday turned that without that brief flash, Barnaby could scarcely have seen the shadowed eyes. He felt an odd little shock within himself when he realized they were very light in colour and were fixed on him.

A great crack of thunder banged out overhead. The black canopy burst and fell out of the sky in a deluge.

There was a stampede. Barnaby snatched up his raincoat, struggled into it and dragged the hood over his head. He had not paid his bill and groped for his pocket-book. The three countrymen blundered towards him and there was some sort of collision between them and the young couple. The young man broke into loud quarrelsome expostulation. Barnaby could find nothing smaller than a thousand-lire note. He turned away, looked round for a waiter and found that they had all retreated under the canvas awning. His own man saw him, made a grand-opera gesture of despair, and turned his back.

'*Aspetti*,' Barnaby shouted in phrase-book Italian waving his thousand-lire note, '*Quanto devo pagare?*'

The waiter placed his hands together as if in prayer and turned up his eyes.

'*Basta!*'

'——*lasci passare*——'

'*Se ne vada ora*——'

'*Non desidero parlarle.*'

'*Non l'ho fatto io*——'

'*Vattene!*'

'*Sciocchezze!*'

The row between the lover and the countrymen was heating up. They now screamed into each other's faces behind Barnaby's back. The waiter indicated, with a multiple gesture, the heavens, the rain, his own defencelessness.

Barnaby thought: After all, I'm the one with a raincoat. Somebody crashed into his back and sent him spread-eagled across his table.

A scene of the utmost confusion followed, accompanied by flashes of lightning, immediate thunder-claps and torrents of rain. Barnaby was winded and bruised. A piece of glass had cut the palm of his hand, and his nose also bled. The combatants had disappeared, but his waiter, now equipped with an enormous orange-and-red umbrella, babbled over him and made ineffectual dabs at his hand. The other waiters, clustered beneath the awning, rendered a chorus to the action. '*Poverino!*' they exclaimed. 'What a misfortune!'

Barnaby recovered an upright posture. With one hand he dragged a handkerchief from the pocket of his raincoat and clapped it to his face. In the other he extended to the waiter his bloodied and rain-sopped thousand-lire note.

'Here,' he said in his basic Italian. 'Keep the change. I require a taxi.'

The waiter ejaculated with evident pleasure. Barnaby sat down abruptly on a chair that had become a bird-bath. The waiter ludicrously inserted his umbrella into a socket in the middle of the table, said something incomprehensible, turned up the collar of his white jacket and bolted into the interior. To telephone, Barnaby hoped, for a taxi.

The Piazza Colonna was rain-possessed. A huge weight of water flooded the street and pavements and spurted off the roofs of cars as if another multiple Roman fountain had been born.

Motorists stared through blurred glass and past jigging windscreen-wipers at the world outside. Except for isolated, scurrying wayfarers, the pavements were emptied.

Barnaby Grant, huddled, alone and ridiculous under his orange-and-red umbrella, staunched his bloody nose. He attracted a certain incredulous attention. The waiter had disappeared and his comrades had got up among themselves one of those inscrutable Italian conversations that appear to be quarrels but very often end in backslaps and roars of laughter. Barnaby never could form the slightest notion of how long he had sat under the umbrella before he made his hideous discovery, before his left arm dangled from his shoulder and his left hand encountered—nothing.

As if it had a separate entity the hand explored, discovered only the leg of his chair, widened its search and found—nothing.

He remembered afterwards that he had been afraid to get into touch with his hand, to duck his head and look down and find a puddle of water, the iron foot of his chair-leg and again —nothing.

The experience that followed could, he afterwards supposed, be compared to the popular belief about drowning, in that an impossible flood of thoughts crowded his brain. He thought, for instance, of how long it had taken him to write his book, of his knowledge that undoubtedly it was the best thing he had done, perhaps would ever do. He remembered his agent had once suggested that it was dangerous to write in longhand

13

with no duplication. He remembered how isolated he was in Rome with virtually no Italian, and how he hadn't bothered to use his introductions. He thought inaccurately of—who? Was it Sir Isaac Newton? 'O, Diamond, Diamond, you little know what you have done!' Above all he thought of the ineffable, the unthinkable, the atrocious boredom of what must now ensue: the awful prospect of taking steps as opposed to the numb desolation of his loss: the rock-bottom horror of the event itself which had caused a thing like a water-ram to pound in his thorax.

A classic phrase stood up in his thoughts: 'I am undone.' And he almost cried it aloud.

Here, now, was the waiter, smirking and triumphant, and here at the kerbside, a horse-carriage with a great umbrella protecting the seats and a wary-looking driver with some sort of tarpaulin over his head.

Grant attempted to indicate his loss. He pointed to where his attaché case had been, he grimaced, he gesticulated. He groped for his phrase-book and thumbed through it. '*Ho perduto,*' he said. '*Ho perduto mia valigia.* Have you got it? My case? *Non trovo. Valigia.*'

The waiter exclaimed and idiotically looked under the table and round about the flooded surroundings. He then bolted into cover and stood there gazing at Barnaby and shrugging with every inch of his person.

Barnaby thought: This is it. This is the worst thing that has ever happened to me.

The driver of the horse-carriage hailed him mellifluously and seemed to implore him to make up his mind. He looked at the desolation around him and got into the carriage.

'*Consolato Britannico,*' Grant shouted. 'O God! *Consolato Britannico.*'

'Now look here,' the Consul had said, as if Barnaby Grant required the information, 'this is a bad business, you know. It's a bad business.'

'You, my dear Consul, are telling me.'

'Quite so. Quite so. Now, we'll have to see what we can do, won't we? My wife,' he added, 'is a great fan of yours. She'll be quite concerned when she hears of this. She's a bit of an egg-head,' he had jokingly confided.

Barnaby had not replied. He contemplated his fellow-Briton over a handful of lint kindly provided by the consular staff and rested his bandaged left hand upon his knee.

'Well, of course,' the Consul continued argumentatively, 'properly speaking it's a matter for the police. Though I must say—However, if you'll wait a moment I'll just put a call through. I've got a personal contact—nothing like approaching at the right level, is there? Now, then.'

After a number of delays there had been a long and virtually incomprehensible conversation during which Barnaby fancied he was being described as Great Britain's most celebrated novelist. With many pauses to refer to Barnaby himself, the Consul related at dictation speed the details of the affair and when that was over showered a number of grateful compliments into the telephone—'E stato molto gentile—Grazie. Molto grazie, Signore,' which even poor Barnaby could understand.

The Consul replaced the receiver and pulled a grimace. 'Not much joy from *that* quarter,' he said.

Barnaby swallowed and felt sick.

He was assured that everything that could be done, would be done, but, the Consul pointed out, they hadn't much to go on, had they? Still, he added more brightly, there was always the chance that Barnaby might be blackmailed.

'Blackmailed?'

'Well, you see, whoever took the case probably expected if, not a haul of valuables or cash, something in the nature of documents for the recovery of which a reward would be offered and a haggling basis thus set up. Blackmail,' said the Consul, 'was not of course, the right word. Ransom would be more appropriate. Although . . .' He was a man of broken sentences and he left this one suspended in an atmosphere of extreme discomfort.

'Then I should advertise and offer a reward?'

'Certainly. Certainly. We'll get something worked out. We'll just give my secretary the details in English and she'll translate and see to the insertions.'

'I'm being a trouble,' said the wretched Barnaby.

'We're used to it,' the Consul sighed. 'Your name and London address were on the manuscript, you said, but the case was locked. Not of course, that *that* amounts to anything.'

'I suppose not.'

'You are staying at——?'

'The Pensione Gallico.'

'Ah yes. Have you the telephone number?'

'Yes—I think so—somewhere about me.'

Barnaby fished distractedly in his breast pocket, pulled out his note-case, passport and two envelopes which fell on the desk, face downwards. He had scribbled the Pensione Gallico address and telephone number on the back of one of them.

'That's it,' he said and slid the envelope across to the Consul, who was already observant of its august crest.

'Ah—yes. Thank you.' He gave a little laugh. 'Done your duty and signed the book, I see,' he said.

'What? Oh—that. Well, no, actually,' Barnaby mumbled. 'It's—er—some sort of luncheon. Tomorrow. I mustn't take up any more of your time. I'm enormously grateful.'

The Consul, beaming and expanding, stretched his arm

16

across the desk and made a fin of his hand. 'No, no, no. Very glad you came to us. I feel pretty confident, all things considered. *Nil desperandum*, you know, *nil desperandum*. Rise above!'

But it wasn't possible to rise very far above his loss as two days trickled by and there was no response to advertisements and nothing came of a long language-haltered interview with a beautiful representative of the Questura.

He attended his Embassy luncheon and tried to react appropriately to ambassadorial commiseration and concern. But for most of the time he sat on the roof-garden of the Pensione Gallico among potted geraniums and flights of swallows. His bedroom had a french window opening on to a neglected corner of this garden and there he waited and listened in agony for every telephone call within. From time to time he half-faced the awful notion of re-writing the hundred thousand words of his novel but the prospect made him physically as well as emotionally sick as he turned away from it.

Every so often he experienced the sensation of an abrupt descent in an infernal lift. He started out of fits of sleep into a waking nightmare. He told himself he should write to his agent and to his publisher but the mere thought of doing so tasted as acrid as bile and he sat and listened for the telephone instead.

On the third morning a heat wave came upon Rome. The roof-garden was like a furnace. He was alone in his corner with an uneaten brioche, a pot of honey and three wasps. He was given over to a sort of fretful lassitude and finally to a condition that he supposed must be that of Despair itself.

'What I need,' he told himself on a wave of nausea, 'is a bloody good cry on somebody's bloody bosom.'

One of the two waiters came out.

'*Finito?*' he sang, as usual. And then, when Barnaby gave his punctual assent, seemed to indicate that he should come indoors. At first he thought the waiter was suggesting that it was too hot where he was, and then that for some reason the manageress wanted to see him.

And then, as a sudden jolt of hope shook him, he saw a fattish man with a jacket hooked over his shoulders come out of the house door and advance towards him. He was between Barnaby and the sun and appeared fantastic, black and insubstantial, but at once Barnaby recognized him.

His reactions were chaotic. He saw the man as if between the inclined heads of two lovers, and to the accompaniment of thunder and lightning. And whether the sensation that flooded him was one solely of terrified relief, or of a kind of blessed anticlimax he could never determine. He merely wondered, when the man advanced into the shade and drew an attaché case from under his jacket, if he himself was going to faint.

'Mr Barnaby Grant?' asked the man. 'I think you will be pleased to see me, will you not?'

FOUR

They escaped from the Gallico, which seemed to be overrun with housemaids, to a very small *caffè* in a shaded by-way off the Piazza Navona, a short walk away. His companion had suggested it. 'Unless, of course,' he said archly, 'you prefer something smarter—like the Colonna, for instance,' and Barnaby had shuddered.

He took his attaché case with him and, at his guest's suggestion, unlocked it.

There, in two loose-leaf folders, lay his book, enclosed by giant-sized rubber bands. The last letter from his agent still lay on top, just as he had left it.

He had rather wildly offered his guest champagne cocktails,

cognac, wine—anything—but when reminded that it was not yet ten o'clock in the morning, settled for coffee.

'Well then,' he said, 'at a more appropriate hour—you will let me—and in the meantime I must—well—of course.'

He slid his hand inside his jacket. His heart still thumped at it like a fist.

'You are thinking of the reward so generously offered,' said his companion. 'But, please—no. No. It is out of the question. To have been of service even on so insignificant a scale, to Barnaby Grant—that really is a golden reward. Believe me.'

Barnaby had not expected this and he at once felt he had committed a gigantic error in taste. He had been misled, he supposed, by general appearances: not only by the shabby alpaca jacket that had replaced the English tweed and like it was hooked over the shoulders, displaying a dingy open shirt with worn cuffs, nor by the black-green hat or the really lamentable shoes, but by something indefinable in the man himself. I wish, he thought, I could take an instant liking to him. I owe him that, at the least.

And as his companion talked, Barnaby found himself engaged in the occupational habit of the novelist: he dwelt on the bullet head, close cropped like an American schoolboy's, and the mouse-coloured sparse fringe. He noted the extreme pallor of the skin, its appearance of softness and fine texture like a woman's: the unexpected fullness and rich colour of the mouth and those large pale eyes that had looked so fixedly into his in the Piazza Colonna. The voice and speech? High but muted, it had no discernible accent but carried a suggestion of careful phrasing. Perhaps English was no longer the habitual language. His choice of words was pedantic as if he had memorized his sentences for a public address.

His hands were plump and delicate and the nails bitten to the quick.

His name was Sebastian Mailer.

19

'You wonder, of course,' he was saying, 'why you have been subjected to this no doubt agonizing delay. You would like to know the circumstances?'

'Very much.'

'I can't hope that you noticed me the other morning in Piazza Colonna.'

'But yes. I remember you very well.'

'Perhaps I stared. You see, I recognized you at once from the photographs on your book-jackets. I must tell you I am a most avid admirer, Mr Grant.'

Barnaby murmured.

'I am also, which is more to the point, what might be described as "an old Roman hand". I have lived here for many years and have acquired some knowledge of Roman society at a number of levels. Including the lowest. You see I am frank.'

'Why not?'

'Why not indeed! My motives in what I imagine some of our compatriots would call muck-raking, are aesthetic and I think I may say philosophical, but with that I must not trouble you. It will do well enough if I tell you that at the same time as I recognized you I also recognized a despicable person known to the Roman riff-raff as—I translate—"Feather-fingers". He was stationed at a short distance from you and behind your back. His eyes were fastened upon your attaché case.'

'God!'

'Indeed, yes. Now, you will recollect that the incipient thunderstorm broke abruptly and that with the downpour and subsequent confusion a fracas arose between some of the occupants of tables adjacent to your own.'

'Yes.'

'And that you received a violent blow in the back that knocked you across your table.'

20

'So it did,' Barnaby agreed.

'Of course you thought that you had been struck by one of the contestants but this was not so. The character I have brought to your notice took advantage of the mêlée, darted forward, delivered the blow with his shoulder, snatched up your case and bolted. It was an admirably timed manœuvre and executed with the greatest speed and precision. The contestants continued to shout at each other, and I, my dear Mr Grant, gave chase.'

He sipped his coffee, made a small inclination, an acknowledgement perhaps of Barnaby's passionate attention.

'It was a long pursuit,' Mailer continued. 'But I clung to his trail and—is the phrase "ran him to earth"? It *is*. Thank you. I ran him to earth, then, in what purveyors of sensational fiction would describe as "a certain *caffè* in such-and-such a little street not a thousand miles from——" etc., etc.— perhaps my phraseology is somewhat dated. In plain terms, I caught up with him at his habitual haunt, and by means with which I shall not trouble you, recovered your attaché case.'

'On the same day,' Barnaby couldn't help asking, 'that I lost it?'

'Ah! As the cornered victim of an interrogation always says: I am glad you asked that question. Mr Grant, with any less distinguished person I would have come armed with a plausible prevarication. With you, I cannot adopt this measure. I did not return your case before because——'

He paused, smiling very slightly, and without removing his gaze from Barnaby's face, pushed up the shirt-sleeve of his left arm which was white-skinned and hairless. He rested it palm upwards on the table and slid it towards Barnaby.

'You can see for yourself,' he said. 'They look rather like mosquito bites, do they not. But I'm sure you will recognize them for what they are. Do you?'

'I—I think I do.'

'Quite. I have acquired an addiction for cocaine. Rather "square" of me, isn't it? I really must change, one of these days, to something groovier. You see I am conversant with the jargon. But I digress. I am ashamed to say that after my encounter with "Feather-fingers", I found myself greatly shaken. No doubt my constitution has been somewhat undermined by my unfortunate proclivity. I am not a robust man. I called upon my—the accepted term is, I believe, fix—and, in short, I rather exceeded my usual allowance and have been out of circulation until this morning. I cannot, of course, hope that you will forgive me.'

Barnaby gave himself a breathing space and then—he was a generous man—said: 'I'm so bloody thankful to have it back I feel nothing but gratitude, I promise you. After all, the case was locked and you were not to know———'

'Oh but I was! I guessed. When I came to myself I guessed. The weight, for one thing. And the way it shifted, you know, inside. And then, of course, I saw your advertisement: "containing manuscript of value only to owner". So I cannot lay that flattering unction to my soul, Mr Grant.'

He produced a dubious handkerchief and wiped his neck and face with it. The little *caffè* was on the shady side of the street but Mr Mailer sweated excessively.

'Will you have some more coffee?'

'Thank you. You are very kind. Most kind.'

The coffee seemed to revive him. He held the cup in his two plump, soiled hands and looked at Barnaby over the top.

'I feel so deeply in your debt,' Barnaby said. 'Is there nothing I can do———?'

'You will think me unbearably fulsome—I have, I believe, become rather Latinized in my style, but I assure you the mere fact of meeting you and in some small manner———'

This conversation, Barnaby thought, is going round in

circles. 'Well,' he said, 'you must dine with me. Let's make a time, shall we?'

But Mr Mailer, now squeezing his palms together, was evidently on the edge of speech and presently achieved it. After a multitude of deprecating parentheses he at last confessed that he himself had written a book.

He had been at it for three years: the present version was his fourth. Through bitter experience, Barnaby knew what was coming and knew, also, that he must accept his fate. The all-too-familiar phrases were being delivered '. . . value, enormously, your opinion . . .' '. . . glance through it.' '. . . advice from such an authority . . .' '. . . interest a publisher . . .'

'I'll read it, of course,' Barnaby said. 'Have you brought it with you?'

Mr Mailer, it emerged, was sitting on it. By some adroit and nimble sleight-of-hand, he had passed it under his rump while Barnaby was intent upon his recovered property. He now drew it out, wrapped in a dampish Roman newsheet and, with trembling fingers, uncovered it. A manuscript, closely written in an Italianate script, but not, Barnaby rejoiced to see, bulky. Perhaps forty thousand words; perhaps, with any luck, less.

'Neither a novel nor a novella in length, I'm afraid,' said its author, 'but so it has befallen and as such I abide by it.'

Barnaby looked up quickly. Mr Mailer's mouth had compressed and lifted at the corners. Not so diffident, after all, Barnaby thought.

'I hope,' said Mr Mailer, 'my handwriting does not present undue difficulties. I cannot afford a typist.'

'It seems very clear.'

'If so, it will not take more than a few hours of your time. Perhaps in two days or so I may——? But I mustn't be clamorous.'

Barnaby thought: And I must do this handsomely. He said: 'Look, I've a suggestion. Dine with me the day after tomorrow and I'll tell you what I think.'

'How kind you are! I am overwhelmed. But, please, you must allow me—if you don't object to—well to somewhere —quite modest—like this, for example. There is a little trattoria, as you see. Their *fettuccini*—really very good and their wine quite respectable. The manager is a friend of mine and will take care of us.'

'It sounds admirable and by all means let us come here but it shall be my party, Mr Mailer, if you please. You shall order our dinner. I am in your hands.'

'Indeed? Really? Then I must speak with him beforehand.' On this understanding they parted.

At the Pensione Gallico Barnaby told everybody he encountered: the manageress, the two waiters, even the chambermaid who had little or no English, of the recovery of his manuscript.

Some of them understood him and some did not. All rejoiced. He rang up the Consulate which was loud in felicitations. He paid for his advertisements.

When all this had been accomplished he re-read such bits of his book as he had felt needed to be re-written, skipping from one part to another.

It crossed his mind that his dominant reaction to the events of the past three days was now one of anticlimax: All that agony and—back to normal, he thought and turned a page.

In a groove between the sheets held by their loose-leaf binder he noticed a smear, and on opening the manuscript more widely found a slight deposit of something that looked like cigarette ash.

He had given up smoking two years ago.

FIVE

On second thoughts (and after a close examination of the lock on his case) he reminded himself that the lady who did for him in London was a chain-smoker and excessively curious and that his manuscript often lay open on his table. This reflection comforted him and he was able to work on his book and, in the siesta, to read Mr Mailer's near-novella with tolerable composure.

'Angelo in August
by
Sebastian Mailer.'

It wasn't bad. A bit jewelled. A bit fancy. Indecent in parts but probably not within the meaning of the act. And considering it was a fourth draft, more than a bit careless: words omitted: repetitions, redundancies. Barnaby wondered if cocaine could be held responsible for these lapses. But he'd seen many a worse in print and if Mr Mailer could cook up one or two shorter jobs to fill out a volume he might very well find a publisher for it.

He was struck by an amusing coincidence and when, at the appointed time, they met for dinner, he spoke of it to Mr Mailer.

'By the way,' he said, refilling Mr Mailer's glass, 'you have introduced a secondary theme which is actually the ground-swell of my own book.'

'Oh no!' his guest ejaculated, and then: 'But we are told, aren't we, that there are only—how many is it? Three?—four?—basic themes?'

'And that all subject-matter can be traced to one or another of them? Yes. This is only a detail in your story, and you don't develop it. Indeed, I feel it's extraneous and might well be dropped. The suggestion is *not*,' Barnaby added, 'prompted by professional jealousy,' and they both laughed, Mr Mailer a great deal louder than Barnaby.

He evidently repeated the joke in Italian to some acquaint-ances of his whom he had greeted on their arrival and had presented to Barnaby. They sat at the next table and were much diverted. Taking advantage of the appropriate moment, they drank Barnaby's health.

The dinner, altogether, was a great success. The food was excellent, the wine acceptable, the proprietor attentive and the *mise en scène* congenial. Down the narrowest of alley-ways they looked into the Piazza Navona, and saw the water-god Il Moro in combat with his Fish, superbly lit. They could almost hear the splash of his fountains above the multiple voice of Rome at night. Groups of youths moved elegantly about Navona and arrogant girls thrust bosoms like those of figureheads at the eddying crowds. The midsummer night pulsed with its own beauty.

Barnaby felt within himself an excitement that rose from a more potent ferment than their gentle wine could induce. He was exalted.

He leant back in his chair, fetched a deep breath, caught Mr Mailer's eye and laughed. 'I feel,' he said, 'as if I had only just arrived in Rome.'

'And, perhaps, as if the night had only just begun?'

'Something of the sort.'

'Adventure?' Mailer hinted.

Perhaps, after all, the wine had not been so gentle. There was an uncertainty about what he saw when he looked at Mailer, as if a new personality emerged. He really had got *very* rum eyes, thought Barnaby, tolerantly.

'An adventure?' the voice insisted. 'May I help you, I wonder? A cicerone?'

May I help you? Barnaby thought. He might be a shop-assistant. But he stretched himself a little and heard himself say lightly: 'Well—in what way?'

'In any way,' Mailer murmured. 'Really, in any way at all. I'm versatile.'

'Oh,' Barnaby said. '*I'm* very orthodox, you know. The largest Square,' he added and thought the addition brilliantly funny, 'in Rome.'

'Then, if you will allow me——'

The proprietor was there with his bill. Barnaby thought that the little *trattoria* had become very quiet but when he looked round he saw that all the patrons were still there and behaving quite normally. He had some difficulty in finding the right notes but Mr Mailer helped him and Barnaby begged him to give a generous tip.

'Very good indeed,' Barnaby said to the proprietor, 'I shall return.' They shook hands warmly.

And then Barnaby, with Mr Mailer at his elbow, walked into narrow streets past glowing windows and pitch-dark entries, through groups of people who shouted and by-ways that were silent, into what was, for him, an entirely different Rome.

2. An Expedition is Arranged

ONE

BARNABY had no further encounter with Sebastian Mailer until the following spring when he returned to Rome after seeing his book launched with much éclat in London. His Pensione Gallico could not take him for the first days so he stayed at a small hotel not far from it in Old Rome.

On his second morning he went down to the foyer to ask about his mail but finding a crowd of incoming tourists milling round the desk, sat down to wait on a chair just inside the entrance.

He opened his paper but did not read it, finding his attention sufficiently occupied by the tourists who had evidently arrived *en masse*: particularly by two persons who kept a little apart from their companions but seemed to be of the same party nevertheless.

They were a remarkable pair, both very tall and heavily built with high shoulders and a surprisingly light gait. He supposed them to be husband and wife but they were oddly alike, having perhaps developed a marital resemblance. Their faces were large, the wife's being emphasized by a rounded jaw and the husband's by a short chin-beard that left his mouth exposed. They both had full, prominent eyes. He was very attentive to her, holding her arm and occasionally her big hand in his own enormous one and looking into her face.

He was dressed in blue cotton shirt, jacket and shorts.

Her clothes, Barnaby thought, were probably very 'good' though they sat but lumpishly on her ungainly person.

They were in some sort of difficulty and consulted a document without seeming to derive any consolation from it. There was a large map of Rome on the wall: they moved in front of it and searched it anxiously, exchanging baffled glances.

A fresh bevy of tourists moved between these people and Barnaby and for perhaps two minutes hid them from him. Then a guide arrived and herded the tourists off, exposing the strange pair again to Barnaby's gaze.

They were no longer alone. Mr Mailer was with them.

His back was turned to Barnaby but there was no doubt about who it was. He was dressed as he had been on that first morning in the Piazza Colonna and there was something about the cut of his jib that was unmistakable.

Barnaby felt an overwhelming disinclination to meet him again. His memory of the Roman night spent under Mr Mailer's ciceronage was blurred and confused but specific enough to give him an extremely uneasy impression of having gone much too far. He preferred not to recall it and he positively shuddered at the mere thought of a renewal. Barnaby was not a prig but he did draw a line.

He was about to get up and try a quick getaway through the revolving doors when Mailer made a half turn towards him.

He jerked up his newspaper and hoped he had done so in time.

This is a preposterous situation, he thought behind his shield. I don't know what's the matter with me. It's extraordinary. I've done nothing really to make me feel like this but in some inexplicable way I do feel—he searched in his mind for a word and could only produce one that was palpably ridiculous—contaminated.

He couldn't help rather wishing that there was a jalousie

29

in his newspaper through which he could observe Mr Mailer and the two strangers and he disliked himself for so wishing. It was as if any thought of Mailer involved a kind of furtiveness in himself and since normally he was direct in his dealings, the reaction was disagreeable to him.

All the same he couldn't resist moving his paper a fraction to one side so that he could bring the group into his left eye's field of vision.

There they were. Mailer's back was still turned towards Barnaby. He was evidently talking with some emphasis and had engaged the rapt attention of the large couple. They gazed at him with the utmost deference.

Suddenly both of them smiled.

A familiar smile. It took Barnaby a moment or two to place it and then he realized with quite a shock that it was the smile of the Etruscan terracottas in the Villa Giulia: the smile of Hermes and Apollo, the closed smile that sharpens the mouth like an arrowhead and—cruel, tranquil or worldly, whichever it may be—is always enigmatic. Intensely lively, it is as knowledgeable as the smile of the dead.

It faded on the mouths of his couple but didn't quite vanish, so that now, thought Barnaby, they had become the Bride and Groom of the Villa Giulia sarcophagus and really the man's gently protective air furthered the resemblance. How *very* odd, Barnaby thought.

Fascinated, he forgot about Sebastian Mailer and lowered his newspaper.

He hadn't noticed that above the map in the wall there hung a tilted looking-glass. Some trick of light from the revolving doors flashed across it. He glanced up, and there, again between the heads of lovers, was Mr Mailer, looking straight into his eyes.

His reaction was indefensible. He got up quickly and left the hotel.

He couldn't account for it. He walked round Navona telling himself how atrociously he had behaved. Without the man I have just cut, he reminded himself, the crowning event of my career wouldn't have happened. I would still be trying to rewrite my most important book and very likely I would fail. I owe everything to him!

What on earth had moved him, then, to behave atrociously? Was he so ashamed of that Roman night that he couldn't bear to be reminded of it? He supposed it must be that, but at the same time he knew that there had been a greater compulsion.

He disliked Mr Mailer. He disliked him very much indeed. And in some incomprehensible fashion he was afraid of him.

He walked right round the great Piazza before he came to his decision. He would, if possible, undo the damage. He would go back to the hotel and if Mr Mailer was no longer there he would seek him out at the *trattoria* where they had dined. Mailer was an habitué and his address might be known to the proprietor.

I'll do that! thought Barnaby.

He had never taken more distasteful action. As he entered by the revolving doors into the hotel foyer he found that all the tourists had gone but that Mr Mailer was still in conference with the 'Etruscan' couple.

He saw Barnaby at once and set his gaze on him without giving the smallest sign of recognition. He had been speaking to the 'Etruscans' and he went on speaking to them but with his eyes fixed on Barnaby's.

Barnaby thought: Now *he's* cut *me* dead, and serve me bloody well right, and he walked steadily towards them.

As he drew near he heard Mr Mailer say:

'Rome *is* so bewildering, is it not? Even after many visits? Perhaps I may be able to help you? A cicerone?'

'Mr Mailer?' Barnaby heard himself say. 'I wonder if you remember me. Barnaby Grant.'

31

'I remember you very well, Mr Grant.'

Silence.

Well, he thought, I'll get on with it, and said: 'I saw your reflection just now in that glass. I can't imagine why I didn't know you at once and can only plead a chronic absence of mind. When I was half-way round Navona the penny dropped and I came back in the hope that you would still be here.' He turned to the 'Etruscans'. 'Please forgive me,' said the wretched Barnaby, 'I'm interrupting.'

Simultaneously they made deprecating noises and then the man, his whole face enlivened by that arrowhead smile, exclaimed: 'But I am right! I cannot be mistaken! This is *the* Mr Barnaby Grant.' He appealed to Mr Mailer. 'I *am* right, am I not?' His wife made a little crooning sound.

Mr Mailer said: 'Indeed, yes. May I introduce: The Baron and Baroness Van der Veghel.'

They shook hands eagerly and were voluble. They had read all the books, both in Dutch (they were by birth Hollanders) and in English (they were citizens of the world). They had his last (surely his greatest?) work actually with them—*there* was a coincidence! They turned to Mr Mailer. He, of course, had read it?

'Indeed, yes,' he said exactly as he had said it before. 'Every word. I was completely riveted.'

He had used such an odd inflection that Barnaby, already on edge, looked nervously at him but their companions were in full spate and interrupted each other in a recital of the excellencies of Barnaby's works.

It would not be true to say that Mr Mailer listened to their raptures sardonically. He merely listened.

His detachment was an acute embarrassment to Barnaby Grant. When it had all died down: the predictable hope that he would join them for drinks—they were staying in the hotel— the reiterated assurances that his work had meant so much to them, the apologies that they were intruding and the tactful withdrawal, had all been executed, Barnaby found himself alone with Sebastian Mailer.

'I am not surprised,' Mr Mailer said, 'that you were disinclined to renew our acquaintance, Mr Grant. I, on the contrary, have sought you out. Perhaps we may move to somewhere a little more private? There is a writing-room, I think. Shall we——?'

For the rest of his life Barnaby would be sickened by the memory of that commonplace little room with its pseudo Empire furniture, its floral carpet and the false tapestry on its wall: a mass-produced tapestry, popular in small hotels, depicting the fall of Icarus.

'I shall come straight to the point,' Mr Mailer said. 'Always best, don't you agree?'

He did precisely that.

Sitting rather primly on a gilt-legged chair, his soft hands folded together and his mumbled thumbs gently revolving round each other, Mr Mailer set about blackmailing Barnaby Grant.

TWO

All this happened a fortnight before the morning when Sophy Jason saw her suddenly bereaved friend off at the Leonardo da Vinci Airport.

She returned by bus to Rome and to the roof-garden of the Pensione Gallico where, ten months ago, Barnaby Grant had received Sebastian Mailer. Here she took stock of her situation.

She was twenty-three years old, worked for a firm of London publishers and had begun to make her way as a children's author. This was her first visit to Rome. She and the bereaved friend were to have spent their summer holidays together in Italy.

They had not made out a hard-and-fast itinerary but had snowed themselves under with brochures, read the indispensable Miss Georgina Masson and wandered in a trance about the streets and monuments.

The friend's so-abruptly-deceased father had a large interest in a printing works near Turin and had arranged for the girls to draw most generously upon the firm's Roman office for funds. They had been given business and personal letters of introduction. Together, they had been in rapture: alone, Sophy felt strange but fundamentally exhilarated. To be under her own steam—and in Rome!

She had Titian hair, large eyes and a generous mouth, and had already found it advisable to stand with her back to the wall in crowded lifts and indeed wherever two or more Roman gentlemen were gathered together at close quarters. 'Quarters', as she had remarked to her friend, being the operative word.

I must make a plan or two, of sorts, she told herself but the boxes on the roof-garden were full of spring flowers, the air shook with voices, traffic, footsteps and the endearing clop of hooves on cobble-stones. Should she blue a couple of thousand lire and take a carriage to the Spanish Steps? Should she walk and walk until bullets and live coals began to assemble on the soles of her feet? What to do?

Really, I *ought* to make a plan, thought crazy Sophy and then—here she was, feckless and blissful, walking down the Corso in she knew not what direction. Before long she was contentedly lost. Sophy bought herself gloves, pink sun-glasses, espadrilles and a pair of footpads, which she put on, there and then, greatly to her comfort.

Leaving the store she noticed a little bureau set up near the entrance. 'DO,' it urged in English on a large banner, 'let US be your Guide to Rome.'

A dark, savage-looking girl sat scornfully behind the counter, doing her nails.

Sophy read some of the notices and glanced at already familiar brochures. She was about to leave when a smaller card caught her eye. It advertised in printed Italianate script: 'Il Cicerone, personally conducted excursions. Something different!' it exclaimed, 'Not too exhausting, sophisticated visits to some of the least-publicized and most fascinating places in Rome. Under the learned and highly individual guidance of Mr Sebastian Mailer. Dinner at a most exclusive restaurant and further unconventional expeditions by arrangement.

'*Guest of honour:* The distinguished British Author, Mr Barnaby Grant, has graciously consented to accompany the excursions from April 23rd until May 7th. Sundays included.'

Sophy was astounded. Barnaby Grant was the biggest of all big guns in her publisher's armoury of authors. His new and most important novel, set in Rome and called *Simon in Latium* had been their prestige event and the best-seller of the year. Already bookshops here were full of the Italian translation.

Sophy had offered Barnaby Grant drinks at a deafening cocktail party given by her publishing house and she had once been introduced to him by her immediate boss. She had formed her own idea of him and it did not accommodate the thought of his trapesing round Rome with a clutch of sightseers. She supposed he must be very highly paid for it and found the thought disagreeable.

In any case could so small a concern as this appeared to be, afford the sort of payment Barnaby Grant would command?

Perhaps, she thought, suddenly inspired, he's a chum of this learned and highly individual Mr Sebastian Mailer.

She was still gazing absent-mindedly at the notice when she became aware of a man at her elbow. She had the impression that he must have been there for some time and that he had been staring at her. He continued to stare and she thought: Oh blast! What a bore you are.

'Do forgive me,' said the man, removing his greenish black hat. 'Please don't think me impertinent. My name is Sebastian Mailer. You had noticed my little announcement I believe.'

The girl behind the counter glanced at him. She had painted her nails and now disdainfully twiddled them in the air.

Sophy faced Mr Mailer. 'Yes,' she said. 'I had.'

He made her a little bow. 'I must not intrude. Please!' and moved away.

Sophy said: 'Not at all,' and because she felt that she had made a silly assumption, added: 'I was so interested to see Barnaby Grant's name on your card.'

'I am indeed fortunate,' Mr Mailer rejoined, 'am I not? Perhaps you would care—but excuse me. One moment. *Would* you mind?'

He said something in Italian to the savage girl who opened a drawer, extracted what seemed to be a book of vouchers and cast it on the counter.

Mr Mailer inspected it.

'Ah yes,' he said. 'Others, also, would seem to be interested. We are fully booked, I see.'

At once Sophy felt an acute disappointment. Of all things now, she wanted to join one of Mr Mailer's highly sophisticated tours. 'Your numbers are strictly limited, are they?' she asked.

'It is an essential feature.' He was preoccupied with his vouchers.

'Might there be a cancellation?'

'I beg your pardon? You were saying?'

'A cancellation?'

'Ah. Quite. Well—possibly. You feel you would like to join one of my expeditions.'

'Very much,' Sophy said and supposed that it must be so.

He pursed up his full mouth and thumbed over his vouchers.

'Ah,' he said. 'As it falls out! There is a cancellation I see. Saturday, the twenty-sixth. Our first tour. The afternoon and evening. But before you make a decision I'm sure you would like to know about cost. Allow me.'

He produced a folder and turned aside in a gentlemanly manner while Sophy examined it. The itinerary was given and the name of the restaurant where the party would dine. In the evening they would take a carriage drive and then visit a nightclub. The overall charge made Sophy blink. It was enormous.

'I *know*,' Mr Mailer tactfully assured her. 'But there are many much, much less expensive tours than mine. The Signorina here would be pleased to inform you.'

Obviously he didn't give a damn whether she went or stayed away. This attitude roused a devil of recklessness in Sophy. After all, mad though it seemed, she *could* manage it.

'I shall be very glad to take the cancellation,' she said and even to herself her voice sounded both prim and defiant.

He said something further in Italian to the girl, raised his hat, murmured, 'Then—*arrivederci*' to Sophy, and left her to cope.

'You paya to me,' said the girl ferociously and when Sophy had done so, presented her with a ticket and a cackle of inexplicable laughter.

Sophy laughed jauntily if senselessly in return, desiring, as always, to be friendly with all and sundry.

She continued to walk about Rome and to anticipate with feelings she would have been quite unable to define, Saturday, the twenty-sixth of April.

THREE

'I must say,' Lady Braceley murmured, 'you don't seem to be enjoying yourself very madly. I never saw such a glum face.'

'I'm sorry, Auntie Sonia. I don't mean to look glum. Honestly, I couldn't be more grateful.'

37

'Oh,' she said, dismissing it, 'grateful! I just hoped that we might have a nice, gay time together in Rome.'

'I'm sorry,' he repeated.

'You're so—odd. Restless. And you don't look at all well, either. What have you been doing with yourself?'

'Nothing.'

'On the tiles, I suppose.'

'I'll be all right. Really.'

'Perhaps you shouldn't have pranced out of Perugia like that.'

'I couldn't have been more bored with Perugia. Students can be such an unutterable drag. And after Franky and I broke up—you know.'

'All the same your parents or lawyers or the Lord Chancellor or whoever it is, will probably be livid with me. For not ordering you back.'

'Does it matter? And anyway—my parents! We know, with all respect to your horrible brother, darling, that the longer his boy-child keeps out of his life the better he likes it.'

'Kenneth—darling!'

'As for Mummy—*what's* the name of that dipso-bin she's moved into? I keep forgetting.'

'Kenneth!'

'So come off it, angel. We're not still in the 'twenties, you know.'

They looked thoughtfully at each other.

His aunt said: 'Were you a very bad lot in Perugia, Kenneth?'

'No worse than a dozen others.'

'What *sort* of lot? What did you do?'

'Oh,' Kenneth said, 'this and that. Fun things.' He became self-suffused with charm. 'You're much too young to be told,' he said. 'What a fabulous dress. Did you get it from that amazing lady?"

'Do you like it? Yes, I did. Astronomical.'

'And looks it.'

His aunt eyed herself over. 'It had better,' she muttered.

'Oh lord!' Kenneth said discontentedly and dropped into a chair. 'Sorry! It must be the weather or something.'

'To tell you the truth I'm slightly edgy myself. Think of something delicious and outrageous we can do, darling. What is there?'

Kenneth had folded his hands across the lower half of his face like a yashmak. His large and melting brown eyes looked over the top at his aunt. There was a kind of fitful affectation in everything he did: he tried-on his mannerisms and discarded them as fretfully as his aunt tried-on her hats.

'Sweetie,' he said. 'There *is* a thing.'

'Well—what? I can't hear you when you talk behind your fingers.'

He made a triangular hole with them and spoke through that. 'I know a little man,' he said.

'What little man? Where?'

'In Perugia and now here.'

'What about him?'

'He's rather a clever little man. Well, not so little, actually.'

'Kenneth, don't go on like that. It's maddening: it's infuriating.' And then suddenly:

'In Perugia. Did you—did you—*smoke*——?'

'There's no need for the hushed tones, darling. You've been handed the usual nonsense, I see.'

'Then you *did*?'

'Of course,' he said impatiently and, after a pause, changed his attitude. He clasped his hands round his knee and tilted his head on one side. 'You're so fabulous,' he said. 'I can tell you anything. As if you were my generation. Aren't we wonderful? Both of us?'

'Are we? Kenneth—what's it like?'

39

'Pot? Do you really want to know?'

'I'm asking, aren't I?'

'Dire the first time and quite fun if you persevere. Kid-stuff really. All the fuss is about nothing.'

'It's done at—at parties, isn't it?'

'That's right, lovey. Want to try?'

'It's not habit-forming. Is it?'

'Of course it's not. It's nothing. It's OK as far as it goes. You don't get hooked. Not on pot. You'd better meet my little man. Try a little trip. In point of fact I *could* arrange a *fabulous* trip. Madly groovy. You'd adore it. All sorts of gorgeous gents. Super exotic pad. The lot.'

She looked at him through her impossible lashes: a girl's look that did a kind of injury to her face.

'I might,' she said.

'Only thing—it's top-bracket for expense. All-time-high and worth it. One needs lots of lovely lolly and I haven't—surprise, surprise—got a morsel.'

'Kenneth!'

'In fact if my rich aunt hadn't invited me I would have been out on my little pink ear. Don't pitch into me, I don't think I can take it.'

They stared at each other. They were very much alike: two versions of the same disastrous image.

'I understand you,' Kenneth said. 'You know that, don't you? I'm a sponge, OK? But I'm not just a sponge. I give back something. Right?' He waited for a moment and when she didn't answer, shouted, 'Don't I? *Don't* I?'

'Be quiet. Yes. Yes, of course you do. Yes.'

'We're two of a kind, right?'

'Yes. I said so, didn't I? Never mind, darling. Look in my bag. I don't know how much I've got.'

'God, you're wonderful! I—I'll go out straight away. I—I'll—I'll get it—' his mouth twisted—'fixed. We'll have such a—what did that old burnt-out Egyptian bag call it?—or her boy-friend?—gaudy night?—won't we?'

Her note-case shook in his hand. 'There isn't much here,' he said.

'Isn't there?' she said. 'They'll cash a cheque downstairs. I'll write one. You'd better have something in hand.'

When he had gone she went into her bedroom, sat in front of her glass and examined the precarious mask she still presented to the world.

Kenneth, yawning and sweating, went in febrile search of Mr Sebastian Mailer.

FOUR

'It's the familiar story,' the tall man said. He uncrossed his legs, rose in one movement, and stood, relaxed, before his companion who, taken by surprise, made a laborious business of getting to his feet.

'The big boys,' said the tall man, 'keep one jump ahead while their henchmen occasionally trip over our wires. Not often enough, however.'

'Excuse me, my dear colleague. Our wires?'

'Sorry. I meant: we do sometimes catch up with the secondary villains but their principals continue to evade us.'

'Regrettably!'

'In this case the biggest boy of all is undoubtedly Otto Ziegfeldt who, at the moment, has retired to a phoney castle in the Lebanon. We can't get him. Yet. But this person, here in Rome, is a key man.'

'I am most anxious that his activities be arrested. We all know, my dear colleague, that Palermo has most regrettably been a transit port. And also Corsica. But that he should have extended his activities to Naples and, it seems, to Rome! No, assure yourself you shall have every assistance.'

41

'I'm most grateful to you, Signor Questore. The Yard was anxious that we should have this talk.'

'*Please!* Believe me, the greatest pleasure,' said Il Questore Valdarno. He had a resonant voice and grand-opera appearance. His eyes melted and he gave out an impression of romantic melancholy. Even his jokes wore an air of impending disaster. His position in the Roman police force corresponded, as far as his visitor had been able to work it out, with that of a Chief Constable.

'We are all so much honoured, my dear Superintendent,' he continued. 'Anything that we can do to further the already cordial relationship between our own Force and your most distinguished Yard.'

'You are very kind. Of course, the whole problem of the drug traffic, as we both know, is predominantly an Interpol affair but as in this instance we are rather closely tied up with them——'

'Perfectly,' agreed Valdarno, many times nodding his head.

'——and since this person is, presumably, a British subject——'

The Questore made a large involved gesture of deprecation: 'Of course!'

'——in the event of his being arrested the question of extradition might arise.'

'I assure you,' said the Questore, making a joke, 'we shall not try to deprive you!'

His visitor laughed obligingly and extended his hand. The Questore took it and with his own left hand dealt him the buffet with which Latin gentlemen endorse their friendly relationships. He insisted on coming to the magnificent entrance.

In the street a smallish group of young men carrying a few inflammatory placards shouted one or two insults. A group of police, gorgeously arrayed, pinched out their cigarettes and moved towards the demonstrators who cat-called and bolted a short way down the street. The police immediately stopped and relit their cigarettes.

'How foolish,' observed the Questore in Italian, 'and yet after all, not to be ignored. It is all a great nuisance. You will seek out this person, my dear colleague?'

'I think so. His sight-seeing activities seem to offer the best approach. I shall enrol myself for one of them.'

'Ah-ah! You are a droll! You are a great droll.'

'No, I assure you. *Arrivederci.*'

'Goodbye. Such a pleasure. Goodbye.'

Having finally come to the end of a conversation that had been conducted in equal parts of Italian and English, they parted on the best of terms.

The demonstrators made some desultory comments upon the tall Englishman as he walked past them. One of them called out, 'Ullo, gooda-day!' in a squeaking voice, another shouted 'Rhodesia! *Imperialismo!*' and raised a cat-call, but a third remarked '*Molto elegante*' in a loud voice and apparently without sardonic intention.

Rome sparkled in the spring morning. The swallows had arrived, the markets were full of flowers, young greens and kaleidoscopic cheap-jackery. Dramatic façades presented themselves suddenly to the astonished gaze, lovely courtyards and galleries floated in shadow and little piazzas talked with the voices of their own fountains. Behind magnificent doorways the ages offered their history lessons in layers.

Like the achievements of a Roman pastrycook, thought the tall man irreverently: modern, renaissance, classic, Mithraic, each under another in one gorgeous, stratified edifice. It would be an enchantment to walk up to the Palatine Hill where the air would smell freshly of young grass and a kind of peace and order would come upon the rich encrustations of time.

Instead he must look for a tourist bureau either in the streets

43

or at the extremely grand hotel he had been treated to by his Department in London. He approached it by the way of the Via Condotti and presently came upon a window filled with blown-up photographs of Rome. The agency was a distinguished one and their London office well-known to him.

He turned into an impressive interior, remarked that its décor was undisturbed by racks of brochures, and approached an exquisite but far from effete young man who seemed to be in charge.

'Good morning, sir,' said the young man in excellent English. 'May I help you?'

'I hope so,' he rejoined cheerfully. 'I'm in Rome for a few days. I don't want to spend them on a series of blanket-tours covering the maximum amount of sights in the minimum amount of time. I have seen as much as I can take of celebrated big-boomers. What I would like now is to do something leisurely and civilized that leads one a little off the beaten way of viewing and yet is really—well, really *of* Rome and not, historically speaking, beside the point. I'm afraid I put that very badly.'

'But not at all,' said the young man looking hard at him. 'I understand perfectly. A personal courier might be the answer but this is the busy season, sir, and I'm afraid we've nobody free for at least a fortnight whom I could really recommend.'

'Somebody told me about something called Il Cicerone. Small parties under the guidance of a—I'm not sure if I've got his name right—Sebastian something? Do you know?'

The young man looked still more fixedly at him and said: 'It's odd—really, it's quite a coincidence, sir, that you should mention Il Cicerone. A week ago I could have told you very little about it. Except, perhaps, that it wasn't likely to be a distinguished affair. Indeed'—he hesitated and then said— 'please forgive me, sir. I've been at our London office for the

44

past three years and I can't help thinking that I've had the pleasure of looking after you before. Or at least of seeing you. I hope you don't mind,' the young man said in a rush, 'I trust you will not think this insufferable cheek: I haven't mastered my Anglo-Saxon attitudes, I'm afraid.'

'You've mastered the language, at least.'

'Oh—that! After an English university and so on, I should hope so.'

'——and have an excellent memory.'

'Well, sir, you are not the sort of person who is all that readily forgotten. Perhaps, then, I am correct in thinking——?'

'You came into the general manager's office in Jermyn Street while I was there. Some two years ago. You were in the room for about three minutes: during which time you gave me a piece of very handy information.'

The young man executed an involved and extremely Italianate gesture that ended up with a smart slap on his own forehead.

'Ah-ah-ah! *Mamma mia!* How could I be such an ass!' he exclaimed.

'It all comes back to you?' observed the tall man dryly.

'But completely. All!'

He fell away a step and contemplated his visitor with an air of the deepest respect.

'Good,' said the visitor, unmoved by this scrutiny. 'Now about the Il Cicerone thing——'

'It is entirely for recreation, sir, that you inquire?'

'Why not?'

'Indeed! Of course! I merely wondered——'

'Come on. What did you wonder?'

'If perhaps there might be a professional aspect.'

'And why did you wonder that? Look, Signor Pace—that *is* your name, isn't it?'

'Your own memory, sir, is superb.'

45

'Signor Pace. Is there, perhaps, something about this enterprise, or about the person who controls it that makes you think I might be interested in it—or him—for other than sight-seeing reasons?'

The young man became pink in the face, gazed at his clasped hands, glanced round the bureau which was empty of other people and finally said, 'The cicerone in question, Signore—a Mr Sebastian Mailer—is a person of a certain, or perhaps I should say, uncertain reputation. Nothing specific you understand, but there are—' he agitated his fingers—'suggestions. Rome is a great place for suggestions.'

'Yes?'

'I remarked that it was quite a coincidence you should inquire about him. That is because he was here earlier today. Not for the first time. He asked to be put on our books some weeks ago but his reputation, his appearance—everything—did not recommend his venture to us and we declined. Then, this morning as a new inducement he brings us his list of patrons. It was quite astonishing, Signore, this list.'

'May I see it?'

'We still have not accepted him. I—I don't quite——'

'Signor Pace, your guess was a good one. My interest in this person is professional.'

'Ah!'

'But I am most anxious to appear simply as a tourist. I remember that in London your chief spoke very highly indeed of your discretion and promise—a promise that is evidently being fulfilled.'

'You are kind enough to say so, sir.'

'I realize that I can't get a booking with Il Cicerone through you but perhaps you can tell me——'

'I can arrange it with another agency and will be delighted to do so. As for the list of patrons: under the circumstances, I think, there is no reason why I should not show it to you.

46

Will you come into the office, if you please. While you examine it I will attend to your booking.'

The list Signor Pace produced was a day-by-day record of people who had put themselves down for Il Cicerone expeditions. It was prefaced by a general announcement that made his visitor blink: 'Under the distinguished patronage of the celebrated author, Mr Barnaby Grant.'

'This *is* coming it strong!'

'Is it not?' Signor Pace said, busily dialling. 'I cannot imagine how it has been achieved. Although——' he broke off and addressed himself elegantly to the telephone. '*Pronto. Chi parla?*'—and, as an aside: 'Look at the patronage, Signore. On the first day, Saturday, the twenty-sixth, for instance.'

Here it was, neatly set out in the Italianate script:

Lady Braceley.	London
The Hon. Kenneth Dorne.	London
Baron and Baroness Van der Veghel.	Geneva
Major Hamilton Sweet.	London
Miss Sophy Jason.	London
Mr Barnaby Grant (Guest of Honour).	London

After further discussion, Signor Pace broke out in a cascade of thanks and compliments and covered the mouthpiece.

'All is arranged,' he cried. 'For whichever tour you prefer.'

'Without hesitation—the first one. Saturday, the twenty-sixth.'

This, evidently, was settled. Signor Pace hung up and swung round in his chair. 'An interesting list, is it not? Lady Braceley —what *chic*!'

'You may call it that.'

'Well, Signore! A certain reputation, perhaps. What is called the "jet set". But from the point of view of the tourist-trade—extremely chic. Great éclat. We always arrange her travel. There is, of course, immense wealth.'

'Quite so. The alimony alone.'

'Well, Signore.'

'And the Hon. Kenneth Dorne?'

'I understand, her nephew.'

'And the Van der Veghels?'

'I am dumb. They have not come our way. Nor have Miss Jason and Major Sweet. But, Signore, the remarkable feature, the really astonishing, as one says, turn-up for the book, is the inclusion of Mr Barnaby Grant. And what is meant, I ask myself, by Guest of Honour?'

' "Prime Attraction", I imagine.'

'Of course! But for him to consent! To lend his enormous prestige to such a very dim enterprise. And, we must admit, it appears evident that the gimmick has worked.'

'I wouldn't have thought Lady Braceley was a natural taker for the intellectual bait.'

'Signore, he is impressive, he is handsome, he is famous, his is prestigious——Am I correct in saying "prestigious"?'

'It really means he's a bit of a conjurer. And so, of course, in a sense, he is.'

'And therefore to be acquired by Lady Braceley. Or, at least, considered.'

'You may be right. I understand she's staying at my hotel. I heard her name at the desk.'

'Her nephew, Mr Dorne, is her guest.'

'Fortunate youth! Perhaps. By the way, what are the charges for these jaunts?'

'In the top bracket and, at that, exceedingly high. I would have said impertinently so but, as you see, he is getting the response. One can only hope the patrons are satisfied.'

'In any case you have given me the opportunity to form an opinion. I'm extremely obliged to you.'

'But, please! Come,' said the jaunty Signor Pace, 'let us make our addition to the list.'

He gaily drew it towards him and at the bottom wrote his addition.

'You see!' he cried in playful triumph. 'I remembered everything! The rank! The spelling!'

'If you don't mind, we'll forget about the rank and the spelling.'

The visitor drew a line through the word 'Superintendent' and another through the letter 'y', so that the entry read:

'R. Allen, London.'

3. Saturday, the Twenty-sixth

ONE

IT BECAME FAIRLY CLEAR from the outset why Mr Sebastian Mailer made extravagant charges for his expeditions.

At three-thirty in the afternoon two superb Lancias arrived at the rendezvous near the Church of the Trinity and therefore within a very short distance of the hotel where three of Mr Mailer's prospects were staying.

From here, as they assembled, his seven guests looked down at April azaleas flaring on the Spanish Steps and at Rome suddenly laid out before them in a wide gesture. There was a sense of opulence and of excitement in the air. Alleyn got there before the appointed time and saw the cars draw up. They had small labels in their windows: 'Il Cicerone'.

Out of one of them stepped a dark man of romantic appearance whom he at once recognized as Barnaby Grant, and out of the other the person he had come to see: Sebastian Mailer. He was smartened up since Barnaby Grant's last encounter with him and was dressed in a black suit of some material that might have been alpaca. This, together with a pair of clumping black shoes gave him a dubiously priestly look and made Alleyn think of Corvo and wonder if he might turn out to be such another. The white silk shirt was clean and the black bow tie looked new. He now wore a black beret on his cropped head and no longer had the appearance of an Englishman.

Alleyn kept his distance among a group of sightseers who milled about taking photographs.

50

He saw that while Sebastian Mailer, half-smiling, talked vivaciously, Grant seemed to make little or no response. He had his back to Alleyn who thought the nape of his neck looked indignant. It looks, Alleyn thought, like the neck of a learner-driver seen from the rear: rigid, cross and apprehensive.

A young woman approached the cars, spotted Mailer and made towards him. She had a glowing air about her as if Rome had a little gone to her head. Miss Sophy Jason, Alleyn said to himself.

He saw her look quickly at Barnaby Grant. Mailer pulled slightly at his beret, made a little bow and introduced her.

The girl's manner was shy, Alleyn thought, but not at all gauche: rather charming, in fact. Nevertheless she said something to Grant that seemed to disconcert him. He glared at her, replied very shortly and turned away. The girl blushed painfully.

This brief tableau was broken by the arrival of two oversized persons hung about with canvas satchels and expensive cameras: a man and a woman. The Van der Veghels, Alleyn concluded and, like Barnaby Grant before him, was struck by their resemblance to each other and their strangely archaic faces.

They were well-dressed in a non-with-it sort of way: both of them in linen and both wearing outsize shoes with great rubber-studded soles and canvas tops. They wore sensibly shady hats and identical sun-glasses with pink frames. They were eager in their greetings and evidently had met Grant before. What great hands and feet you have, Baron and Baroness, thought Alleyn.

Lady Braceley and her nephew were still to come. No doubt it would be entirely in character for them to keep the party waiting. He decided it was time for him to present himself and did so, ticket in hand.

Mailer had the kind of voice Alleyn had expected: a rather

fluting alto. He was a bad colour and his hands were slightly tremulous. But he filled his role very competently: there was the correct degree of suavity and assurance, the suggestion that everything was to be executed at the highest level.

'So glad you are joining us, Mr Allen,' said Sebastian Mailer. 'Do come and meet the others, won't you? May I introduce——'

The Baron and Baroness were cordial. Grant looked hard at him, nodded with what seemed to be an uneasy blend of reluctance and good manners, and asked him if he knew Rome well.

'Virtually, not at all,' Alleyn said. 'I've never been here for more than three or four days at a time and I'm not a systematic sightseer.'

'No?'

'No. I want things to occur and I'm afraid spend far too much time sitting at a *caffè* table waiting for them to do so, which of course they don't. But who knows? One of these days the heavens may open and big drama descend upon me.'

Alleyn was afterwards to regard this as the major fluke-remark of his career. At the moment he was merely astonished to see what an odd response it drew from Barnaby Grant. He changed colour, threw an apprehensive glance at Alleyn, opened his mouth, shut it and finally said, 'Oh,' without any expression at all.

'But today,' Alleyn said, 'I hope to improve my condition. Do we, by any chance, visit one of your Simon's haunts? That would be a wonderful idea.'

Again Grant seemed to be about to speak and again he boggled. After a sufficiently awkward pause he said: 'There's some idea of it. Mailer will explain. Excuse me, will you.'

He turned away.

All right, Alleyn thought. But if you hate it as much as all this, why the hell do you do it?

He moved on to Sophy Jason, who was standing apart and seemed to be glad of his company. We're all too old for her, Alleyn thought. Perhaps the nephew of Lady Braceley will meet the case, but one doubts it.

He engaged Sophy in conversation and thought her a nice intelligent girl with a generous allowance of charm. She looked splendid against the background of azaleas, Rome and a pontifical sky.

Before long, Sophy found herself telling Alleyn about her suddenly-bereaved friend, about this being her first visit to Rome, about the fortunate accident of the cancellation and finally about her job. It really was extraordinary, she suddenly reflected, how much she was confiding to this quiet and attentive stranger.

She felt herself blushing. 'I can't imagine why I'm gabbling away like this!' she exclaimed.

'It's obliging of you to talk to me,' Alleyn said. 'I've just been not exactly slapped back but slightly edged off by the Guest of Honour.'

'Nothing to what I was!' Sophy ejaculated. 'I'm still cringing.'

'But—isn't he one of your publisher's authors?'

'He's our great double-barrel. I was dumb enough to remind him that I had been presented by my boss. He took the news like a dose of poison.'

'How very odd of him.'

'It was really a bit of a facer. He'd seemed so un-fierce and amiable on the earlier occasion and has the reputation in the firm of being a lamb. Aren't we rather slow getting off our mark? Mr Mailer is looking at his watch.'

'Major Sweet's twenty minutes late and so are Lady Braceley and the Hon. Kenneth Dorne. They're staying at the——' He broke off. 'Here, I fancy, they come.'

And here, in fact, they came and there was Mr Mailer, his

beret completely off, advancing with a winning and proprietary air towards them.

Alleyn wondered what first impression they made on Sophy Jason. For all her poise and obvious intelligence he doubted if the like of Sonia Braceley had ever come her way.

Alleyn knew quite a lot about Sonia Braceley. She began life as the Hon. Sonia Dorne and was the daughter of a beer-baron whose children, by and large, had turned out disastrously. Alleyn had actually met her, many years ago, when visiting his Ambassadorial elder brother, George, at one of his official Residences. Even then she had what his brother, whom Alleyn tolerantly regarded as a bit of an ass, alluded to as 'a certain reputation'. With the passage of time, this reputation had consolidated. 'She has experienced everything,' Sir George had weightily quipped, 'except poverty.'

Seeing her now it was easy to believe it. It's the legs, Alleyn thought. More than the precariously maintained mask or the flabby underarm or the traitorous neck. It's the legs. Although the stockings are tight as a skin they look as if they should hang loose about these brittle spindleshanks; and how hazardously she's balanced on her golden kid sandals. It's the legs.

But the face was not too good either. Even if one discounted the ruches under the eyes and the eyes themselves, there was still that dreadfully slack mouth. It was painted the fashionable livid colour but declared itself as unmistakably as if it had been scarlet: the mouth of an elderly Maenad.

Her nephew bore some slight resemblance to her. Alleyn remembered that his father, the second Lord Dorne, had been rapidly divorced by two wives and that the third, Kenneth's mother, had been, as George would have said, 'put away'. Not much of a start, Alleyn thought, compassionately, and wondered if the old remedy of 'live on a quid-a-day and earn it,' would have done anything for Kenneth Dorne.

As they advanced, he noticed that the young man watched

54

Mailer with an air that seemed to be made up of anxiety, furtiveness and perhaps subservience. He was restless, pallid, yellow and damp about the brow. When Mailer introduced him and he offered his hand it proved to be clammy as to the palm, and tremulous. Rather unexpectedly, he had a camera slung from his shoulder.

His aunt also shook hands. Within the doeskin glove the fingers contracted, momentarily retained their clasp and slowly withdrew. Lady Braceley looked fixedly into Alleyn's eyes. So she still, he thought, appalled, gives it a go.

She said: 'Isn't this *fun*?' Her voice was beautiful.

Mailer was at her elbow with Grant in tow: 'Lady Braceley, may I present? Our guest of honour—Mr Barnaby Grant.'

She said: 'Do you know you're the sole reason for my coming to this party? Kenneth, with a team of wild horses, wouldn't have bullied me into sightseeing at this ghastly hour. *You're* my "sight".'

'I don't know,' Grant said rapidly, 'how I'm meant to answer that. Except that I'm sure you'll find the Church of S. Tommaso in Pallaria much more rewarding.'

'Is that where we're going? Is it a *ruin*?' she asked, opening her devastated eyes very wide and drawling out the word 'I can't tell you how I hate roo-ins.'

There was perhaps one second's silence and then Grant said: 'It's not exactly that. It's—well, you'll see when we get there.'

'Does it come in your book? I've read your book—that Simon one—which is a great compliment if you only knew it because you don't write my sort of book at all. Don't be huffy. I adored this one although I haven't a clue, really, what it's about. You shall explain it to me. Kenneth tried, didn't you, darling, but he was even more muddling than the book. Mr Allen, come over here and tell me—have *you* read the last Barnaby Grant and if you have, did you know what it was about?'

55

Alleyn was spared the task of finding an answer to this by the intervention of Sebastian Mailer who rather feverishly provided the kind of raillery that seemed to be invited and got little reward for his pains. When he archly said: 'Lady Braceley, you're being very naughty. I'm quite sure you didn't miss the last delicate nuance of *Simon in Tuscany*,' she merely said 'What?' and walked away before he could repeat his remark.

It was now the turn of the Baron and Baroness. Lady Braceley received the introduction vaguely. 'Aren't we going to start?' she asked Alleyn and Grant. 'Don't you rather hate hanging about? Such a bore, don't you think? Who's missing?'

Upon this cool inquiry, Sebastian Mailer explained that Major Sweet was joining them at the basilica and proceeded to outline the programme for the afternoon. They would drive round the Colosseum and the Forum and would then visit the basilica of S. Tommaso in Pallaria which, as they all knew, was the setting for the great central scene in Mr Barnaby Grant's immensely successful novel, *Simon in Latium*. He had prevailed upon the distinguished author, Mr Mailer went on, to say a few words about the basilica in its relation to his book which, as they would hear from him, was largely inspired by it.

Throughout this exposition Barnaby Grant, Alleyn noticed, seemed to suffer the most exquisite embarrassment. He stared at the ground, hunched his shoulders, made as if to walk away and, catching perhaps a heightened note in Mr Mailer's voice, thought better of this and remained, wretchedly it appeared, where he was.

Mr Mailer concluded by saying that as the afternoon was deliciously clement they would end it with a picnic tea on the Palatine Hill. The guests would then be driven to their hotels to relax and change for dinner and would be called for at nine o'clock.

He now distributed the guests. He, with Lady Braceley,

Alleyn and Barnaby Grant would take one car; the Van der Veghels, Sophy Jason and Kenneth Dorne would take the other.

The driver of the second car was introduced. 'Giovanni is fluent in English,' said Mr Mailer, 'and learned in the antiquities. He will discourse upon matters of interest en route. Come, ladies and gentlemen,' said Mr Mailer, 'let us embark. *Pronto!*'

TWO

The four arches that lead into the porch of S. Tommaso in Pallaria are of modest proportion, and their pillars, which in classic times adorned some pagan temple, are slender and worn. The convolvulus tendrils that their carver twined about them have broken in many places but the work is so delicate that the stone seems to tremble.

In the most shadowed corner of the porch sat a woman with a tray of postcards. She wore a black head-scarf pulled forward over her face and a black cotton dress. She shouted something, perhaps at Mr Mailer. Her voice was strident which may have caused her remark to sound like an insult. He paid no attention to it.

He collected his party about him and looked at his watch. 'Major Sweet,' he said, 'is late. We shall not wait for him but before we go in I should like to give you, very shortly, some idea of this extraordinary monument. In the fourth century before Christ——'

From the dark interior there erupted an angry gentleman who shouted as he came.

'Damned disgusting lot of hanky-panky,' shouted this gentleman. 'What the hell——' He pulled up short on seeing the group and narrowed his blazing eyes in order to focus upon it. He had a savage white moustache and looked like an

57

improbable revival of an Edwardian warrior. 'Are you Mailer?' he shouted. 'Sweet,' he added, in explanation.

'Major Sweet, may I——'

'You're forty-three minutes late. Forty-three minutes!'

'Unfortunately——'

'Spare me,' begged Major Sweet, 'the specious excuses. There is no adequate explanation for unpunctuality.'

Lady Braceley moved in. '*All* my fault, Major,' she said. 'I kept everybody waiting and I've no excuses: I never have and I always do. I dare say you'd call it "ladies' privilege", wouldn't you? Or would you?'

Major Sweet turned his blue glare upon her for two or three seconds. He then yapped 'How do you do' and seemed to wait for further developments.

Mr Mailer with perfect suavity performed the introductions. Major Sweet acknowledged them by making slight bows to the ladies and an ejaculation of sorts to the men. 'Hyah,' he said.

'Well,' said Mr Mailer. 'To resume. When we are inside the basilica I shall hand over to our most distinguished guest of honour. But perhaps beforehand a very brief historical note may be of service.'

He was succinct and adequate, Sophy grudgingly admitted. The basilica of San Tommaso, he said, was one of a group of monuments in Rome where the visitors could walk downwards through the centuries into Mithraic time. At the top level, here where they now stood, was the twelfth-century basilica which in a moment they would enter. Beneath it, was the excavated third-century church which it had replaced. 'And below that— imagine it——' said Mr Mailer, 'there has lain sleeping for over eighteen hundred years a house of the Flavian period: a classic "gentleman's residence" with its own private chapel dedicated (and Mr Grant will tell you more about this) dedicated to the god Mithras.'

He paused, and Sophy, though she regarded him with the most profound distaste, thought: He's interested in what he's talking about. He knows his stuff. He's enjoying himself.

Mr Mailer went on to describe briefly the enormous task of nineteenth-century excavation that had so gradually disclosed first, the earlier basilica and then, deep down beneath it, the pagan household. 'Rome has risen, hereabout, sixty feet since those times,' he ended. 'Does that surprise you? It does me, every time I think of it.'

'It doesn't me,' Major Sweet announced. 'Nothing surprises me. Except human gullibility,' he added darkly. 'However!'

Mr Mailer shot him an uneasy glance. Sophy gave a little snort of suppressed amusement and caught Barnaby Grant looking at her with something like appreciation. Lady Braceley, paying no attention to what was said, let her ravaged eyes turn from one man's face to another. The Van der Veghels, standing close together, listened intently.

Kenneth Dorne, Sophy noticed, was restless and anxious-looking. He shuffled his feet and dabbed at his face with his handkerchief. And the tall man, what was his name—Allen?—stood a little apart, politely attentive and, Sophy thought, extremely observant.

'But now,' Mr Mailer said, 'shall we begin our journey into the past?'

The woman with the postcards had sidled between the group and the entrance. She had kept her face down and it was still shadowed by her black head-scarf. She muttered, almost inaudibly, '*Cartoline? Posta-carda?*' edging towards Sebastian Mailer. He said generally to his company, 'There are better inside. Pay no attention,' and moved forward to pass the woman.

With extraordinary swiftness she pushed back her head-scarf, thrust her face up at him and whispered: '*Brutto! Farabutto! Traditore!*' and added what seemed to be a stream

59

of abuse. Her eyes burned. Her lips were retracted in a grin and then pursed together.

She's going to spit in his face, thought Sophy in alarm and so she was, but Mr Mailer was too smart for her. He dodged and she spat after him and stood her ground with the air of a grand-opera virago. She even gave a hoarse screech of eldritch laughter.

Mr Mailer entered the basilica. His discomforted flock divided round the postcard-seller and slunk after him.

'Kenneth, darling,' Lady Braceley muttered. 'Honestly! *Not* one's idea of a gay little trip!'

Sophy found herself between Barnaby Grant and Alleyn. 'Was that lady,' Alleyn asked Grant, 'put in as an extra touch of atmosphere? Does she recur, or was she a colourful accident?'

Grant said, 'I don't know anything about her. Mad, I should think. Ghastly old bag, wasn't she?' and Sophy thought: Yes, but he hasn't answered the question.

She said to Alleyn, 'Would you suppose that all that carry-on, if translated into Anglo-Saxon terms, would amount to no more than a cool glance and an indrawn breath?'

Grant looked across Alleyn at her, and said with a kind of eagerness, 'Oh, rather! You have to make allowances for their sense of drama.'

'Rather excessive in this instance,' she said coolly, giving, she said to herself, snub for snub.

Grant moved round and said hurriedly, 'I know who you are, now. I didn't before. We met at Koster Press didn't we?' Koster Press was the name of his publisher's house in London.

'For a moment,' Sophy said and then: 'Oh, but how lovely!' They were in the basilica.

It glowed sumptuously as if it generated its own light. It was alive with colour: 'mediterranean' red, clear pinks, blues and greens; ivory and crimson marble, tingling gold mosaic. And dominant in this concourse of colour the great vermilion that cries out in the backgrounds of Rome and Pompeii. Sophy moved away from the group and stared with delight at this enchantment. Grant, who had been left with Alleyn, abruptly joined her.

'I've got to talk about this,' he muttered. 'I wish to God I hadn't.'

She looked briefly at him. 'Then why do it?' said Sophy.

'You think that was an affectation. I'm sorry.'

'Really, it couldn't matter less what I think.'

'You needn't be so snappish.'

They stared at each other in astonishment.

'I can't make this out,' Grant said unexpectedly. 'I don't know you.' And Sophy in a panic, stammered, 'It's nothing. It's none of my business, I'm sorry I snapped.'

'Not at all.'

'And now,' fluted Sebastian Mailer, 'I hand over to my most distinguished colleague, Mr Grant.'

Grant made Sophy an extremely stuffy little bow and moved out to face his audience.

Once he was launched he too did his stuff well and with considerable charm, which was more than could be said for Mr Mailer. For one thing, Sophy conceded, Grant looked a lot nicer. His bony face was really rather beautifully shaped and actually had a carved, medieval appearance that went handsomely with its surroundings.

He led them further into the glowing church. There were two or three other groups of sightseers, but compared with the traffic in most celebrated monuments these were few.

Grant explained that even in this, the most recent of the three levels of San Tommaso, there was a great richness of time sequences. When in the twelfth century the ancient church below it was filled in, its treasures, including pieces from the pagan household underneath it, were brought up into this new basilica so that now classical, medieval and renaissance works mingled. 'They've kept company,' Grant said, 'for a long time and have grown together in the process. You can see how well they suit each other.'

'It happens on the domestic level too,' Alleyn said, 'don't you think? In houses that have belonged to the same family for many generations? There's a sort of consonance of differences.'

'Exactly so,' Grant agreed with a quick look at him. 'Shall we move on?'

A wave of scent announced the arrival of Lady Braceley at Alleyn's elbow. 'What a marvellous way of putting it,' she murmured. 'How clever you are.'

The doeskin glove with its skeletal enclosure touched his arm. She tipped her head on one side and was looking up at him.

Sophy, watching, thought a shutter had come down over his face and indeed Alleyn suffered a wave of revulsion and pity and a recognition of despair. I'd give a hell of a lot, he thought, to be shot of this lady.

Sebastian Mailer had come up on the far side of Lady Braceley. He murmured something that Alleyn couldn't catch. Grant was talking again. The hand was withdrawn from Alleyn's arm and the pair turned away and moved out of sight behind the junction of two pilasters.

Now, Alleyn speculated, was Mailer doing a rescue job or had he something particular and confidential to say to Lady Braceley?

Grant led his party into the centre of the nave and through the enclosed *schola cantorum*, saying, Sophy thought, neither too much nor too little but everything well. She herself was caught up in wonder at the great golden bowl-shaped mosaic of the apse. Acanthus and vine twined tenderly together to enclose little groups of everyday persons going about their medieval business. The Cross, dominant though it was, seemed to have grown out of some pre-Christian tree.

'I shall say nothing about the apse,' Grant said. 'It speaks for itself.'

Mailer and Lady Braceley had reappeared. She sat down on a choir bench and whether by some accident of lighting or because she was overtaken by one of those waves of exhaustion that unexpectedly fall upon the old, she looked as if she had shrunk within her own precarious façade. Only for a moment, however. She straightened her back and beckoned her nephew who fidgeted about on the edge of the group, half-attentive and half-impatient. He joined her and they whispered together, he yawning and fidgeting, she apparently in some agitation.

The party moved on round the basilica. The Van der Veghels took photographs and asked a great many questions. They were laboriously well-informed in Roman antiquities.

Presently the Baron, with an arch look, began to inquire about the particular features that appeared so vividly in Grant's novel. Were they not standing, at this very moment, in the place where his characters assembled? Might one not follow, precisely, in the steps they had taken during that wonderful climactic scene?

'O-o-oah!' cried the Baroness running her voice up and down a chromatic scale of enthusiasm. 'It will be so farskinating. Yes?'

Grant reacted to this plea as he had to earlier conversations: with a kind of curbed distaste. He gave Sophy and Alleyn one each of his sharp glances, darted a look of something like pure hatred at Sebastian Mailer and suggested, confusedly, that an author seldom reproduced in scrupulous detail, an actual *mise en scène* any more than he used unadulterated human material. 'I don't mean I didn't start off with San Tommaso,' he shot out at Sophy. 'Of course I did. But I gave it another name and altered it to my purpose.'

'As you had every right to do,' Sophy said boldly and Alleyn

63

thought the two of them were united for the moment in their common field of activity.

'Yes, but do *show* us.' Lady Braceley urged. 'Don't be beastly. *Show* us. You promised. You know you did.'

Kenneth Dorne said, 'Isn't that why we came? Or not? I thought you were to be the great attraction.'

He had approached Grant and stood in an attitude of some elegance, his left arm extended along one of the closure-slabs of the *schola*, his right hand on his hip. It was not a blatant pose but it was explicit nevertheless and at least one aspect of Kenneth was now revealed. He looked at Grant and widened his eyes.

'Is it all a sell-out?' he asked. 'Or have I made a muddle? Or am I merely being impertinent?'

A rabid oath, instantly stifled, burst from Major Sweet. He shouted, 'I beg your pardon,' and glared at a wall-painting of the Foolish Virgins.

'Oh dear,' Kenneth said, still to Grant. 'Now the Major's cross. What *have* I said?' He yawned again and dabbed at his face with his handkerchief.

Grant gave him a comprehensive look. 'Nothing to the purpose,' he said shortly and walked away. Mr Mailer hurried into the breach.

'Naughty!' he tossed at Kenneth and then, vindicating Grant to his disconcerted customers, told them he was unbelievably modest.

Lady Braceley eagerly supported this view as did the Van der Veghels. Grant cut short their plaudits by adopting, with a great effort, it seemed to Alleyn, a brisk and business-like air and by resuming his exposition.

'Of course,' he said, 'if you'd really like to see the equivalent places to those in the book I'll be delighted to point them out, although I imagine if you've read it they declare themselves pretty obviously. There, in the right-hand aisle, for instance, is the picture so much admired by Simon and, I may add, by me. Doubting Saint Thomas, himself, by Masolino da Panicale. Look at those pinks and the "Pompeian" red.'

'Fabulous!' Kenneth restlessly offered. 'Psychedelic, aren't they?'

Grant disregarded this. He said to Sophy. 'He's so *very* doubtful, isn't he? Head on one side, lips pursed up and those gimlet fingers! How right that enormous hospital in London was to adopt him: he's the very pith and marrow of the scientific man, don't you think?'

Sebastian Mailer gave a shrill little cackle of appreciation: perhaps of surprise.

'While we are in this aisle of the basilica,' Grant said, leading them along it for a short distance, 'you may like to see something that I'm afraid I did adopt holus-bolus.'

He showed them a railed enclosure, about six feet by three in size. They collected round it with little cries of recognition.

It encompassed an open rectangular hole like the mouth of a well. Fixed to the rails was a notice, saying in five languages that climbing them was strictly forbidden.

'Listen,' Grant said. 'Can you hear?'

They stood still. Into the silence came the desultory voices of other sightseers moving about the basilica: the voice of a guide out in the atrium, footfalls on marble and a distant rumour of the Roman streets.

'Listen,' Grant repeated and presently from under their feet, scarcely recognizable at first but soon declaring itself, rose the sound of running water, a steady, colloquial voice, complex and unbroken.

'The Cloaca Maxima?' Major Sweet demanded.

'A pure stream leading into it,' Grant rejoined. 'More than sixty feet below us. If you lean over the rail you may be able to see that there is an equivalent opening immediately beneath this one, in the floor of the earlier church. Yet another thirty feet below, out of sight unless someone uses a torch, is a third opening and far down *that*, if a torch is lowered, it's possible to see the stream that we can hear. You may remember that Simon dropped a pebble from here and that it fell down through the centuries into the hidden waters.'

The Van der Veghels broke into excited comment.

Grant, they warmly informed him, had based the whole complex of imagery in his book upon this exciting phenomenon. 'As the deeper reaches of Simon's personality were explored——' on and on they went, explaining the work to its author. Alleyn, who admired the book, thought that they were probably right but laid far too much insistence on an essentially delicate process of thought.

Grant fairly successfully repressed whatever embarrassment he felt.

Suddenly the Baron and Baroness burst out in simultaneous laughter and cries of apology. How ridiculous! How impertinent! Really, what could have possessed them!

Throughout this incident, Major Sweet had contemplated the Van der Veghels with raised eyebrows and a slight snarl. Sophy, stifling a dreadful urge to giggle, found herself observed by Alleyn and Grant, while Lady Braceley turned her huge, deadened lamps from one man to another, eager to respond to whatever mood she might fancy she detected.

Kenneth leant far over the rail and peered into the depths. 'I'm looking down through the centuries,' he announced. His voice was distorted as if he spoke into an enormous megaphone. 'Boom! Boom!' he shouted and was echoed far below. '*Ghost beneath: Swear*,' he boomed, and then: 'Oh God!' He straightened up and was seen to have turned a sickly white. 'I'd forgotten,' he said. 'I'm allergic to heights. What a revolting place.'

'Shall we move on?' said Grant.

Sebastian Mailer led the way to a vestibule where there

was the usual shop for postcards, trinkets and colour slides. Here he produced tickets of admission into the lower regions of San Tommaso.

THREE

The first descent was by way of two flights of stone stairs with a landing between. The air was fresh and dry and smelt only of stone. On the landing was a map of the underground regions and Mailer drew their attention to it.

'There's another one down below,' he said. 'Later on, some of you may like to explore. You can't really get lost: if you think you are, keep on going up any stairs you meet and sooner or later you'll find yourself here. These are very beautiful, aren't they?'

He drew their attention to two lovely pillars laced about with convolvulus tendrils. 'Pagan,' Mr Mailer crooned, 'gloriously pagan. Uplifted from their harmonious resting place in the Flavian house below. By industrious servants of the Vatican. There are ways and ways of looking at the Church's appropriations are there not?'

Major Sweet astonished his companions by awarding this remark a snort of endorsement and approval.

Mr Mailer smiled and continued.

'Before we descend—look, ladies and gentlemen, behind you.'

They turned. In two niches of the opposite wall were terra-cotta sculptures: one a male, ringleted and smiling, the other a tall woman with a broken child in her arms. They were superbly lit from below and seemed to have, at that instant, sprung to life.

'Apollo, it is thought,' Mr Mailer said, 'and perhaps Athena. Etruscan, of course. But the archaic smiles are Greek. The

67

Greeks, you know, despised the Etruscans for their cruelty in battle and there are people who read cruelty into these smiles, transposed to Etruscan mouths.' He turned to Grant: 'You, I believe——' he began and stopped. Grant was staring at the Van der Veghels with an intensity that communicated itself to the rest of the party.

They stood side by side admiring the sculptures. Their likeness, already noticed by Grant, to the Etruscan terra-cottas of the Villa Giulia startlingly declared itself here. It was as if their faces were glasses in which Apollo and Athena smiled at their own images. Sharp arrowhead smiles, full eyes and that almost uncanny liveliness—the lot, thought Alleyn.

It was obvious that all the company had been struck by this resemblance, except, perhaps, Lady Braceley who was uninterested in the Van der Veghels. But nobody ventured to remark on it apart from Sebastian Mailer who, with an extraordinary smirk, murmured as if to himself: 'How *very* remarkable. *Both.*'

The Van der Veghels, busy with flashlights, appeared not to hear him and Alleyn very much doubted if any of the others did. Barnaby Grant was already leading them down a further flight of steps into a church that for fifteen hundred years had lain buried.

In excavating it a number of walls, arches and pillars had been introduced to support the new basilica above it. The ancient church apart from the original apse, was now a place of rather low, narrow passages, of deep shadows and of echoes.

Clearly heard, whenever they all kept still, was the voice of the subterranean stream. At intervals these regions were most skilfully lit so that strange faces with large eyes floated out of the dark: wall-paintings that had been preserved in their long sleep by close-packed earth.

'The air,' Barnaby Grant said, 'has done them no good. They are slowly fading.'

68

'They enjoyed being stifled,' Sebastian Mailer said from somewhere in the rear. He gave out a little whinnying sound.

'More than I do,' Lady Braceley said. 'It's horribly stuffy down here, isn't it?'

'There are plenty of vents,' Major Sweet said: 'The air is noticeably fresh, Lady Braceley.'

'I don't think so,' she complained. 'I don't think I'm enjoying this part, Major. I don't think I want——' She screamed.

They had turned a corner and come face to face with a nude, white man wearing a crown of leaves in his curls. He had full, staring eyes and again the archaic smile. His right arm stretched towards them.

'Auntie darling, what *are* you on about!' Kenneth said. 'He's fabulous. Who is he, Seb?'

'Apollo again. Apollo shines bright in the Mithraic mystery. He was raised up from below by recent excavators to garnish the Galalian corridors.'

'Damn highfalutin' poppycock,' Major Sweet remarked. It was impossible to make out in what camp he belonged.

So Kenneth, Alleyn noted, calls Mailer 'Seb'. Quick work!

'And they are still digging?' the Baron asked Grant as they moved on. 'The Apollo had not risen when your Simon came to S. Tommaso? He is then a contemporary resurrection?'

'A latter-day Lazarus,' fluted Mr Mailer. 'But how *much* more attractive!'

Somewhere in the dark, Kenneth echoed his giggle.

Sophy, who was between Alleyn and Grant, said under her breath, 'I wish they wouldn't,' and Grant made a sound of agreement that seemed to be echoed by Major Sweet.

They continued along the cloister of the old church.

It was now that Baron Van der Veghel developed a playful streak. Holding his camera at the ready and humming a little air, he outstripped the party, turned a corner and disappeared into shadow.

69

Mr Mailer, at this juncture, was in full spate. 'We approach another Etruscan piece,' he said. 'Thought to be Mercury. One comes upon it rather suddenly: on the left.'

It was indeed a sudden encounter. The Mercury was in a deep recess: an entrance, perhaps to some lost passage. He was less strongly lit than the Apollo but the glinting smile was sharp enough.

When they came up with him, a second head rose over his shoulders and smirked at them. A flashlight wiped it out and the echoes rang with Baron Van der Veghel's uninhibited laughter. Lady Braceley gave another scream.

'It's too much,' she cried. 'No. It's too much!'

But the elephantine Van der Veghels, in merry pin, had frisked ahead. Major Sweet let fly anathema upon all practical jokers and the party moved on.

The voice of the subterranean stream grew louder. They turned another corner and came upon another railed well. Grant invited them to look up and there, directly overhead, was the under-mouth of the one they had already examined in the basilica.

'But what were they *for*,' Major Sweet demanded. 'What's the idea? Grant?' he added quickly, apparently to forestall any comment from Mr Mailer.

'Perhaps,' Grant said, 'for drainage. There's evidence that at some stage of the excavations seepage and even flooding occurred.'

'Hah,' said the Major.

The Baroness leant over the rail of the well and peered down.

'Gerrit!' she exclaimed. 'L-oo-ook! There is the sarcophagus! Where Simon sat and meditated!' Her voice, which had something of the reedy quality of a schoolboy's, ran up and down the scale. 'See! Down there! Belo-oow.' Her husband's flashlight briefly explored her vast stern as he gaily snapped her.

70

Heedless, she leant far over the railing.

'Be careful, my darlink!' urged her husband. 'Mathilde! Not so far! Wait till we descend.'

He hauled her back. She was greatly excited and they laughed together.

Alleyn and Sophy approached the well-railing and looked downwards. The area below was illuminated from some unseen source and the end of a stone sarcophagus was clearly visible. From their bird's-eye position they could see that the stone lid was heavily carved.

As they looked, a shadow, much distorted, moved across the wall behind it, disappeared, and was there again, turning this way and that.

Sophy cried out: 'Look! It's—it's that woman!' But it had gone.

'What woman!' Grant asked, behind her.

'The one with the shawl over her head. The postcard-seller. Down there.'

'Did you see her?' Mr Mailer asked quickly.

'I saw her shadow.'

'My dear Miss Jason! Her shadow! There are a thousand Roman women with scarves over their heads who could cast the same shadow.'

'I'm sure not. I'm sure it was she. It looked as if—as if—she wanted to hide.'

'I agree,' Alleyn said.

'Violetta is not permitted to enter the basilica, I assure you. You saw the shadow of someone in another party, of course. Now—let us follow Mr Grant down into the temple of Mithras. He has much to relate.'

They had completed their circuit of the cloisters and entered a passage leading to a spiral iron stairway. The ceiling was lower here and the passage narrow. Grant and Mailer led the way and the others trailed behind them.

71

The head of the little procession had reached the stairhead when Lady Braceley suddenly announced that she couldn't go on.

'I'm frightfully sorry,' she said, 'but I want to go back. I'm afraid you'll think it too dreary of me but I can't, I can't, *I can't* stay in this awful place another moment. You must take me back, Kenneth. I didn't know it'd be like this. I've never been able to endure shut-up places. At once. *Kenneth! Where are you? Kenneth!'*

But he wasn't with them. Her voice flung distorted echoes about the hollows and passages.

'Where's he gone?' she cried out and the whole region replied '—gone—on—on.'

Mailer had taken her by the arm. 'It's all right, Lady Braceley. I assure you. It's perfectly all right. Kenneth went back to photograph the Apollo. In five minutes I will find him for you. Don't distress yourself. No doubt I'll meet him on his way here.'

'I won't wait for him. Why's he suddenly taking photographs? I gave him a camera costing the earth and he never uses it. I won't wait for him, I'll go now. *Now.'*

The Baron and Baroness swarmed gigantically about her making consoling noises. She thrust them aside and made for Grant, Major Sweet and Alleyn who were standing together.

'Please! *Please!'* she implored, and after a quick look round, latched with great determination on to the Major. 'Please take me away!' she implored. 'Please do.'

'My dear lady,' Major Sweet began in tones more consistent with 'My good woman'—'My dear lady, there's no occasion for hysteria. Yes—well, of course, if you insist. Be glad to. No doubt,' said the Major hopefully, 'we'll meet your nephew on our way.'

Clinging to him, she appealed to Grant and Alleyn. 'I

know you think me too hopeless and silly,' she said. 'Don't you?'

'Not at all,' Alleyn said politely, and Grant muttered something that might have been 'claustrophobia'.

Mr Mailer said to the Major: 'There's a continuation of this stairway that goes up into the basilica. If you'll take Lady Braceley that way I'll go back and find Mr Dorne and send him to her.'

Lady Braceley said, 'It's maddening of him. *Honestly!*'

Sophy said, 'Would you like me to come with you, Lady Braceley?'

'Oh, no,' she said. 'No. Thank you. Too kind but——' her voice trailed away.

She still gazed at Alleyn and Grant. She wants an entourage, Sophy thought.

'Well,' Major Sweet said crossly. 'Shall we go?'

He piloted her towards the upper flight of the spiral stairway. 'I'll come back,' he shouted, 'as soon as that young fellow presents himself. Hope he's quick about it.'

'You'll carry on, won't you?' Mr Mailer said to Grant.

'Very well.'

Grant, Alleyn and Sophy embarked on the downward flight. They could hear Lady Braceley's heels receding up the iron treads together with the duller clank of Major Sweet's studded brogues.

Behind them the Van der Veghels shouted excitedly to each other.

'It is only,' roared the Baroness, 'that I do not wish to miss a word, my darlink, that he may let fall upon us.'

'Then on! Go and I will join you. One more picture of the Mercury. Joost one!' cried the Baron.

She assented and immediately fell some distance down the iron stairs. A cry of dismay rose from her husband.

'Mathilde! You are fallen.'

73

'That is so.'

'You are hurt.'

'No. I am uninjured. What a joke.'

'On, then.'

'So.'

The descending spiral made some two or three turns. The sound of running water grew louder. They arrived at a short passage. Grant led them along it into a sort of ante-room.

'This is the insula,' he said. 'You might call it a group of flats. It was built for a Roman family or families somewhere about the middle of the first century. They were not, of course, Christians. You will see in a moment how they worshipped their god. Come into the Triclinium. Which is also the Mithraeum.'

He motioned them into a cave-like chamber. The roof was vaulted and studded with small stones. Massive stone benches ran along the sides and in the centre was an altar.

Grant said, 'You know about the Mithraic cult. There's no need for me——'

'Please! But *please*,' implored the Baroness. 'We would like so much! Everythink! Please!'

Alleyn heard Grant say 'Oh God!' under his breath and saw him look, almost as if he asked for her support, at Sophy Jason. And, for her part, Sophy received this appeal with a ripple of warmth that bewildered her.

'Only if he wants to,' she said.

But Grant, momentarily shutting his eyes, embarked on his task. The Baroness, all eyes and teeth, hung upon his every word. Presently she reached out an imploring hand and whispered, 'Excuse! Forgive me. But for my husband to miss this is too much. I call for him.' She did so with a voice that would have done credit to Brünhilde.

He came downstairs punctually and nimbly and in response to her finger on her lips, fell at once into a receptive attitude.

Grant caught Sophy's eye, scowled at her, momentarily shut his own eyes, and, in an uneven voice told them about the cult of the god Mithras. It was, he said, a singularly noble religion and persisted, literally underground, after other pagan forms of worship had been abolished in Christian Rome.

'The god Mithras,' he said, and although at first he used formal, guide-book phrases, he spoke so directly to Sophy that they might have been alone together, 'the god Mithras was born of a rock. He was worshipped in many parts of the ancient world including England and was, above all, a god of light. Hence his association with Apollo who commanded him to kill the Bull which is the symbol of fertility. In this task he was helped by a Dog and a Snake but a Scorpion double-crossed him and spilled the bull's blood from which all life was created. And in that way evil was let loose upon mankind.'

'Yet another expulsion from Eden?' Sophy said.

'Sort of. Strange, isn't it? As if blind fingers groped about some impenetrable, basic design.'

'Curse of mankind!' Major Sweet proclaimed.

He had rejoined the party unnoticed and startled them by this eruption. 'Religions,' he announced, 'Bally-hoo! The lot of them! Scoundrels!'

'Do you think so?' Grant asked mildly. 'Mithras doesn't seem so bad, on the whole, His was a gentle cult for those days. His worship was Mystery and the initiates passed through seven degrees. It was tough going. They underwent lustral purification, long abstinence and most severe deprivation. Women had no part of it. You wouldn't have been allowed,' he told Sophy, 'to enter this place, still less to touch the altar. Come and look at it.'

'You make me feel I shouldn't.'

'Ah, no!' cried the Baroness. 'We must not be superstitious,

75

Miss Jason. Let us look, because it is very beautiful, see, and most interestink.'

The altar was half-way down the Mithraeum. The slaughter of the Bull was indeed very beautifully carved on one face and the apotheosis of Mithras assisted by Apollo on another.

To Grant's evident dismay Baron Van der Veghel had produced out of his vast canvas satchel, a copy of *Simon*.

'We must,' he announced, 'hear again the wonderful passage. See, Mr Grant, here is the book. Will the author not read it for us? How this English Simon finds in himself some equivalent to the Mithraic powers. Yes?'

'Ah, no!' Grant ejaculated. 'Please!' He looked quickly about and beyond the group of six listeners as if to assure himself that there were no more. 'That's *not* in the bargain,' he said. 'Really.' And Alleyn saw him redden. 'In any case,' said Grant. 'I read abominably. Come and look at Mithras himself.'

And at the far end of the chamber, there was the god in a grotto, being born out of a stony matrix: a sturdy person with a Phrygian cap on his long curls and a plumpish body: neither child nor man.

Alleyn said: 'They made sacrifices, didn't they? In here.'

'Of course. On the altar,' Grant said quickly. 'Can you imagine! A torch-lit scene, it would be, and the light would flicker across those stone benches and across the faces of initiates, attenuated and wan from their ordeal. The altar fire raises a quivering column of heat, the sacrificial bull is lugged in: perhaps they hear it bellowing in the passages. There is a passage, you know, running right round the chamber. Probably the bull appears from a doorway behind Mithras. Perhaps it's garlanded. The acolytes drag it in and the priest receives it. Its head is pulled back, the neck exposed and the knife plunged in. The reek of fresh blood and the stench of

76

the burnt offering fills the Mithraeum. I suppose there are chanted hymns.'

Sophy said dryly: 'You gave us to understand that the Mithraic cult was a thoroughly nice and, did you say, gentle religion.'

'It was highly moral and comparatively gentle. Loyalty and fidelity were the ultimate virtues. Sacrifice was a necessary ingredient.'

'Same idea,' Major Sweet predictably announced, 'behind the whole boiling. Sacrifice. Blood, Flesh. Cannibalism. More refinement in one lot, more brutality in another. Essentially the same.'

'You don't think,' Alleyn mildly suggested, 'that this might indicate pot-shots at some fundamental truth?'

'Only fundamental truth it indicates—humans are carnivores,' shouted the Major in triumph. 'Yak-yak-yak,' he added and was understood to be laughing.

'It is so unfortunate,' said Baron Van der Veghel, 'that Lady Braceley and Mr Dorne are missing all this. And where is Mr Mailer?'

'Did you see them?' Alleyn asked Major Sweet.

'I did not. I put *her* in the—what d'you call it? Garden? Courtyard?'

'Atrium?'

'Whatever it is. On the bench. She didn't much like it, but still . . . silly woman.'

'What about young Dorne?' Alleyn said.

'Didn't see 'im. Frightful specimen.'

'And Mailer?'

'No. Damn casual treatment, I call it. What do we do now?'

Grant said with that air of disengagement that clung about him so persistently: 'I understand it was thought that you might like to look round here under your own steam for a few minutes. We can meet again here, or if you prefer it, up above in the atrium. I'll stay here for ten minutes in case there's anything you want to ask and then I'll go up and wait in the atrium. We'll probably meet on the way and in any case you can't get lost. There are "out" notices everywhere. I'm sure Mailer——' He broke off. Somebody was approaching down the iron stairway.

'Here he is,' Grant said.

But it was only Kenneth Dorne.

He had sounded to be in a hurry and made a precipitate entry but when he came out of the shadows and saw the others he halted and slouched towards them. His camera dangled from his hand. It struck Sophy that he was, in some unsatisfactory way, assuaged and comforted.

'Hullo,' he said. 'Where's my aunt?'

Grant informed him. He said 'Oh dear!' and giggled.

'Hadn't you better take a look at her?' Major Sweet asked.

'What?'

'Your aunt. She's up top. In the garden.'

'May she flourish,' Kenneth said, 'like the Green Bay Tree. Dear Major.'

Major Sweet contemplated him for one or two seconds. 'Words,' he then said, 'fail me.'

'Well,'' Kenneth rejoined, 'thank God for that.'

This produced a kind of verbal stalemate.

It was broken by the Van der Veghels. They had, they excitedly explained, hoped so much (ah, *so* much, interpolated the Baroness), that Mr Grant would be persuaded to read aloud the Mithraic passage from *Simon* in its inspirational environment. As everybody saw, they had brought their copy—was it too much, even, to ask for a signature?— to that end. They understood, none better, the celebrated Anglo-Saxon reticence. But after all, the terms of the brochure, not of course to be insisted upon *au pied de la lettre*, had encouraged them to believe . . .

They went on along these lines with a sort of antiphonal reproachfulness and Grant's face, even in that dim light, could be seen to grow redder and redder.

At last he turned helplessly to Sophy, who muttered, 'Hadn't you better?' and was strangely gratified when he said at once and at large, 'If you really want it, of course. I didn't mean to be disobliging. It's only that I'll feel such an ass.'

The Van der Veghels broke into delighted laughter and the Baron developed a more extravagant flight of fancy. They would take a photograph; a group at the centre of which would be Grant, reading aloud. In the background, the god Mithras himself would preside over the work he had inspired. This extraordinary variant on Victorian group-photography was put into operation after a playful argument between the Van der Veghels about their active and passive roles. Finally they agreed that the Baroness would take the first picture and she went excitedly into action. The wretched Grant, with open book, was placed upon an obscure stone protrusion to the left of Mithras, Alleyn on his one hand and Sophy, who was beginning to get the giggles, on the other. Behind Sophy posed Major Sweet and behind Alleyn, Kenneth Dorne.

'And you, Gerrit, my darlink,' the Baroness instructed her husband, 'because you are so big, yes? at the rear.'

'Afterwards we exchange,' he urged.

'So.'

'And all to concentrate upon the open page.'

'Ach. So.'

Major Sweet always unpredictable, took a serious view of this business. 'How,' he objected, 'are we to concentrate on something we can scarcely see.'

And indeed, it was well-urged. The head of the little god, like the altar and all the other effigies in these regions, was

79

cleverly lit from a concealed niche but his surroundings were deep in shadow, none more so than the area in which the group was deployed. The Van der Veghels explained that all would be revealed by the flashlamp. Their great desire was that the god should be incorporated in the group and to this end a little make-believe was to be excused.

Grant's discomfiture had become so evident that Alleyn and Sophy Jason, simultaneously but without consultation, decided upon a note of high comedy.

'I see,' Alleyn suddenly offered. 'Even if we can't see it, we're to gaze upon the book? Fair enough. And I expect Mr Grant knows the passage by heart. Perhaps he could recite it for us in the dark.'

'I can do nothing of the sort, damn you,' Grant said warmly.

The Baroness explained. Afterwards they would move into a more luminous spot and Grant would then, without subterfuge, read the appropriate passage.

In the meantime, the Baroness reiterated, would they all concentrate upon the almost imperceptible page.

After a good deal of falling about in the dark the group assembled. 'Would it be pretty,' Alleyn suggested, 'if Miss Jason were to point out a passage in the book and I were to place my arm about the author's shoulders, eagerly seeking to read it?'

'*What* a good suggestion,' Sophy cried. 'And Major Sweet could perhaps bend over on the other side.'

'Delighted, I'm sure,' said the Major with alacrity and did bend very closely over Sophy. 'Damn good idea, what,' he whistled into her ear.

'It recalls,' Alleyn remarked, 'Tchekov reading aloud to Stanislavsky and the Moscow Arts players.'

This observation was received with loud applause from the Baroness.

Sophy and Alleyn crowded up to Grant.

'You shall suffer for this,' Grant said between his teeth. 'Both of you.'

'On the book, on the book, all on the book!' gaily chanted the Baroness. 'Nobody to move. Gerrit, you must step a little back and Mr Dorne, are you there, please?'

'Oh God, yes, I'm here.'

'Good. Good. And so, all are ready? Freeze, please. I shoot.'

The camera clicked but the darkness was uninterrupted. The Baroness who had uttered what was no doubt a strong expletive in her own language now followed it up with a reproach to her husband. 'What did I tell you, my darlink! They are useless these local bulps. No! Do not answer. Do not move. I have another in my pocket. Not to move anybody, please, or speak. I find it.'

Sophy giggled. Major Sweet immediately groped for her waist.

'Serve you bloody well right,' whispered Grant to Sophy. He had detected this manœuvre. From somewhere not far away but beyond the Mithraeum there came the sound, distorted as all sounds were in that region, by echoes, as of a high-pitched voice.

There followed a seemingly interminable interval broken after a time by a distant thud as of a heavy door being shut. The Baroness fiddled and muttered. Kenneth detached himself from the group and took a flashlight shot of the god. He was urged back into position and at last the Baroness was ready.

'Please. Please. Attention. Freeze, please. Again, I shoot.'

This time the light flashed, they were all blinded and the Baroness gave out loud cries of satisfaction and insisted upon taking two more.

Against mounting impatience the group was then re-formed

with the Baroness replacing her husband and over-hanging Major Sweet like some primitive earthmother. The Baron had better luck with his flashlamp and all was accomplished.

'Although,' he said. 'it would have been nicer to have included our cicerone, would it not?'

'Must say he's taking his time,' Major Sweet grumbled. 'Damned odd sort of behaviour if you ask me.'

But Kenneth pointed out that Sebastian Mailer was probably keeping his aunt company in the atrium. 'After all,' he said to Grant, 'he handed over to you, didn't he?'

Grant, under pressure from the Van der Veghels, now moved into the area of light and with every sign of extreme reluctance read the Mithraic passage from *Simon* to this most strangely assorted audience. He read rapidly and badly in an uninflected voice but something of the character of his writing survived the treatment.

'——Nothing had changed. The dumpy god with Phrygian cap, icing-sugar ringlets, broken arms and phallus rose from his matrix of stony female breasts. A rather plebeian god one might have said, but in his presence fat little Simon's ears heaved with the soundless roar of a sacrificial bull, his throat and the back of his nose were stung by blood that nineteen centuries ago had boiled over white-hot stone, and his eyes watered in the reek of burning entrails. He trembled and was immeasurably gratified.'

The reading continued in jerks to the end of the appropriate passage.

Grant shut the book with a clap, passed it like a hot potato to the Baroness and hitched his shoulders against obligatory murmurs from his audience. These evaporated into an uneasy silence.

Sophy felt oppressed. For the first time claustrophobia threatened her. The roof seemed lower, the walls closer, the regions beyond them very much quieter as if the group had been deserted, imprisoned almost, so many fathoms deep in the ground. For tuppence, she thought, I could do a bolt like Lady Braceley.

Grant repeated his suggestion that the others might like to explore and that he himself would remain for ten minutes in the Mithraeum in case anyone preferred to rejoin him there before returning to the upper world. He reminded them that there were side openings and an end one, leading into surrounding passages, and the insula.

Kenneth Dorne said he would go up and take a look at his aunt. He seemed to be more relaxed and showed a tendency to laugh at nothing in particular. 'Your reading was m-a-a-r-vellous,' he said to Grant and smiled from ear to ear. 'I adore your Simon.' He laughed immoderately and left by the main entrance.

Major Sweet said he would take a look-see round and rejoin them above. 'I have,' he threatened, 'a bone to pick with Mailer. Extraordinary behaviour.' He stared at Sophy. 'Thinking of looking round at all?' he invited.

'I think I'll stay put for a moment,' she said. She did not at all fancy roaming in a Mithraic gloaming with the Major.

Alleyn said he, too, would find his own way back and the Van der Veghels who had been photographing each other against the sacrificial altar decided to join him, not, Sophy thought, entirely to his delight.

Major Sweet left by one of the side doors. Alleyn disappeared behind the god, enthusiastically followed by the Van der Veghels. They could be heard ejaculating in some distant region. Their voices died and there was no more sound except, Sophy fancied, the cold babble of that subterranean stream.

'Come and sit down,' Grant said.

She joined him on one of the stone benches.

'Are you feeling a bit oppressed?'

'Sort of.'

'Shall I take you up? There's no need to stay. That lot are all right under their own steam. Say the word.'

'How kind,' Sophy primly rejoined, 'but, thank you, no. I'm not all that put out. It's only——'

'Well?'

'I've got a theory about walls.'

'*Walls?*'

'Surfaces. Any surfaces.'

'Do explain yourself.'

'You'll be profoundly unimpressed.'

'One never knows. Try me.'

'Mightn't surfaces—wood, stone, cloth, anything you like —have a kind of physical sensitivity we don't know about? Something like the coating on photographic film? So that they retain impressions of happenings that have been exposed to them. And mightn't some people have an element in their physical make-up—their chemical or electronic arrangements or whatever—that is responsive to this and aware of it?'

'As if other people were colour-blind and only they saw red?'

'That's the idea.'

'That would dispose rather neatly of ghosts, wouldn't it?'

'It wouldn't be only the visual images the surfaces retained. It'd be emotions too.'

'Do you find your idea an alarming one?'

'Disturbing, rather.'

'Well—yes.'

'I wonder if it might fit in with your Simon.'

'Ah,' ejaculated Grant, 'don't remind me of that, for God's sake!'

'I'm sorry,' Sophy said, taken aback by his violence.

He got up, walked away and with his back turned to her

said rapidly, 'All right, why don't you say it! If I object so strongly to all this show-off, why the hell do I do it? That's what you're thinking, isn't it? Come on. *Isn't it?*'

'If I am it's no business of mine. And anyway I *did* say it. Up above.' She caught her breath. 'It seems ages ago,' said Sophy. 'Ages.'

'We've dropped through some twenty centuries, after all. And I'm sorry to have been so bloody rude.'

'Think nothing of it,' Sophy said. She looked up at the sharply lit head of Mithras. 'He is not very formidable after all. Plump and placid, really, wouldn't you say? Isn't it odd, though, how those blank eyes seem to stare? You'd swear they had pupils. Do you suppose——'

She cried out. The god had gone. Absolute darkness had closed down upon them like a velvet shutter.

'It's all right,' Grant said. 'Don't worry. They do it as a warning for closing time. It'll go on again in a second.'

'Thank the Lord for that. It's—it's so completely black. One might be blind.'

'"All dark and comfortless"?'

'That's from *Lear*, isn't it? Not exactly a reassuring quotation, if I may say so.'

'Where are you?'

'Here.'

In a distant region there was a rumour of voices: distorted, flung about some remote passage. Grant's hand closed on Sophy's arm. The god came into being again, staring placidly at nothing.

'There you are,' Grant said. 'Come on. We'll climb back into contemporary Rome, shall we?'

'Please.'

He moved his hand up her arm and they embarked on the return journey.

Through the insula, a left turn and then straight towards

85

the iron stairway, passing a cloistral passage out of which came the perpetual voice of water. Up the iron stairway. Through the second basilica, past Mercury, and Apollo, and then up the last flight of stone steps towards the light, and here was the little shop: quite normal and bright.

The people in charge of the postcard and holy trinket stalls, a monk and two youths, were shutting them up. They looked sharply at Grant and Sophy.

'No more,' Grant said to them. 'We are the last.'

They bowed.

'There's no hurry,' he told Sophy. 'The upper basilica stays open until sunset.'

'Where will the others be?'

'Probably in the atrium.'

But the little garden was quite deserted and the basilica almost so. The last belated sightseers were hurrying away through the main entrance.

'He's mustered them outside,' Grant said. 'Look—there they are. Come on.'

And there, in the outer porch where they had originally assembled, were Mr Mailer's guests in a dissatisfied huddle: the Van der Veghels, the Major, Lady Braceley, Kenneth and, removed from them, Alleyn. The two sumptuous cars were drawn up in the roadway.

Grant and Alleyn simultaneously demanded of each other: 'Where's Mailer?' and then, with scarcely a pause: 'Haven't *you* seen him?'

But nobody, it transpired, had seen Mr Mailer.

4. Absence of Mr Mailer

'NOT SINCE he slouched off to find *you*,' Major Sweet shouted, glaring at Kenneth. 'Down below, there.'

'Find *me*,' Kenneth said indifferently. 'I don't know what you're talking about. I haven't seen him.'

Alleyn said, 'He went back to find you when you returned to photograph the Apollo.'

'He must have changed his mind then. Last I saw of him was—you know—it was—you know, it was just before I went back to Apollo.'

Kenneth's voice dragged strangely. He gave an aimless little giggle, closed his eyes and reopened them sluggishly. By the light of day, Alleyn saw that the pupils had contracted. 'Yes, that's right,' Kenneth drawled, 'I remember. It was then.'

'And he didn't follow you and Lady Braceley, Major Sweet?'

'I imagined that to be perfectly obvious, sir. He did not.'

'And he didn't join you, Lady Braceley, in the atrium?'

'If that's the rather dismal little garden where the gallant Major dumped me,' she said, 'the answer is no. Mr Mailer didn't join me there or anywhere else. I don't know why,' she added, widening her terrible eyes at Alleyn, 'but that sounds vaguely improper, don't you think?'

Major Sweet, red in the face, said unconvincingly that he had understood Lady Braceley would prefer to be alone in the atrium.

'That,' she said, 'would have rather depended on what was offering as an alternative.'

'I must say——' he began in a fluster, but Alleyn interrupted him.

'Would you stay where you are, all of you,' Alleyn said. And to Grant, 'You're in charge, aren't you? Be a good chap and see they stay put, will you?'

He was gone—back into the church.

'By God, that's pretty cool I must say,' fumed the Major. 'Ordering people about, damn it, like some blasted policeman. Who the devil does he think he is!'

'I fancy,' Grant said, 'we'd better do as he suggests.'

'Why?'

'Because,' Grant said with a half-smile at Sophy, 'he seems to have what Kent recognized in Lear.'

'What the hell's that?'

'Authority.'

'How right you are,' said Sophy.

'I think he's gorgeous,' Lady Braceley agreed, '*too* compulsive and masterful.'

A long and uneasy silence followed this appraisal.

'But what's he *doing*?' Kenneth suddenly asked. 'Where's he gone?'

'I'm blasted well going to find out,' the Major announced.

As he was about to carry out this threat, Alleyn was seen, returning quickly, through the basilica.

Before Major Sweet could launch, as he clearly intended to do, a frontal attack, Alleyn said:

'Do forgive me, all of you. I'm afraid I was insufferably bossy but I thought it as well to go back and ask at the shop if Mr Mailer had come through.'

'All right, all right,' said the Major. 'Had he?'

'They say not.'

'They might not have noticed him,' Grant offered.

'It's possible, of course, but they know him by sight and say they were waiting for him to go out. They check the numbers of tickets for the lower regions in order to guard against shutting someone in.'

'What's he doing, skulking down there?' the Major demanded. 'I call it a damn poor show. Leaving us high and dry.' He attacked Grant. 'Look here, Grant, you're on the strength here, aren't you? Part of the organization, whatever it is.'

'Absolutely not. I've nothing to do with it. Or him,' Grant added under his breath.

'My dear fellow, your name appears in their literature.'

'In a purely honorary capacity.'

'I suppose,' Kenneth said, 'it's publicity for you, isn't it?'

'I'm not in need——' Grant began and then turned white. 'Isn't all this beside the point?' he asked Alleyn.

'I'd have thought so. The people in charge have gone down to find him. There's a complete system of fluorescent lighting kept for maintenance, excavation and emergencies. If he's there they'll find him.'

'He may have been taken ill or something,' Sophy hazarded.

'That is so, that is so,' cried the Van der Veghels like some rudimentary chorus. They often spoke in unison. 'He is of a sickly appearance,' the Baroness added. 'And sweats a great deal,' said her husband, clinching the proposition.

The two drivers now crossed the road. Giovanni, the one who spoke English and acted as an assistant guide, invited the ladies and gentlemen to take their seats in the cars. Alleyn asked if they had seen Mr Mailer. The drivers put their heads on one side and raised their hands and shoulders. No.

'Perhaps,' Lady Braceley said in an exhausted voice, 'he's fallen down those horrid-awful stairs. Poorest Mr Mailer.

Do you know, I think I will sit in the car. I'm no good at standing about on my gilded pins.'

She swivelled one of her collective stares between Grant, Alleyn and the Baron and got into the car, finding a moment to smile into the face of Giovanni as he opened the door. Established, she leant out of the window. 'The offer of a cigarette,' she said, 'would be met in the spirit in which it was made.'

But only Kenneth, it seemed, could oblige and did so, leaning his face down to his aunt's as he offered his lighter. They spoke together, scarcely moving their lips and for a moment or two looked alike.

Grant muttered to Alleyn, 'This is a bloody rum turn-up for the books, isn't it?'

'Rum enough, yes.'

Sophy said, 'Of course, they'll find him, won't they? I mean they must.'

'You were together, weren't you, after the rest of us left?'

'Yes,' they said.

'And returned together?'

'Of course,' Grant said. 'You saw us. Why?'

'You were the last out by some moments. You didn't hear anything? Mailer's wearing rather heavy shoes. They made quite a noise, I noticed, on the iron steps.'

No, they said. They hadn't heard a thing.

'I think I'll go back, Grant. Care to come?'

'Back? You mean—down below again?'

'If necessary.'

'I'll come,' Grant said, 'as far as the office—the shop. I'm not madly keen to traipse round the nether regions after Mailer. If he's there the staff'll find him.'

'All right. But don't you think something ought to be done about this lot?'

'Look here,' Grant said angrily, 'I've already said I accept no responsibility for this turn-out. Or for anyone in it——' his voice wavered and he glanced at Sophy. 'Except Miss Jason who's on her own.'

'I'm all right,' Sophy said airily and to Alleyn, 'What should we do? Can you suggest anything?'

'Suppose you all carry on with your picnic on the Palatine Hill? The drivers will take you there. The one that speaks English—Giovanni—seems to be a sort of second-in-command. I'm sure he'll take over. No doubt they'll unpack hampers and lay on the charm: they're wonderful at that. I'll unearth Mailer and if he's all right we'll follow you up. It'll be a lovely evening on the Palatine Hill.'

'What do you think?' Sophy asked Grant.

'It's as good an idea as any other.' He turned to Alleyn. 'Sorry to be bloody-minded,' he said. 'Shall we go back in there, then?'

'On second thoughts I won't bother you. If you wouldn't mind fixing things with Giovanni—I suggest that even if I don't reappear with Mailer in hand, you carry on with the programme. The alfresco tea, then back to your hotels and the cars will pick you all up again at nine o'clock. You're at the Gallico, aren't you? You might be very kind and just make a note of where the others are staying. There I go, bossing again. Never mind.'

He gave Sophy a little bow and as Major Sweet bore down upon them, neatly side-stepped him and returned to the basilica.

'I'll be damned,' said Barnaby Grant.

'I dare say,' Sophy said. 'But all the same you'll do it. It's like what you said.'

'*What* did I say, smarty-pants?'

'He's got authority.'

When Alleyn got back to the vestibule he found the shop still in process of closure. An iron lattice gate with a formidable padlock shut off the entrance to the lower regions. S. Tommaso in Pallaria, like its sister basilica, S. Clemente, is in the care of Irish Dominicans. The monk in charge—Father Denys, it transpired—spoke with a superb brogue. Like so many Irishmen in exile, he had the air of slightly putting it on as if he played his own part in some pseudo-Hibernian comedy. He greeted Alleyn like an old acquaintance.

'Ah, it's yourself again,' he said. 'And I have no news for you. This fellow Mailer's not below. We've had the full power of the lighting on and it's enough to dazzle the eyes out of your head. I'm after looking beneath with these two young chaps——' he indicated his assistants. 'We made a great hunt of it, every nook and cranny. He's not there, at all, no doubt of it.'

'How very odd,' Alleyn said. 'He's in charge of our party, you know. What can have happened to him?'

'Well now, it's a strange occurrence and no mistake. I can only suggest he must have slipped through here at a great pace when we were all occupied and never noticed 'um. Though that's not an easy thing to credit, for as I've mentioned we keep a tally ever since a Scandinavian lady twisted a fetlock and got herself locked in five years ago and she screeching all night to no avail and discovered clean demented, poor soul, in the morning. And another thing. Your party was the only one beneath, for the one or two odd visitors had come out before you arrived. So he would have been on his own and the more noticeable for it.'

'I don't want to make a nuisance of myself, Father, and I don't for a moment suggest your search wasn't thorough but would you mind if I——?'

'I would not but I can't permit it. It's the rule of the place, d'ye see. No visitors beneath under any pretext after closure.'

'Yes, I see. Then—is there a telephone I could use?'

'There is and welcome. In here. You can go, now,' he said over his shoulder to his assistants and repeated it in Italian.

He opened a door into a store-cupboard, pointed to a telephone and switched on a light.

There wasn't much room or air when the door was shut. Alleyn backed gingerly into an open box of holy trinkets, eased himself into a crouch supported by the edge of a shelf, examined his memory and dialled the resulting number.

Il Questore Valdarno had not left his office. He listened to Alleyn's story with an animation that was almost tangible but with few interruptions.

When Alleyn had finished, Valdarno said in English: 'He has run.'

'Run?'

'Flown. He has recognized you and decamped.'

'They seem pretty sure, here, that he couldn't have got past them.'

'Ah, ah, ah,' said the Questore contemptuously, 'who are they? a monk and two pale shop boys. Against this expert! Pah! He has run away at the double-up behind the show-cases.'

'Speaking of postcards, there was a savage elderly postcard lady in the entrance who made a scene with Mailer.'

'A scene? How?'

'Yelling abuse at him. It was not in the sort of Italian we learnt in my Diplomatic days but the general drift was invective and fury.'

Alleyn could almost hear the Questore's shrug.

'He has done something to annoy her, perhaps,' he suggested in his melancholy voice.

'She spat at him.'

93

'Ah,' sighed the Questore. 'He had irritated her.'

'No doubt,' Alleyn faintly agreed. 'She's called Violetta,' he added.

'Why do you concern yourself with this woman, my dear colleague?'

'Well, if I understood her at all, she threatened to kill him.'

'Evidently a short-tempered woman. Some of these street-vendors are in fact badly-behaved persons.'

'I thought he was greatly disturbed by the encounter. He made light of it but he turned very white.'

'Ah.' There was a brief silence. 'She sells postcards outside S. Tommaso?'

'Yes. One of our party thought she saw her shadow on the wall of a passage down in the Mithraeum.'

'They are not permitted to enter.'

'So I gathered.'

'I will have inquiries made. I will also have the airports, omnibus and railway stations watched. I feel there is a strong probability Mailer has recognized you and will attempt an escape.'

'I am deeply obliged to you, Signor Questore.'

'Please!'

'But I confess the chances of his recognizing me—we have never met—do seem a bit thin.'

'Some contact of his, an English contact, may have seen you and informed him. It is most possible.'

'Yes,' Alleyn said, 'it's possible of course.'

'We shall see. In the meantime, my dear Superintendent, may I have a little speech with this Dominican?'

'I'll call him.'

'And we keep in close touch, isn't it?'

'Of course.'

'With my compliments, then,' said Il Questore Valdarno sadly.

Alleyn returned to the shop and delivered his message.

'Il Questore Valdarno, is it?' said Father Denys. 'You didn't let on this was a pollis affair but it doesn't surprise me at all. Wait, now, and I'll talk to 'um.'

He did so in voluble Italian and returned looking perturbed. 'It's a queer business,' he said, 'and I don't say I fancy the turn it's taking. He wants to send in some of his fellows to search below and is going to talk to my Superior about it. I told 'um we'd overlooked every inch of the place but that doesn't satisfy the man. He says will I tell you you're welcome to join in. Eight sharp in the morning.'

'Not tonight?'

'Ah, why would it be tonight and himself if he's below, which he's not, locked up like a fish in a tin.' Father Denys looked pretty sharply at Alleyn. 'You're not the cut of a policeman, yourself,' he said. 'None of my business, of course.'

'Do I look like a harmless visitor? I hope I do. Tell me, do you know anything about the woman called Violetta who sells postcards here?'

Father Denys clapped his hand to his forehead. 'Violetta, is it!' he ejaculated. 'A terrible pest, that one, God forgive me, for she's touched in her wits, poor creature. Sure, this other business put her clean out of my mind. Come into the atrium till I tell you. We'll lock up this place.'

He did lock up the vestibule and pretty securely, too, fetching a great key out of a pocket in his habit. Nobody else had that one or a key to the iron grille he said, except Brother Dominic who opened up in the morning.

The basilica was now deserted and the time six o'clock. All the bells in Rome rang the Ave Maria and Father Denys took time off to observe it. He then led the way into the atrium and settled beside Alleyn on a stone bench, warm with the westering sun. He was a cosy man and enjoyed a gossip.

Violetta, he said, had sold postcards in the entrance to

95

S. Tommaso for some months. She was a Sicilian of dubious origins, was not as old as Alleyn may have supposed and when she first appeared carried upon her the remnants of ferocious good looks. Her story, which she never ceased to pour out, was that her husband had deserted her and in doing so had betrayed her to the police.

'For doing what?' Alleyn asked.

'Ah, she never lets on exactly. Something to do with passing prohibited articles. Likely enough stolen, though she makes out she'd no notion what mischief was in it till the pollis came down upon her and destroyed her. She's very wild in her conversation and the saints themselves wouldn't know which was fact and which was fantasy.'

She had behaved herself reasonably well, however, reserving her outbursts for the Dominicans and sticking to her legal postcard-vending territory until about two days ago when he had found her squatting in a corner of the porch letting out the most frightful animadversions in a hissing torrent and shaking her fists. She literally foamed at the mouth and was quite incoherent, but after Father Denys had rebuked her for blasphemy and, Alleyn gathered, sorted her out in a pretty big way, she became slightly more comprehensible.

Her rage, it emerged, had been directed at a person who had visited the Sacristy to discuss arrangements for sightseeing trips by a newly-formed enterprise called——

'Don't tell me,' Alleyn said as Father Denys paused for dramatic effect. 'Let me guess. Called "Il Cicerone".'

'Right for you.'

'In the person of Mr Sebastian Mailer?'

'Right again,' cried Father Denys, clapping his hands together. 'And the poor creature's husband or if he's not he ought to be, God help him.'

It was past five o'clock on that very warm afternoon when two cars arrived at the Palatine Hill. The air smelt of sunny earth, grass, myrtle and resin. In lengthening shadows poppies made little scarlet exclamations, and legions of acanthus marched down the contours of the hill. The skies had deepened behind broken columns and arches: the bones of classic Rome.

Giovanni, the driver, had responded with gusto to the role of guide. He said that he had no notion of what had befallen Mr Mailer but suggested that a sudden onslaught of the affliction known to tourists as Roman Tummy might have overtaken him. By its nature, Giovanni delicately reminded them, it necessitated an immediate withdrawal. He then led his party across the ruins of Domus Augustana and down a little flight of steps towards a grove of pines. Back again and here and there he led them giving names to ruins and with sweeps of his arms laying Rome at their feet.

Sophy looked and dreamed and ached with pleasure and did not listen very closely to Giovanni. She was suddenly tired and vaguely happy.

Barnaby Grant walked beside her in companionable silence, the Van der Veghels thundered about with cries of appreciation, a thousand inquiries and much photography. Lady Braceley, arm-in-arm with Kenneth and the reluctant Major, trailed and hobbled in the rear and could be heard faintly lamenting the rough going.

'I've a low saturation point for sights,' Sophy remarked. 'Or rather for information about sights. I stop listening.'

'Well,' Grant said kindly, 'at least you admit it.'

'I'd have you know, it doesn't mean that I'm insensible to all this.'

'All right. I didn't suppose you were.'

'On the contrary, I'm knocked dumb. Or nearly dumb,' Sophy amended. 'You may say: *visually* speechless.'

He looked at her with amusement. 'I daresay you're hungry,' he offered.

'And I dare say you're right,' she agreed in surprise. 'Thirsty, anyway.'

'Look, we're settling for our tea.'

They had come to a terrain called the Belvedere and looked beyond the tops of a pine grove to the monstrous splendour of the Colosseum. Spires, roofs, gardens, an obelisk, insubstantial in the late afternoon haze, swam into the distance and dissolved against the Alban Hills.

Giovanni and his assistant, having found a place by a fallen column, spread rugs and cloths and opened hampers.

It was, as Sophy said, an exquisite snack: delicate little sandwiches of smoked salmon and caviare: Roman and Neapolitan pastries, fruit and a chilled white wine. There was also, surprisingly, whisky and soda. And tea for anybody who preferred it as Sophy herself did, iced with lemon, and very fragrant.

What a rum little lot we are, she thought indulgently. A light breath of air brought a stronger whiff of myrtle and pine needles with it and momentarily lifted her hair from her forehead.

She found that Grant looked fixedly at her and she said hurriedly: 'We none of us seem to be worrying about poor Mr Mailer, do we?'

He made a sharp movement of his hands. 'No doubt our authoritative friend has coped,' he said.

Major Sweet, having eaten very heartily and made smart work of two whiskies-and-soda, appeared to be in a mollified condition. He said: 'Most extraordinary chap. My opinion.' But lazily and without rancour. '"Strordinary good tea,' he added.

'*I* think,' Lady Braceley said, 'we're all getting along very nicely as we are—with Giovanni,' and gave Giovanni a sufficiently lingering glance. 'Although,' she said, 'it's a pity that other gorgeous brute's deserted us.'

'What exactly,' Kenneth asked restlessly, 'is the programme for tonight? Cars at nine—for where? Where do we dine?'

'At the Gioconda, sir,' Giovanni said.

'Good God!' the Major ejaculated. As well he might. The Gioconda is the most exclusive as it is undoubtedly the most expensive restaurant in Rome.

'Really?' Lady Braceley said. 'Then I must make up my quarrel with Marco. We had a row about tables last week. He turfed out a Mexican attaché or somebody thought to be rather grand, and gave his table to me. There was almost an international incident. I told him I hated that sort of thing. Actually it was too naughty of him.'

'This time,' Kenneth said, 'darling Auntie, you'll find yourself with a set dinner at a back table near the service door. If I know anything about escorted tours.'

'Excuse me, but no, sir,' Giovanni said. 'This is not such an arrangement. The service is in all ways as for the best. You will order, if you please, what you wish.'

'And pay for it?' Kenneth asked rudely.

'On the contrary, sir, no. I will attend to the settlement.' He turned to Grant. 'When you are ready to leave, sir,' he said, 'will you please ask your waiter to send for me? I will make the tipping also, but of course if any of you is inclined—' he made an eloquent gesture. 'But it will not be necessary,' he said.

'Well!' the Major ejaculated, 'I must say this is—ah—it seems—ah—' he boggled slightly—'quite in order,' he said. 'What?'

The Van der Veghels eagerly concurred. 'At first,' the Baron confided to Sophy, 'my wife and I thought perhaps the

99

charge was too much—a ridiculous amount—but Mr Mailer impressed us so greatly, and then'— he gaily bowed to Grant —'there was the unique opportunity to meet the creator of *Simon*. We were captured! And now, see, how nicely it develops, isn't it, providing all is well with the excellent Mailer.'

'Ah, pooh, ah pooh, ah pooh!' cried the Baroness rather as if she invoked some omnipotent Chinese. 'He will be very well, he will be up and bobbing. There will be some easy explaining and all laughing and jolly. We should not allow our pleasures to be dim by this. Not at all.'

'I must tell you,' the Baron waggishly said to Grant, 'that I have a professional as well as an aesthetic pleasure in meeting Mr Barnaby Grant. I am in the publishing trade, Mr Grant. Ah-ha, ah-ha!'

'Ah-ha, ah-ha!' confirmed the Baroness.

'Really?' Grant said, politely whipping up interest. 'Are you indeed!'

'The firm of Adriaan and Welker. I am the editor for our foreign productions.'

Sophy had given a little exclamation and Grant turned to her.

'This is your field,' he said, and to the Van der Veghels: 'Miss Jason is with my own publishers in London.'

There were more ejaculations and much talk of coincidence while Sophy turned over in her mind what she knew of the firm of Adriaan and Welker and afterwards as they drove away from the Palatine, confided to Grant.

'We've done a few of their juvenile and religious books in translation. They're predominantly a religious publishing firm, the biggest, I fancy, in Europe. The angle is Calvinistic and as far as children's books go, rather nauseatingly pi. The head of the firm, Welker, is said to be the fanatical king-pin of some extreme sect in Holland. As you may imagine, they do *not* publish much contemporary fiction.'

'Not, one would venture, a congenial milieu for the romping Van der Veghels.'

'Oh, I don't know,' Sophy said vaguely. 'I dare say they manage to adjust.'

'What a world-weary child!' Grant observed and shook his head at her.

Sophy turned pink and fell silent.

They were in the second car with Major Sweet who was asleep. The other four had seated themselves, smartly, with Giovanni. Lady Braceley, offering the plea that she suffered from car-sickness, had placed herself in the front seat.

The horrific evening welter of Roman traffic surged, screeched and hooted through the streets. Drivers screamed at each other, removed both hands from the wheel to fold them together in sarcastic prayer at the enormities perpetrated by other drivers. Pedestrians, launching themselves into the maelstrom, made grand opera gestures against oncoming traffic. At pavement tables, Romans read their evening papers, made love, argued vociferously, or, over folded arms, stared with portentous detachment at nothing in particular.

Major Sweet lolled to and fro with his mouth open and occasionally snorted. Once he woke and said that what was wanted here was a London bobby.

'Out there,' said Grant, 'he wouldn't last three minutes.'

'Balls,' said the Major and fell asleep again. He woke when they stopped suddenly and added, 'I'm most frightfully sorry, can't think what's come over me,' and slept again immediately.

Grant found to his surprise that Sophy, too, was at the Pensione Gallico. He himself had only moved in the day before and had not yet eaten there. He asked her if he might give her a drink at Tre Scalini in Navona. 'They could pick us both up there,' he said.

'Nice idea. Thank you.'

'At half past eight then?'

He managed to make this clear to the driver.

The Major was decanted at his hotel and Sophy and Gran at the Gallico.

Grant's room was like an oven. He bathed, lay down for an hour in a state of nature and extreme perturbation and then dressed. When he was ready he sat on his bed with his head in his hands.

If only, he thought, this could be the definitive movement. If only it all could stop: *now*. And the inevitable reference floated up: '*the be-all and the end-all here, but here upon this bank and shoal of time———*'

He thought of Sophy Jason, sitting on the Palatine Hill, her hair lifted from her forehead by the evening breeze and a look of pleased bewilderment in her face. A remote sort of girl, a restful girl who didn't say anything silly, he thought, and then wondered if, after all, 'restful' was quite the word for her.

He leant over his window-sill and looked at the façades and roofs and distant cupolas.

The clock struck eight. A horse-carriage rattled through the cobbled street below, followed by a succession of motor-bicycles and cars. In an upstairs room across the street an excited babble of voices erupted and somewhere deep inside the house a remorseless, untrained tenor burst into song.

Further along the second floor of the Pensione Gallico a window was thrown up and out looked Sophy, dressed in white.

He watched her rest her arms on the window ledge, dangle her hands and sniff the evening air. How strange it was to look at someone who was unaware of being observed. She was turned away from him and craned towards the end of their street where spray from a fountain in Navona could just be seen catching the light in a feathered arc. He watched her with a sense of guilt and pleasure.

After a moment or two he said: 'Good evening.'

She was still for a moment and then slowly turned to him. 'How long have you been there?' she asked.

'No time at all. You're ready, I see. Shall we go?'

'If you like: yes, shall we?'

It was cooler out of doors. As they entered Navona the splashing of water, by its very sound, freshened the evening air. The lovely piazza sparkled, lights danced in cascades of water, glared from headlamps and glowed in Tre Scalini *caffè*.

'There's a table,' Grant said. 'Let's nab it, quickly.'

It was near the edge of the pavement. Their view of Navona was minimal. To Sophy this was of small matter. It suited her better to be here, hemmed in, slightly jostled, bemused, possibly bamboozled in some kind of tourist racket, than to be responding to Rome with scholarly discretion and knowledgeable good taste and a reserve which in any case she did not command.

'This is magic,' she said, beaming at Grant. 'That's all. It's magic. I could drink it.'

'So you shall,' he said, 'in the only possible way,' and ordered champagne cocktails.

At first they did not have a great deal to say to each other but were not troubled by this circumstance. Grant let fall one or two remarks about Navona. 'It was a circus in classical times. Imagine all these strolling youths stripped and running their courses by torchlight or throwing the discus in the heat of the day.' And after one of their silences. 'Would you like to know that the people in the middle fountain are personifications of the Four Great Rivers? Bernini designed it and probably himself carved the horse, which is a portrait.' And later: 'The huge church was built over the site of a brothel. Poor St Agnes had her clothes taken off there and in a burst of spontaneous modesty, instantly grew quantities of luxurious and concealing hair.'

'She must have been the patron saint of Lady Godiva.'

'And of the librettists of *Hair*.'

'That's right.' Sophy drank a little more champagne cocktail. 'I suppose we really ought to be asking each other whatever could have happened to Mr Mailer,' she said.

Grant was motionless except that his left hand, resting on the table, contracted about the stem of his glass.

'Oughtn't we?' Sophy said vaguely.

'I feel no obligation to do so.'

'Nor I really. In fact, I think it's very much nicer without him. If you don't mind my saying so?'

'No,' Grant said heavily. 'No, I don't mind. Here comes the car.'

FOUR

When Alleyn got back to his fine hotel at ten past six he found a message asking him to telephone Il Questore Valdarno.

He did so and was told with a casual air that scarcely concealed the Questore's sense of professional gratification, that his people had already traced the woman called Violetta to her lair which was in a slum. When he said they had traced her, the Questore amended, he did not mean precisely in person since she was not at home when his man called. He had, however, made rewarding inquiries among her neighbours who knew all about her war with Sebastian Mailer and said, variously, that she was his cast-off mistress, wife or shady business associate, that he had betrayed her in a big way and that she never ceased to inveigh against him. Violetta was not popular among the ladies in her street, being quarrelsome, vindictive and unpleasant to children. She was also held to poach on certain begging preserves in the district. It emerged that Mr Mailer in his salad days had abandoned Violetta in Sicily, 'Where, my dear Superintendent,' said the Questore, 'she may well have been one of his contacts in the smuggling of heroin. Palermo is a port of transit as we well know.'

'Yes, indeed.'

'All are agreed that she is a little mad.'

'Ah.'

It appeared, the Questore continued, that for an unspecified time, years perhaps, Mailer had eluded Violetta, but getting wind of his being first in Naples and then in Rome she had chased him, finally establishing herself on the postcard beat outside S. Tommaso.

'I have spoken with this Irish Dominican,' said the Questore. 'It is nonsense for him to say that no one could escape their vigilance going or coming from the places below. It is ridiculous. They sell their cards, they sell their rosaries, they add up their cashes, they visit their stores, they sleep, they talk, they say their prayers. A man of Mailer's talents would have no difficulty.'

'What about a woman of Violetta's talents?'

'Ah-ah. You speak of the shadow on the wall? While I am sure that she *could* elude the vigilance of these gentlemen, I doubt if she did so. And if she did, my dear colleague, where was she when they made their search? I have no doubt the search was thorough: of *that* they are perfectly capable and the lighting is most adequate. They know the terrain. They have been excavating there for a century. No, no, I am persuaded that Mailer recognized you and, being aware of your most formidable and brilliant record in this field, took alarm and fled.'

'Um,' Alleyn said, 'I'm not at all sure I struck terror in that undelicious breast. Mailer seemed to me to be, in a subfusc sort of way, cocksure. Not to say gloating!'

'*Scusi?* Subfusc?'

'Dim. It doesn't matter. Do you mean you think that at some moment when we were groping about in the underworld, recognition came upon him like a thunder-clap and he fled. There and then?'

'We shall see, we shall see. I spread my net. The airports, the wharves, the *stazioni*.'

Alleyn hurriedly congratulated him on all this expedition.

'But nevertheless,' Valdarno said, 'we make our examination of these premises. Tomorrow morning. It is, of course, not my practice personally to supervise such matters. Normally if a case is considered important enough one of my subordinates reports to one of my immediate staff.'

'I assure you, Signor Questore——'

'But in this case, where so much may be involved, where there are international slantings and above all, where so distinguished a colleague does us the honour—*Ecco!*'

Alleyn made appropriate noises and wondered how great a bore Valdarno really thought him.

'So tomorrow,' the Questore summed up. 'I leave my desk and I take the fields. With my subordinates. And you accompany us, is it not?'

'Thank you. I shall be glad to come.'

They whipped through the routine of valedictory compliments and hung up their receivers.

Alleyn bathed and dressed and wrote a letter to his wife.

'——so you see it's taken an odd turning. I'm supposed to be nudging up to Mailer with the object of finding out just how vital a cog he is in the heroin game and whether, through him, I can get a line on his bosses. My original ploy was to be the oblique approach, the hint, the veiled offer, the striking-up of an alliance and finally the dumping upon him of a tidy load of incriminating evidence and so catching him red-handed. And now, damn him, he disappears and I'm left with a collection of people some of whom may or may not be his fall guys. Consider, if you're not fast asleep by this time, my darling—consider the situation.

'To launch this Il Cicerone business, Mailer must have had access to very considerable funds. You can't do this sort of thing on HP. The cars, the drivers, the food and, above all, the quite phenomenal arrangement that seems to have been made with the Gioconda Restaurant who as a general rule would look upon package diners, on however exalted a scale, as the Caprice would look upon coach-loads from the Potteries. It appears that we dine *à la carte* at the best tables and drink distilled gold if they've got it in their cellars. And Mailer pays all. Well, I know we've paid him through the nose but that's another story.

'And then—this lot. This lot who've stumped up fifty quid each for the pleasure of hearing Barnaby Grant, with evident reluctance, read aloud, very badly, from his own best-seller. Next attraction: a walk round an ancient monument that's open to the public followed by tea or whatever they had on the Palatine Hill, and dinner at the Gioconda which could set them back anything up to £20 a nob if they went under their own steam, and then on to a further entertainment coyly unspecified in the brochure. Probably a very expensive strip and champagne show with possibly a pot party to follow. Or worse.

'All right. Take Lady B. She's rolling in money. One of her husbands was an Italian millionaire and she may have alimony paid out to her in Rome. She could obviously afford this show. She's rich, raffish, pretty bloody awful and all for *la dolce vita*. No doubt she's paying for the egregious Kenneth who looks to me very much as if he's hooked and may therefore turn out to be a useful lead into Mailer's activities. I gather from something young Sophy Jason, who is an enchanter, let fall that she just suddenly decided to blue fifty quid out of the Italian funds available to her through business connections.

'The Van der Veghels are a couple of grotesques and

interest me enormously as I think they would you. Grotesques?
No, not the right word. We both go for the Etruscan thing,
don't we? Remember? Remember that male head, bearded
and crowned with leaves in the Museo Barraco? Remember
the smiling mouth, shaped, now I come to think of it, exactly
like a bird in flight with the thin moustache repeating and
exaggerating the curve of the lips? And the wide open eyes?
What an amusing face, we thought, but it is perhaps atrociously
cruel? I assure you, a portrait of the Baron Van der Veghel.
But against this remember the tender and fulfilled couple of
that sarcophagus in the Villa Giulia: the absolute in satisfied
love? Recall the protective hand of the man. The extraordinary marital likeness, the suggestion of heaviness in the
shoulders, the sense of completion. Portrait, I promise you,
of the Van der Veghels. They may be Dutch by birth but
blow me down flat if they're not Etruscan by descent. Or
nature. Or something.

'The overall effect of the Van der Vs is, however, farcical.
There's always an easy laugh to be won from broken English
or, come to that, fractured French. Remember the de
Maupassant story about an English girl who became increasingly boring as her command of French improved? The
Baroness's lapses are always, as I'm sure beastly Kenneth
would say, good for a giggle.

'I suppose their presence in the set-up is the least surprising.
They're avid and merciless sightseers and photographers and
their fund of enthusiasm is inexhaustible. Whether one can
say the same of their fund of cash is anyone's guess.

'Major Sweet. Now, why has Major Sweet coughed up
fifty quid for this sort of jaunt? On the face of it he's a cari-
cature, a museum piece: the sort of Indian Army officer who,
thirty years ago, was fair game for an easy laugh shouting
Qui-hi at a native servant and saying By George, what? I find
it unconvincing. He's bad-tempered, I should imagine pretty

hard on the bottle, and amorous. As the young Sophy found to her discomfort in the Mithraic underworld. He's violently, aggressively and confusingly anti-religion. Religion of any kind. He lumps them all together, turns purple in the face and, deriving his impenetrable argument from the sacraments, pagan or Christian, says the whole lot are based on cannibalism. Why should he pay through the nose to explore two levels of Christianity and a Mithraic basement? Just to have a good jeer?

'Finally—Barnaby Grant. To my notion, the prime puzzle of the party. Without more ado I would say, quite seriously, that I can think of no earthly reason why he should subject himself to what is clearly the most exquisite torture, unless Mailer put the screws on him in another sense. Blackmail. It might well be one of Mailer's subsidiary interests and can tie in very comfortably with the drug racket.

'And as a *bonne-bouche* we have the antic Violetta. If you could have seen Violetta with her "*Cartoline—Posta-cardas*" and harpy's face, foaming away under a black headpiece! Il Questore Valdarno can shrug her off with remarks about short-tempered postcard ladies but never trust me again if that one isn't possessed of a fury. As for Sophy Jason saying it was Violetta's shadow she saw on the wall by the stone sarcophagus, I think it's odds-on she's right. I saw it, too. It was distorted but there was the tray, the shawl and the hitched up shoulder. Clear as mud or my name's Van der Veghel.

'And I think Valdarno's right when he says Mailer could have nipped out under the noses of Father Denys and his boys. There's plenty of cover.

'But without any justification for saying so, I don't believe he did.

'On the same premise Violetta could have nipped in and I do believe *she* did. And out again?

'That too is another story.

'It's now a quarter past eight of a very warm evening. I am leaving my five-star room for the five-star cocktail bar where I rather hope to hob-nob with the Lady B. and her nephew. From there we shall be driven to La Gioconda where we shall perhaps eat quails stuffed with pâté and washed down with molten gold. At Mailer's expense? Well—allegedly.

'More of the continuing story of Anyone's Guess tomorrow. Bless you, my dear love, My——'

5. Evening Out

ONE

THEY HAD DINED by candlelight at a long table in the garden.

Between leafy branches of trees and far below, shone Rome. It might have been its own model, laid out on a black velvet cloth and so cunningly illuminated that its great monuments glowed in their setting like jewels. At night the Colosseum is lit from within and at this distance it was no longer a ruin but seemed so much alive that a mob might have spewed through its multiple doorways, rank with the stench of the circus. It was incredibly beautiful.

Not far from their table was a fountain, moved there at some distant time from its original site down in Old Rome. At its centre lolled Neptune: smooth, luxurious and naked, idly fingering the long ringlets of his beard. He was supported by tritons and all kinds of monsters. They spouted, jetted and dribbled into basins that overflowed into each other making curtains of water-drops. The smell of water, earth and plants mingled with cigar-smoke, coffee, cosmetics and fumes of wine.

'What is all this *like*?' Sophy asked Grant. 'All this magnificence? I've never read Ouida, have you? And anyway this is not at all Victorian.'

'How about Antonioni?'

'Well—all right. But not *La Dolce Vita*. I don't think I get any whiffs of social corruption, really. Do you?'

He didn't answer and she looked across the table at Alleyn. 'Do you?' she asked him.

Alleyn's glance fell upon Lady Braceley's arm, lying as if discarded on the table. Emeralds, rubies and diamonds encircled that flaccid member, veins stood out on the back of the hand, her rings had slipped to one side and her talons— does she have false ones, he wondered, and saw that she did— made little dents in the table-cloth.

'Do *you*,' Sophy persisted, 'sniff the decadent society?' and then, evidently aware of Lady Braceley and perhaps of Kenneth, she blushed.

Sophy had the kind of complexion Jacobean poets would have praised, a rose-blush that mounted and ebbed very delicately under her skin. Her eyes shone in the candlelight and there was a nimbus round her hair. She was as fresh as a daisy.

'At the moment,' Alleyn said, smiling at her, 'not at all.'

'Good!' said Sophy and turned to Grant. 'Then I needn't feel apologetic about enjoying myself.'

'Are you liking it so much? Yes, I see you are. But why should you apologize?'

'Oh—I don't know—a streak of puritan, I suppose. My grandpa Jason was a Quaker.'

'Does he often put in an appearance?'

'Not all that often but I thought he lurked just now. "Vanity, vanity," you know, and the bit about has one any right to buy such a sumptuous evening, the world being as it is.'

'Meaning you should have spent the cash on doing good?'

'Yes. Or not spent it at all. Grandpapa Jason was also a banker.'

'Tell him to buzz off. You've done a power of good.'

'I? How? Impossible.'

'You've turned what promised to be a perfectly hellish evening into——'

Grant stopped short, waited for a moment and then leant towards her.

'Yes, well, all right,' Sophy said in a hurry. 'You needn't bother about that. Silly conversation.'

'——into something almost tolerable,' Grant said.

On the other side of the table Alleyn thought: No doubt she's very well able to take care of herself but I wouldn't have thought her one of the easy-come easy-go sort. On the contrary. I hope Grant isn't a predatory animal. He's a god in her world and a romantic-looking, ravaged sort of god, at that. Just the job to fill in the Roman foreground. Twenty years her senior, probably. He's made her blush again.

Major Sweet, at the head of the table, had ordered himself yet another cognac but nobody followed his example. The champagne bottles were upside down in the coolers and the coffee cups had been removed.

Giovanni appeared, spoke to the waiter and retired with him, presumably to pay the bill. The *maître-d'hôtel*, Marco, swept masterfully down upon them and not for the first time inclined, smiled and murmured over Lady Braceley. She fished in her golden reticule and when he kissed her hand, left something in his own. He repeated this treatment with subtle modulations, on the Baroness, worked in a gay salute to Sophy, included the whole table in a comprehensive bow and swept away with the slightest possible oscillation of his hips.

'Quite a dish, isn't he?' Kenneth said to his aunt.

'Darling,' she replied, 'the things you say! Isn't he too frightful, Major?' She called up the table to Major Sweet, who was staring congestedly over the top of his brandy glass at Sophy.

'What!' he said. 'Oh. Ghastly.'

Kenneth laughed shrilly.

'When do we move?' he asked at large. 'Where do we go from here?'

113

'Now we are gay,' cried the Baroness. 'Now we dance and all is hip and night-life. To the Cosmo, is it not?'

'Ah-ha, ah-ha, to the Cosmo!' the Baron echoed.

They beamed round the table.

'In that case,' Lady Braceley said, picking up her purse and gloves, 'I'm for the *ritirata*.'

The waiter was there in a flash to drop her fur over her shoulders.

'I too, I too,' said the Baroness and Sophy followed them out.

The Major finished his brandy. 'The Cosmo, eh?' he said. 'Trip a jolly old measure, what? Well, better make a move, I suppose——'

'No hurry,' Kenneth said. 'Auntie's best official clocking in *la ritirata* is nineteen minutes and that was when she had a plane to catch.'

The Baron was in deep consultation about tipping with the Major and Grant. Their waiter stood near the door into the restaurant. Alleyn strolled over to him.

'That was a most excellent dinner,' he said and over-tipped just enough to consolidate his follow-on. 'I wonder if I may have a word with Signor Marco? I have a personal introduction to him which I would like to present. Here it is.'

It was Valdarno's card with an appropriate message written on the back. The waiter took a quick look at it and another at Alleyn and said he would see if the great man was in his office.

'I expect he is,' Alleyn said cheerfully. 'Shall we go there?'

The waiter, using his restaurant walk, hurried through the foyer into a smaller vestibule where he begged Alleyn to wait.

He tapped discreetly at a door marked *Il direttore*, murmured something to the elegant young man who opened it, and handed in the card. The young man was gone for a very short time and returned with a winning smile and an invitation to enter. The waiter scuttled off.

Marco's office was small but sumptuous. He advanced upon Alleyn with ceremony and a certain air of guarded cordiality.

'Good evening, again, Mr——' he glanced at the card. 'Mr Alleyn. I hope you have dined pleasantly.' His English was extremely good. Alleyn decided to be incapable of Italian.

'Delightfully,' he said. 'A superb evening. Il Questore Valdarno told me of your genius, and how right he was.'

'I am glad.'

'I think I remember you some years ago in London, Signore. At the Primavera.'

'Ah! My "salad days". Thirty-one different salads, in fact. Perhaps five are worth remembering. Can I do anything for you, Mr Alleyn? Any friend of Il Questore Valdarno——?'

Alleyn made a quick decision.

'You can, indeed,' he said. 'If you will be so kind. I think I should tell you, Signore, that I am a colleague of the Questore's and that I am not in Rome entirely for pleasure. May I——'

He produced his own official card. Marco held it in his beautifully manicured fingers and for five seconds was perfectly motionless. 'Ah, yes,' he said at last. 'Of course. I should have remembered from my London days. There was a *cause célèbre*. Your most distinguished career. And then—surely—your brother—he was Ambassador in Rome, I think, some time ago?'

Alleyn normally reacted to remarks about his brother George by falling over backwards rather than profit by their relationship. He bowed and pressed on.

'This is an affair of some delicacy,' he said and felt as if he spoke out of an Edwardian thriller or, indeed, from No. 221B Baker Street. 'I assure you I wouldn't have troubled you if I could have avoided doing so. The fact is Il Questore Valdarno and I find ourselves in something of a quandary. It's come to our knowledge that a certain unsavoury character whose identity has hitherto been unknown is living in Rome. He has formed associations with people of the highest standing who would be appalled if they knew about him. As I think you yourself would be.'

'I? Do you suggest——?'

'He is one of your patrons. We think it proper that you should be warned.'

If Marco had seemed, for an Italian, to be of a rather florid complexion he was so no longer. His cheeks were wan enough to make his immaculately shaven jaws look, by contrast, a cadaverous purple.

There was a kind of scuffling noise behind Alleyn. He turned and saw the beautiful young man who had admitted him seated behind a table and making great play with papers.

'I didn't realize——' Alleyn said.

'My secretary. He does not speak English,' Marco explained and added in Italian, 'Alfredo, it might be as well for you to leave us.' And still in Italian, to Alleyn: 'That will be better, will it not?'

Alleyn looked blank. 'I'm sorry,' he said and spread his hands.

'Ah, you do not speak our language?'

'Alas!'

The young man said rapidly in Italian: '*Padrone*, is it trouble? It is——?' and Marco cut him short. 'It is nothing. You heard me. Leave us.'

When he had gone Alleyn said, 'It won't take long. The man I speak of is Mr Sebastian Mailer.'

A short pause and Marco said, 'Indeed? You are, I must conclude, certain of your ground?'

'Certain enough to bring you the information. Of course you will prefer to check with the Questore himself. I assure you, he will confirm what I've said.'

Marco inclined and made a deprecatory gesture. 'But of

course, of course. You have quite taken me aback, Mr Alleyn, but I am most grateful for this warning. I shall see that Mr Mailer's appearances at La Gioconda are discontinued.'

'Forgive me, but isn't it rather unusual for La Gioconda to extend its hospitality to a tourist party?'

Marco said rapidly and smoothly, 'A normal tourist party —a "package"—would be out of the question. A set meal and a *fiasco* of wine—with little flags on the table—unthinkable! But this arrangement, as you found, is entirely different. The guests order individually, *à la carte*, as at a normal dinner-party. The circumstance of the *conto* being settled by the host —even though he is a professional host—is of little significance. I confess that when this Mailer first approached me I would not entertain the proposal but then—he showed me his list. It was a most distinguished list. Lady Braceley alone—one of the most elegant of our clientèle. And Mr Barnaby Grant—a man of the greatest distinction.'

'When *did* Mailer first approach you?'

'I believe—about a week ago.'

'So tonight was the first of these dinner-parties?'

'And the last, I assure you, if what you tell me is true.'

'You noticed, of course, that he did not appear?'

'With some surprise. But his assistant, Giovanni Vecchi, is a courier of good standing. He informed us that his principal was unwell. Am I to understand——?'

'He may be unwell, he has undoubtedly disappeared.'

'*Disappeared?*' The colour seeped back, unevenly, into Marco's cheeks. 'You mean——?'

'Just that. Vanished.'

'This is very confusing. Should I understand that you believe him to have'—— Marco's full lips seemed to frame and discard one or two words before they chose—'absconded?'

'That is the Questore's theory.'

'But not yours?' he asked quickly.

117

'I have none.'

'I conclude, Mr Alleyn, that your attendance here tonight which must have followed your enrolment in today's tour, is professional rather than recreational.'

'Yes,' Alleyn agreed cheerfully. 'That's about it. And now I mustn't take up any more of your time. If—and the chances I believe are remote—if Mr Mailer should put in an appearance here'— Marco gave an ejaculation and a very slight wince—'Il Questore Valdarno and I would be most grateful if you would say nothing to him about this discussion. Simply telephone at once to—but the number is on the Questore's card, I think.'

'The Questore,' said Marco in a hurry, 'will I am sure appreciate that any kind of unpleasantness, here, in the restaurant, would be——' he flung up his hands.

'Unthinkable,' Alleyn filled in. 'Oh yes. It would all be done very tactfully and quite behind the scenes, you know.' He held out his hand. Marco's was damp and exceedingly cold.

'But you think,' he persisted, 'you yourself think, isn't it, that he will not come back?'

'For what it's worth,' Alleyn agreed, 'that's my idea. Not, at any rate, of his own volition. Goodbye.'

On his way out he went to the telephone booth and rang Il Questore Valdarno, who reported that he had set up further inquiries but had no news. Mailer's flat had been found. The porter said Mailer left it at about three o'clock and had not returned. The police briefly examined the flat, which seemed to be in order.

'No signs of a sudden departure?'

'None. Yet I am still persuaded——'

'Signor Questore, may I ask you to add to the many favours you have already granted? I am not familiar with your police regulations and procedures but I understand you are less restricted than we are. Would it be possible to put a man in

Mailer's flat at once and could that man answer the telephone and make a careful note of any calls, if possible tracing their origin? I think it's highly probable that Marco of La Gioconda will at this moment be trying to get him and will try again. And again.'

'*Marco!* Indeed? But—yes of course. But——'

'I have spoken to him. He was discreet but his reaction to the disappearance was interesting.'

'In what way? He was distressed?'

'Distressed—yes. Not, I think, so much by Mailer's disappearance as by the thought of his return. That prospect, unless I'm very much mistaken, terrifies him.'

'I shall attend to this at once,' said Il Questore.

'If Mailer is still missing tomorrow, would you allow me to have a look at his rooms?'

'But of course. I will instruct my people.'

'You are too kind,' said Alleyn.

When he returned to the vestibule of La Gioconda he found all the party there except Lady Braceley.

He noticed that Giovanni was having little conferences with the men. He spoke first with Kenneth Dorne, who responded with an air of connivance and cast furtive looks about him. Giovanni moved on to the Major who, ignoring Kenneth, listened avidly but with an affectation of indifference much at odds with the grin that twitched the corners of his mouth.

Giovanni seemed to send out a call of some sort to Baron Van der Veghel, who joined them. He too listened attentively, the Etruscan smile very much in evidence. He said little and presently rejoined his wife, linked his arm in hers and stooped towards her. She put her head on one side and gazed at him. He took the tip of her nose between his fingers and gently, playfully waggled it. She beamed at him and tapped his cheek. He pulled her hand down to his mouth. Alleyn thought he had never seen a more explicit display of physical love.

The Baron slightly shook his head at Giovanni, who bowed gracefully and looked at Grant, who was talking to Sophy Jason. Grant at once said quite loudly, 'No, thank you,' and Giovanni moved on to Alleyn.

'Signore,' he said. 'We go now to the Cosmo, a very elegant and exclusive night-club where the guests will remain for as long as they wish. Perhaps until two when the Cosmo closes. That will conclude the programme for this tour. However, Signor Mailer has arranged that a further expedition is available for those who are perhaps a little curious and desire to extend their knowledge of Roman night-life. Some drinks. A smoke. Congenial company. Boys and girls, very charming. Everything very discreet. The cars will be available without further charge but the entertainment is not included in the tour.'

'How much?' Alleyn asked.

'Signore, the fee is fifteen thousand lire.'

'Very well,' Alleyn said. 'Yes.'

'You will not be disappointed, Signore.'

'Good.'

Lady Braceley re-entered the vestibule.

'Here I am!' she cried. 'High as a kite and fit for the wide, wild way-out. Bring on the dancing girls.'

Kenneth and Giovanni went to her. Kenneth put his arm round her waist and said something under his breath.

'Of course!' she said loudly. 'Need you ask, darling? I'd adore to.' She advanced her face towards Giovanni and widened her eyes.

Giovanni bowed and gave her a look, so overtly deferential and subtly impertinent that Alleyn felt inclined either to knock him down or tell Lady Braceley what he thought of her. He saw Sophy Jason looking at her with something like horror.

'And now, ladies and gentlemen,' said Giovanni, 'to Il Cosmo.'

The Cosmo was a night-club with a lavish floor-show. As soon as the party was seated, bottles of champagne were clapped down on their tables.

They hadn't been there long before the members of the orchestra left their dais and walked severally to the front tables. The bass and 'cello players actually planted their instruments on the tables and plucked the strings. The fiddlers and saxophonists came as close as possible. The tympanist held his cymbals poised above the shrinking Major Sweet's head. Eight marginal nudes trimmed with tropical fruit, jolted round the floor space. 'Black lighting,' was introduced and they turned into Negresses. The noise was formidable indeed.

'Well,' Grant asked Sophy. 'Still keeping Grandpapa Jason at bay?'

'I'm not so sure he doesn't ride again.'

The uproar was such that they were obliged to shout into each other's ears.

Lady Braceley was jerking her shoulders in time with the saxophonist at her table. He managed to ogle her while continuing his exertions.

'She seems,' Grant said, 'to be on the short list of *persona grata* here as well as at the Gioconda.'

'It's a bit hard to take, I find.'

'Say the word if you'd like to go. We could, you know. Or do you want to see the rest of the show?'

Sophy shook her head vaguely. She tried to get her reactions into some kind of perspective. It was odd to reflect that less than twelve hours ago she had met Grant for virtually the first time. It was not the first time by many that she made an instant take but she had never before experienced so sharp an antagonism followed for no discernible reason by so complete a sense of familiarity. At one moment they had blackguarded each other to heaps and at another, not fifteen minutes later, they had gossiped away in the shrine of Mithras as if they had not only known but understood each other for years. Me, thought Sophy, and Barnaby Grant. Jolly odd when you come to think of it. It would have been quite a thing if she could put it all down to the violent antagonism that sometimes precedes an equally violent physical attraction but that was no go. Obviously they were under no compulsion to fall into each other's arms.

'If we stay,' Grant was saying, 'I can snatch you up in my arms.'

Sophy gaped at this uncanny distortion of her thoughts.

'In a cachucha, fandango, bolero or whatever,' he explained. 'On the other hand—*do* pay attention,' he said crossly. 'I'm making a dead set at you.'

'How lovely,' Sophy rejoined. 'I'm all ears.'

The rumpus subsided, the orchestra returned to its dais, the Negresses were changed back into naked pink chicks and retired.

A mellifluous tenor, all eyes, teeth and sob-in-the-voice, came out and sang 'Santa Lucia' and other familiar pieces. He, too, moved among his audience. Lady Braceley gave him a piece of everlasting greenery from her table decorations.

He was followed by the star of the programme, a celebrated black singer of soul music. She was beautiful and disturbing and a stillness came over the Cosmo when she sang. One of her songs was about hopelessness, injury and degradation and she made of it a kind of accusation. It seemed to Sophy that her audience almost disintegrated under her attack and she thought it strange that Lady Braceley, for instance, and Kenneth, could sit and look appreciative and join so complacently in the applause.

When she had gone, Grant said, 'That was remarkable, wasn't it?'

Alleyn, overhearing him, said, 'Extraordinary. Do modern audiences find that the pursuit of pleasure is best satisfied by having the rug jerked from under their feet?'

'Oh,' Grant said, 'hasn't that always been so? We like to be reminded that something is rotten in the State of Denmark. It makes us feel important.'

The programme ended with a very stylish ensemble, the lights were subdued, the band insinuated itself into dance music and Grant said to Sophy, 'Come on. Whether you like it or not.'

They danced: not saying very much, but with pleasure.

Giovanni appeared and Lady Braceley danced with him. They did intricate things with great expertise.

The Van der Veghels, half-smiling, closely embraced, swayed and turned on sixpence keeping to the darkened perimeter of the floor.

Major Sweet, who had made a willing but belated attempt upon Sophy, sank bank in his chair, drank champagne and moodily discoursed with Alleyn. He was, Alleyn concluded, the sort of practised drinker who, while far from being sober, would remain more or less in control for a long time. 'Lovely little girl, that,' he said. 'Natural. Sweet. But plenty of spunk, mind you. Looks you bang in the eye, what?' He maundered on rather gloomily: 'Just a nice, sweet, natural little girl—as I was saying.'

'Are you going on to this other show?' Alleyn asked.

'What about yourself?' countered the Major. 'Fair's fair. No names,' he added more obscurely, 'no pack-drill that I'm aware of. Other things being equal.'

'I'm going, yes.'

'Shake,' invited the Major, extending his hand. But finding that it encountered the champagne bottle he refilled his glass. He leant across the table. 'I've seen some curious things in my time,' he confided. 'You're a broadminded man. Everyone to his own taste and it all adds up to experience. Not a word to the ladies: what they can't grieve about they won't see. How old am I? Come on. You say. How old jer say I am?'

'Sixty?'

'And ten. Allotted span, though that's all my eye. See the rest of you out tonight, my boy.' He leant forward and looked dolefully at Alleyn with unfocused eyes. 'I say,' he said. '*She's* not going on, is she?'

'Who?'

'Old Bracegirdle.'

'I believe so.'

'Gawd!'

'It's pretty steep,' Alleyn suggested. 'Fifteen thousand lire.'

'Better be good, what? I'm full of hopes,' leered the Major. 'And I don't mind telling you, old boy, I wouldn't have been within coo-ee of this show tonight in the orinry way. You know what? Flutter. Green baize. Monte. And—phew!' He made a wild gesture with both arms. 'Thassall:—phew!'

'A big win?'

'Phew!'

'Splendid.'

And that, Alleyn supposed, explained the Major. Or did it? 'Funny thing about Mailer, don't you think?' he asked.

'Phew!' said the Major, who seemed to be stuck with this ejaculation. ''Strordinary conduct,' he added. 'Conduct unbecoming if you ask me, but let it go.' He slumped into a moody silence for some moments and then shouted so loudly that people at the neighbouring table stared at him: 'Bloody good riddance. 'Scuse language.'

After this he seemed disinclined for conversation and Alleyn joined Kenneth Dorne.

With the departure of the soul-singer, Kenneth had slumped back into what seemed to be chronic inertia interrupted by fidgets. He made no attempt to dance but fiddled with his

124

shirt ruffles and repeatedly looked towards the entrance as if he expected some new arrival. He gave Alleyn one of his restless, speculative glances. 'You look marvellous,' he said. 'Are you having a gay time?'

'An interesting time, at least. This sort of thing is quite out of my line. It's an experience.'

'Oh!' Kenneth said impatiently. 'This!' He shuffled his feet about. 'I thought you were terrific,' he said. 'You know. The way you managed everybody after Seb vanished. Look. Do you think he's—you know—I mean to say—what *do* you think?'

'I've no notion,' Alleyn said. 'I've never set eyes on the man before. You seem to be quite friendly with him.'

'Me?'

'You call him Seb, don't you?'

'Oh well. You know. Just one of those things. Why not?'

'You find him helpful, perhaps.'

'How d'you mean?' Kenneth said, eyeing him.

'In Rome. I rather hoped—I may be quite wrong, of course.'

Alleyn broke off. 'Are you going on to this late party?' he asked.

'Of course. And I don't care how soon.'

'Really?' Alleyn said. And hoping he introduced the jargon correctly and with the right inflection, he asked, 'May one expect to meet "a scene"?'

Kenneth swept his hair from his eyes with a fingertip.

'What sort of a scene?' he said cautiously.

'A group—a—have I got it wrong? I'm not turned on—is that right?—as yet. I want to "experience". You know?'

Kenneth now undisguisedly inspected him. 'You look fabulous, of course,' he said. 'You know: way up there. But——' He drew a rectangle with his forefinger in the air. 'Let's face it. Square, sweetheart. Square.'

'Sorry about that,' Alleyn said. 'I was depending on Mr Mailer to make the change.'

'Don't let that trouble you. Toni's terrific.'

'Toni?'

'Where we're going. Toni's Pad. It's the greatest. Groovy. You know? Grass, hard stuff, the lot. Mind you, he plays it cool. There'll be a freak-out.'

'A——?'

'A happening. Psychedelic.'

'A floor show?'

'If you like—but way-out. Ever so trendy. Some people just go for giggles and come away. But if it sends you, which is what it's *for*, you move on to the buzz.'

'Obviously you've been there before?'

'Not to deceive you, I have. Seb took us.'

'Us?'

'Auntie came too. She's all for experience. She's fabulous —honestly. I mean it.'

With considerable effort Alleyn said casually, 'Did Seb— turn you on?'

'That's right. In Perugia. I'm thinking,' Kenneth said, 'of making the move.'

'To——?'

'The big leap. Pothead to main-liner. Well, as a matter of fact I've had a taste. You know. Mind you, I'm not hooked. Just the odd pop. Only a fun thing.'

Alleyn looked at a face that not so long ago might have been attractive. Policemen are as wary of reading character into other people's faces as they are of betraying their thoughts in their own, but it occurred to him that if Kenneth was a less repellent colour and if he would shut his mouth instead of letting it droop open in a flaccid smirk he wouldn't be a bad-looking specimen. He might, even at this stage, be less dissolute than his general behaviour suggested. And whatever has happened or is about to happen to Mr Sebastian Mailer, Alleyn thought, it cannot be one millionth fraction of what he most richly deserves.

Kenneth broke the silence that had fallen between them.

'I say,' he said, 'it's idiotic of course but wouldn't it be a yell if after being on about Seb and Toni's Pad and all that bit, you were The Man?'

'The Man?'

'Yes. You know. A plain-clothes fuzz.'

'Do I look like it?'

'Nobody less. You look gorgeous. That might be your cunning, though, mightn't it? Still, you couldn't have me busted when we're not on British soil. Or could you?'

'*I* don't know,' Alleyn said. 'Ask a policeman.'

Kenneth gave an emaciated little laugh. 'Honestly, you kill me,' he said, and after another pause: 'If it's not going too far, what *do* you do?'

'What do you think?'

'I don't know. Something frightfully high-powered and discreet. Like diplomacy. Or has that gone out with the Lord Chamberlain?'

'Has the Lord Chamberlain gone out?'

'Gone in, then. I suppose he still potters about palatial corridors with a key on his bottom.' A disturbing thought seemed to strike Kenneth. 'Oh God!' he said faintly. 'Don't tell me you *are* the Lord Chamberlain.'

'I am not the Lord Chamberlain.'

'It would have been just my luck.'

The dance band came to an inconclusive halt. Barnaby Grant and Sophy Jason returned to the table. Giovanni elegantly steered Lady Braceley to hers where the Major sat in a trance. The Van der Veghels, hand-linked, joined them.

Giovanni explained that the second driver would return Sophy, the Van der Veghels and Grant to their hotels whenever they wished and that he himself would be responsible for the other members of the party.

Alleyn noticed that Toni's Pad had not been named by Giovanni and that there had been no general, open announcement of the extra attraction. Only those rather furtive approaches to the male members of the party. And through Kenneth to Lady Braceley.

The Van der Veghels said they would like to dance a little more and then go home. Sophy and Grant agreed to this and, when the band struck up again, returned to the floor. Alleyn found himself alone with the Van der Veghels, who contentedly sipped champagne.

'I'm not much good, Baroness,' Alleyn said. 'But will you risk it?'

'Of course.'

She herself, like many big women, was very good—steady and light. 'But you dance well,' she said after a moment. 'Why do you say not so? It is this British self-deprecation we hear about?'

'It would be hard to blunder with you as one's partner.'

'Ah-ha, ah-ha, a compliment! Better and better!'

'You are not going on to this other party?'

'No. My husband thinks it would not suit us to go. He did not very much care for the style of the suggestion. It is more for the men, he said, so I tease him and say he is a big square and I am not so unsophisticate.'

'But he remains firm?'

'He remains firm. So you go?'

'I've said yes, but now you alarm me.'

'No!' cried the Baroness with a sort of obligatory archness. 'That I do not believe. You are a cool one. A sophisticate. That I see very clearly.'

'Change your mind. Come and take care of me.'

This brought peals of jollity from the Baroness. She floated

128

expertly and laughed up and down the scale and then, when he persisted, suddenly adopted an air of gravity. Her voice deepened and she explained that though she was sure Alleyn would not believe her, she and the Baron were in fact quite puritanical in their outlook. They came, she said, of Lutheran stock. They did not at all fancy, for instance, Roman night-life as portrayed by Italian films. Had Alleyn ever heard of the publishing firm of Adriaan and Welker? If not, she must tell him that they took a very firm stand in respect of moral tone and that the Baron, their foreign representative, upheld this attitude.

'In our books all is clean, all is honest and healthful,' she declared and elaborated upon this high standard of literary hygiene with great enthusiasm.

It was not a pose, Alleyn thought, it was an attitude of mind: the Baroness Van der Veghel (and evidently her husband, too) was a genuine pietist and, he thought, with a sidelong look at that Etruscan smile, in all probability she was possessed of the calm ruthlessness that so often accompanies a Puritanical disposition.

'My husband and I,' she said, 'are in agreement on the—I think you call it "permissive" society, do you not? In all things,' she added with stifling effrontery, 'we are in absolute accord. We are sure of ourselves. Always we are happy together and agreeing in our views. Like twins, isn't it?' and again she burst out laughing.

In her dancing, in her complacency, in her sudden bursts of high spirits she bore witness to her preposterous claims: she was a supremely contented woman, Alleyn thought; a physically satisfied woman. Intellectually and morally satisfied, too, it would appear. She turned her head and looked towards the table where her husband sat. They smiled at each other and twiddled their fingers.

'Is this your first visit to Rome?' Alleyn asked.

When people dance together and there is concord in their dancing, however alien they may be in other respects, they are in physical agreement. Alleyn felt at once a kind of withdrawal in the Baroness but she answered readily that she and her husband had visited Italy and in particular, Rome, on several previous occasions. Her husband's publishing interests brought him there quite often and when it was convenient she accompanied him.

'But this time,' Alleyn mentioned, 'it is for fun?' and she agreed.

'For you also?' she asked.

'Oh absolutely,' said Alleyn and gave her an extra twirl. 'Have you made any of the Il Cicerone trips on previous visits?' he asked. Again—it was unmistakable—a withdrawal.

She said, 'I think they are of recent formink. Quite new and of the greatest fun.'

'Does it strike you as at all odd,' asked Alleyn, 'that we none of us seem to be particularly bothered about the non-appearance of our cicerone?'

He felt her massive shoulders rise. 'It is strange, perhaps,' she conceded, 'that he disappears. We hope all is well with him, do we not? That is all we can do. The tour has been satisfactory.'

They moved past their table. The Baron cried, 'Good, good!' and gently clapped his enormous hands in praise of their dancing.

Lady Braceley removed her gaze from Giovanni and gave them a haggard appraisal. The Major slept.

'We think,' said the Baroness, resuming their conversation, 'that there was perhaps trouble for him with the postcard woman. The Violetta.'

'She certainly made him a scene.'

'She was down there, we think. Below.'

'Did you see her?'

130

'No. Miss Jason saw her shadow. We thought that Mr Mailer was unhappy when she said so. He made the big pooh pooh but he was unhappy.'

'She's a pretty frightening lady, that one.'

'She is terrible. Such hatred so nakedly shown is terrible. All hatred,' said the Baroness, deftly responding to a change of step, 'is very terrible.'

'The monk in charge had the place searched. Neither Mailer nor Violetta was found.'

'Ah. The monk,' Baroness Van der Veghel remarked and it was impossible to read anything at all into this observation. 'Possibly. Yes. It may be so.'

'I wonder,' Alleyn presently remarked, 'if anyone has ever told you how very Etruscan you are.'

'I? I am a Dutchwoman. We are Netherlanders, my husband and I.'

'I meant, if you'll forgive me, in looks. You are strikingly like the couple on that beautiful sarcophagus in the Villa Giulia.'

'My husband's is a very old Netherlands family,' she announced, apparently without any intention of snubbing Alleyn but merely as a further statement of fact.

Alleyn thought he also could pursue an independent theme. 'I'm sure you won't mind my saying so,' he said, 'because they are so very attractive. They have that strong marital likeness that tells one they, too, are in perfect accord.'

She offered no comment unless her next remark could be construed as such. 'We are distantly related,' she said. 'We are in fact descended upon the distaff side from the Wittelsbachs. I am called Mathilde Jacobea after the so celebrated Countess. But it is strange, what you say, all the same. My husband believes that our family had its origins in Etruria. So perhaps,' she added playfully, 'we are backthrows. He thinks of writing a book on the subject.'

'How very interesting,' said Alleyn politely and entered upon a spinning manœuvre of some virtuosity. It rather irritated him that she followed with perfect ease. 'Yes,' she said, confirming her own pronouncement, 'you dance well. That was most pleasant. Shall we return?'

They went back to her husband, who kissed her hand and contemplated her with his head on one side. Grant and Sophy joined them. Giovanni asked if they were ready to be driven to their hotels and on learning that they were, summoned the second driver.

Alleyn watched them leave and then, with the resignation that all policemen on duty command, addressed himself to the prospect of Toni's Pad.

THREE

'Pad' was not, he discovered, included in the official title. It was simply 'Toni's' and the name was not displayed on the façade. The entrance was through a wrought-iron gate, opened, after a subdued exchange with Giovanni, by a porter. Then across a paved courtyard and up five floors in a lift. Giovanni had collected fifteen thousand lire from each member of his party. He handed these amounts to someone who peered through a trap in a wall. A further door was then opened from the inside and the amenities of Toni's Pad were gradually disclosed.

They were everything and more that might be expected on a pretty elaborate scale and they catered for all tastes at predictable levels.

The patrons were ushered into a pitch-dark room and seated on velvet divans round the wall. It was impossible to discover how many were there but cigarette ends pulsed in many places and the room was full of smoke.

Giovanni's party seemed to be the last arrivals. They were guided to their places by someone with a small blue torch-light. Alleyn contrived to settle near the door.

A voice murmured: 'A "Joint", Signore?' and a box with a single cigarette in it was displayed by the torch. Alleyn took the cigarette. Every now and then people murmured and often giggling broke out.

The Freak-Out was introduced by Toni himself, holding a torch under his face. He was a smooth man who seemed to be dressed in floral satin. He spoke in Italian and then halt-ingly in English. The name of the performance, he said, was 'Keenky Keeks'.

A mauve light flooded the central area and the show was on.

Alleyn was not given to subjective comment where police fieldwork was concerned but in a report that he subsequently drew up on the case-in-hand he referred to Toni's Kinky Kicks as 'infamous' and, since a more explicit description was unnecessary, he did not give one.

The performers were still in action when his fingers found the doorhandle behind a velvet curtain. He slipped out.

The porter who had admitted them was in the vestibule. He was big, heavy and lowering and lay back in a chair placed across the entrance. When he saw Alleyn he did not seem surprised. It might be supposed that rebellious stomachs were not unknown at Toni's.

'You wish to leave, Signore?' he asked in Italian and ges-tured towards the door. 'You go?' he added in basic English.

'No,' Alleyn said in Italian. 'No, thank you. I am looking for Signor Mailer.' He glanced at his hands, which were trembling, and thrust them in his pockets.

The man lowered his feet to the floor, gave Alleyn a pretty hard stare and got up.

'He is not here,' he said.

Alleyn withdrew his hand from his trouser pocket and

looked absent-mindedly at the L.50,000 note. The porter slightly cleared his throat. 'Signor Mailer is not here this evening,' he said. 'I regret.'

'That is disappointing,' Alleyn said. 'I am very surprised. We were to meet. I had an arrangement with him: an arrangement for special accommodation. You understand?' He yawned widely and used his handkerchief.

The porter, watching him, waited for some moments. 'Perhaps he has been delayed,' he said. 'I can speak to Signor Toni on your behalf, Signore. I can arrange the accommodation.'

'Perhaps Signor Mailer will come. Perhaps I will wait a little.' He yawned again.

'There is no need. I can arrange everything.'

'You don't even know——'

'You have only to speak, Signore. Anything!'

The porter became specific. Alleyn affected restlessness and discontent. 'That's all very fine,' he said. 'But I wish to see the Padrone. It is an appointment.'

Alleyn waited for the man to contradict the term 'padrone' but he did not. He began to wheedle. Mellifluously he murmured and consoled. He could see, he said, that Alleyn was in distress. What did he need? Was it perhaps H. and C.? And the equipment? He could provide everything at once and a sympathetic couch in privacy. Or did he prefer perhaps to take his pleasure in his apartment?

Alleyn realized after a minute or two that the man was trading on his own account and had no intention of going to Toni for the cocaine and heroin he offered. Perhaps he stole from the stock in hand. He himself kept up his display of 'withdrawal' symptoms. The L.50,000 note shook in his grasp; he gaped, dabbed at his nose and mopped his neck and brow. He affected to mistrust the porter. How did he know that the porter's stuff was of good quality? Mr Mailer's supplies were of the best: unadulterated, pure. He understood Mr Mailer was a direct importer from the Middle East. How was he to know——?

The porter said at once that it would be from Mr Mailer's stock that he would produce the drugs. Mr Mailer was indeed an important figure in the trade. He became impatient.

'In a moment, Signore, it will be too late. The performance will end. It is true that Toni's guests will retire to other rooms and other amusements. To be frank, Signore, they will not receive the service that I can provide.'

'You guarantee that it is of Signor Mailer's supply?'

'I have said so, Signore.'

Alleyn consented. The man went into a sort of cubby-hole off the vestibule that was evidently his office. Alleyn heard a key turn. A drawer was shut. The porter returned with a sealed package neatly wrapped in glossy blue paper. The cost was exorbitant: about thirty per cent on the British black-market price. He paid and said agitatedly that he wanted to go at once. The man opened the door, took him down in the lift and let him out.

A car was drawn up in the alley and at its wheel, fast asleep, Giovanni's second-in-command. Alleyn concluded that Giovanni found himself fully occupied elsewhere.

He walked to the corner, found the name of the main street—the Via Aldo—and took his bearings. He returned to the car, woke the driver and was driven to his hotel. He maintained his withdrawal symptoms for the driver's benefit, made a muddle over finding his money and finally overtipped lavishly with a trembling hand.

After Toni's Pad the hotel vestibule might have been in the Austrian Tyrol, so healthful did its quietude, its subdued luxury, its tinkling fountains and its emptiness appear. Alleyn went to his room, bathed, and for a minute or two stood on his small balcony and looked down at Rome.

Eastward there was a faint pallor in the sky. In those churches, shut like massive lids, over the ancient underworld, they would soon be lighting candles for the first offices of the day.

Perhaps the lay brother at S. Tommaso in Pallaria was already awake and preparing to go slap-slap in his sandals through the empty streets with a key to the underworld in his habit.

Alleyn locked the cigarette and the package of cocaine and heroin in his briefcase, and telling himself to wake at seven o'clock went to bed and to sleep.

FOUR

Much earlier in the night Barnaby Grant and Sophy Jason from the top of the Pensione Gallico had also looked at Rome.

'It's not very late,' Grant had said. 'Shall we go out on the roof-garden for a minute or two? Would you like a drink?'

'I don't want any more alcohol, thank you,' Sophy said.

'I've got some oranges. We could squeeze them out and add cold water, couldn't we? Fetch your tooth mug.'

The roof-garden smelt of night-scented stocks, watered earth and fern. They made their orange drinks, pointed out the silhouettes of Rome against the sky and spoke very quietly because bedrooms opened on to the roof-garden. This gave their dialogue an air of conspiracy.

'I wish I had one of them,' Sophy said.

'I did last time I was here. That one over there with the french windows.'

'How lovely.'

'I—suppose it was.'

'Didn't you like it?'

'Something rather off-putting happened that time.'

If Sophy had asked 'what' or indeed had shown any kind

of curiosity Grant would probably have fobbed her off with a vague sentence or two, but she said nothing. She looked at Rome and sipped her drink.

'You have the gift of Virgilia, Sophy.'

'What was that?'

'A gracious silence.'

She didn't answer and suddenly he was telling her about the morning of the thunderstorm in the Piazza Colonna and the loss of his manuscript.

She listened with horror, her fingers at her lips. 'Simon,' she muttered. 'You lost Simon!' And then: 'Well—but obviously you got it back.'

'After three days' sweltering hell spent largely on this roof-garden. Yes. I got it back.' He turned away and sat in one of the little wrought-iron chairs. 'At this table, actually,' he said indistinctly.

'I wonder you can face it again.'

'You don't ask how I got it back.'

'Well—how, then?'

'Mailer—brought it here.'

'Mailer? Did you say Mailer? Sebastian Mailer?'

'That's right. Come and sit here, Please.'

She took the other chair at his table, as if, she thought, the waiter was going to bring their breakfast. 'What is it?' she asked. 'You're worried about something. Do you want to talk about it?'

'I suppose I must. To this extent, at least. Do you believe me when I tell you that at the moment I can almost wish he had never recovered the thing?'

Sophy said, after a pause, 'If you say so, I believe you, but it's a monstrous idea. For you to wish Mailer hadn't found it— yes. That I can imagine.'

'And that is what I meant. You're too young to remember when my first book came out. You were a child, of course.'

137

'*Aquarius?* Well, I was about fourteen, I think. I read it with goggling eyes and bated breath.'

'But afterwards. When you came into Koster Press? You heard about—the scandal? Well, didn't you? You can't tell me they don't still thumb it over in those august premises.'

'Yes,' Sophy said. 'I heard about the coincidence bit.'

'The "*coincidence*" bit! Did you, by God! And did you believe that I could have repeated in exact detail the central theme of a book I'd never read?'

'Certainly. That's the general opinion at Koster's.'

'It wasn't the opinion of twelve good, bloody men and true.'

'Token damages, though, weren't they? And there's a long list of proven literary coincidences. I write children's books. I found last year that I'd lifted the entire story-line of Mrs Molesworth's *Cuckoo Clock*. Actually it wasn't coincidence. My grandmother had read her copy aloud to me when I was six. I suppose it was stowed away in my subconscious and bobbed up unbeknownst. But I swear I didn't know.'

'What did you do when you found out?'

'Scrapped it. I was just in time.'

'You were lucky.'

'Does it still hurt so much?'

'Yes,' Grant said. 'Yes, my girl, it does.'

'Why, though? Because people may still believe you cribbed?'

'I suppose so—yes. The whole thing's a nightmare.'

'I'm sorry,' Sophy said. 'That's beastly for you. But I can't quite see——'

'What it's got to do with this book—and Mailer?'

'Yes.'

Grant said: 'Was it at half past three last afternoon that we met for the first time?'

'We've been thrown together. Like people in ships,' Sophy

138

said with a practical air that was invalidated by the circumstance of her being obliged to murmur.

'Mailer kept the manuscript for three days.'

'Why?'

'He says because he flaked out. Cocaine. He showed me his arm to prove it. I don't believe it for a moment.'

'Was he waiting for a reward to be offered?'

'He wouldn't take it.'

'Amazing!' said Sophy.

'I don't think so. I don't think he's an addict. I think he's a pusher in a big way and they never are. He took me to the place they've gone on to, tonight. Toni's. It's a highly tarted-up junk and flop shop. Caters for all tastes. It's outrageous. Where was I?'

'You were going to say——'

'Why he waited three days. Because it took him that amount of time to cook up a novella with a resemblance in theme to an incident in *Simon*. He asked me to read it and give him a criticism. I'm certain *now* that he'd opened my case, read the MS and deliberately concocted this thing. It had all the characteristics, only I was too dumb to spot them. I gave him an opinion and mentioned, as an amusing coincidence, the resemblance. We were in a restaurant and he told some friends about it. Later on in that damnable evening he told other people. He made a great story of it.'

Grant stopped speaking.

A belated horse-carriage clopped down the street under their garden. Much farther away a babble of Italian voices broke out, topped by a whistle, laughter and a snatch of song. A driver in Navona changed gears and revved up his engine.

'Do I begin to see,' Sophy said, 'why you put up with—this afternoon?'

'Do you begin to see!' he burst out. 'Yes, you do begin to

see. You haven't heard half of it yet, but—my God—you do begin to see.'

He brought his clenched fist down on the table with a crash and their tooth mugs clattered together.

'Pardon *me*,' said a shrill lady behind the french windows, 'but is it too much to ask for a mite of common courtesy and consideration?' And then in an access of rage. 'If you can't keep your voices down you can belt up and get out.'

FIVE

Morning was well-established when Giovanni and Kenneth Dorne with Lady Braceley, maintained by lateral pressure and support from the armpits and not so much propelled as lifted, crossed the foyer of the hotel and entered the lift.

Cleaning women with black-currant eyes exchanged looks with the night porter, who was preparing to go off duty. The man with the vacuum cleaner watched their progress to the lift and then joined them and, with back turned and averted glance, took them up to their floor. A chambermaid, seeing their approach, opened the door into their suite and hurried away.

They put Lady Braceley into a chair.

Kenneth fumbled in his pocket for his note-case. 'You're sure, aren't you?' he said to Giovanni. 'It's going to be OK. I mean—you know——?'

Giovanni, indigo about the jaws but otherwise impeccable, said, 'Perfectly, Signore. I am fully in Signor Mailer's confidence.'

'Yes—but—you know? This thing about—well, about the police—did he——?'

'I will be pleased to negotiate.'

They both looked at Lady Braceley.

'We'll have to wait,' Kenneth said. 'It'll be all right, I promise. Later. Say this afternoon when she's—you know?'

'As soon as possible. A delay is not desirable.'

'All right. All right. I know. But—see for yourself, Giovanni.'

'Signore, I have already perceived.'

'Yes. Well, in the meantime—here.'

'You are very kind,' Giovanni said, taking his dirt-money with infinite aplomb. 'I will return at two-thirty, Signore. *Arrivederci.*'

Left alone, Kenneth bit his knuckles, looked at his aunt and caught back his breath in a dry sob. Then he rang for her maid and went to his room.

SIX

'You have enjoyed yourself, my beloved?' the Baron had asked the Baroness in their own language as they prepared for bed.

'Very much. The tall Englishman is a good dancer and clearly a person of some distinction. He what the English call "*funned*" me about not going on to the other place. To take care of him, he said. He is a flirt.'

'I am jealous.'

'Good-good. Almost, I wish we had decided to go.'

'Now, you tease me, my love. It is quite unthinkable that I should take you to one of these places, Mathilde. You would be insulted. I wonder that this person, Allen, suggested it.'

'He was "*funning*" me, my darling.'

'He had no business to do so on that subject.'

The Baroness turned her back to her husband, who deftly unzipped her dress and awarded her a neat little slap.

'The relief,' she said, 'is so enormous, Gerrit. I dare not believe in it. Tell me, now, fully, what happened.'

141

'In effect—nothing. As you know, I hoped to negotiate. I kept the appointment. He did not. It is very strange.'

'And, for the moment at least, we are free of our anxiety?'

'I think we are free altogether, darling. I think we shall not see this Mailer again.'

'No?'

'My feeling is that he is in trouble with the police. Perhaps he was recognized. Perhaps the woman who threatened him has some hold over him. I am sure he has bolted. We shall not be troubled by him again, my poor love.'

'And our secret—our secret, Gerrit?'

'Remains our secret.'

The Baron's winged smile tilted his mouth. He opened his eyes and put his head on one side. 'And as for our financial disaster,' he said. 'It is vanished. Look.'

He unlocked a cupboard, removed from it the great satchel in which he carried his photographic equipment, unlocked that and displayed a large sealed package.

'Such a business it was,' he said, 'getting it all together. And now—back to Geneva and lock it all up again. What a farce!'

'What a farce,' she echoed obediently.

He put the satchel away, locked the cupboard, turned and opened wide his arms.

'So,' he said. 'And now——! Come to me, my beloved.'

SEVEN

Major Sweet was the last of his party to return to his lodging. He was taken to his room by the second driver, being in a trance-like condition from which he neither passed into oblivion nor wholly recovered. The second driver watched him make a pretty good hash of withdrawing money from his pockets and did not attempt to conceal his own chagrin when given a worse than conservative tip.

Alone, the Major was at laborious pains to retrieve the money he had dropped on the carpet. He was reduced to crawling after it like a botanist in search of some rare specimen.

Having achieved several pieces of cash and two notes he sat on the floor with his back to the bed, stared at his gleanings with astonishment and then, inconsistently, threw them over his shoulder.

He rolled over, climbed up to his bed, fell on it, removed his tie and slept.

6. Reappearance of a Postcard Vendor

ONE

AT SEVEN O'CLOCK Alleyn obeyed his own orders and woke.
He ordered breakfast, bathed, shaved and was ready for the
day when the hotel office rang to say a car had called for him.

It was Il Questore Valdarno's car and in it, exuding his
peculiar brand of melancholy and affability, was the Questore
himself.

He welcomed Alleyn and in doing so contrived to establish
the awesome condescension of his being there at all. It was a
long time, Alleyn understood, since the Questore had risen
at this hour, a long time since his association with fieldwork
had taken any form other than the august consideration of
material pre-filtered by his subordinates.

Alleyn expressed, not for the first time, his deep sense of
obligation.

The air was fresh, Rome sparkled, the streets swam with
shoals of early workers. Above them and against a pontifical
blue, giant personages in marble looked downwards, their
arms frozen in benediction. Under the streets, behind façades,
in still-dominant monuments the aspirations of senators,
Caesars and Emperors held their ground. And nowhere more
strangely, Alleyn thought, than in S. Tommaso in Pallaria.

When they arrived they were met by three of the Questore's
'people': Agenti di Questura, which Alleyn took to be the
equivalent of constables, and by Father Denys and the
Sacristan, Brother Dominic, a dour man who drew the key

to the underworld from his habit as if it was a symbol of mortality.

Valdarno was rather high and remote with the clergy, but complaisant too, and not ungracious.

Father Denys greeted Alleyn as an old friend.

'It's yourself again, is it, and you not letting on what was your true function. Sure, I thought to myself there was something about you that was more than met the eye, and here you are, they tell me, a great man in the CID.'

'I hope it was an innocent—reservation, Father.'

'Ah well,' said Father Denys with a tolerance, Alleyn felt, reserved for heretics, 'we'll let you off this time. Now what is all this? A wild-goose chase you and the Questore are on over the head of this queer fellow. Be sure he's given us the slip and away on his own devices.'

'You're persuaded he did give you the slip, Father?'

'What else could it be? He's not beneath.' He turned to Valdarno. 'If you're ready, Signor Questore, we may proceed.'

Cleaners were busy in the upper basilica, which in common with most Latin churches, had the warm air of always being in business and ready for all comers. A Mass had been said and a small congregation of old women and early workers were on their way out. Three women and one man knelt in prayer before separate shrines. The Sacristy was open. The celebrant had concluded his after-Mass observances and was about to leave.

They moved on into the vestibule and shop. Brother Dominic opened the great iron grille and he, with Valdarno, Alleyn and three attendant policemen, began their search of the underworld.

Father Denys remained above, being, as he pointed out, entirely satisfied of the non-presence of Mr Mailer in the basements and having a job to do in the shop.

As they descended Brother Dominic turned on the fluorescent

lighting used by the monks in their maintenance and excavation. It completely changed the atmosphere and character of the underworld, which had become a museum with no shadows and its exhibits remorselessly displayed. Nothing could reduce the liveliness, beauty and strangeness of the Etruscan terra-cottas but they no longer disconcerted.

Little heaps of rubble, tools and rope, tidily disposed, stood at entrances to passages that were still being explored. The Agenti poked into all these and re-emerged dusting their knees and shoulders. Brother Dominic looked on with his hands in his sleeves and an expression of disfavour on his face. The Questore lost no opportunity of telling Alleyn in a stagy aside that this, undoubtedly, was merely a routine search and they might expect nothing from it.

Alleyn asked him if any results had come through from Mailer's flat and learnt that somebody had telephoned immediately after he himself had done so, that the man seemed to be in some agitation, refused to give his name and rang again several times enabling the number to be traced. It was that of La Gioconda. Marco, without a doubt.

'And the woman, Violetta?'

Certainly. Naturally the matter of the woman Violetta had been followed up. Curiously, it must be admitted, she had not returned to her lodging and so far had not been found.

'It is possible,' Valdarno said, 'that they are together.'

'You think so?'

'One cannot tell. She may be implicated. He may have informed her of your identity and frightened her into taking flight. This is mere speculation, my dear Superintendent, and I know your views. I have read your book. In English, I have read it.'

'Well, I'll break my rule and indulge in a bit of speculation on my own account. It occurs to me there is another possible explanation for their double disappearance.'

'Indeed? Please tell me of it.'

Alleyn did so.

Valdarno stared straight in front of him and nursed his splendid moustache. When Alleyn had finished, he turned an incredulous gaze upon him and then decided to be arch. He shook his finger at Alleyn. 'Ah-ah-ah, you pull my leg,' he said.

'I don't, you know.'

'No? Well,' said the Questore, thinking it over, 'we shall see. Yet I fear,' he added, giving Alleyn a comradely clap on the shoulder, 'that we shall see—nothing in particular.'

They moved laboriously onwards and down. To the church on the second level. To the first smiling Apollo and the tall woman with the broken child, to the white Apollo with a crown of leaves, to the Mercury behind whom Baron Van der Veghel had so playfully hidden.

The men flashed torchlights into the recesses and niches. Alleyn looked into them a little more closely.

Behind the white Apollo he found a screwed-up piece of glossy blue paper which he retrieved and wrapped in his handkerchief, sharply observed by Valdarno, to whom he scrupulously confided his reasons for doing so.

Behind the Mercury he found a sealing tab from an un-developed film, left there no doubt by Baron Van der Veghel when he played his little joke and frightened Lady Braceley into fits.

On to the railed hole in the floor of the second-level cloister where Baroness Van der Veghel had peered into the under-world and where Sophy Jason and Alleyn, also looking down, had seen the shadow of a woman they took to be Violetta.

Alleyn reminded Valdarno of this and invited him to stand where Sophy had stood while he himself looked over the Questore's shoulder. There was no lighting down below and they stared into a void.

'You see, Signor Questore, we are looking straight down

into the well-head on the bottom level. And there to the right is the end of the sarcophagus with the carved lid. You can, I think, just make it out. I wonder—could one of your men go down there and switch on the normal lighting. Or perhaps——'

He turned with diffidence to the Dominican. 'I wonder,' he said, 'if you would mind going down, Brother Dominic? Would you? You are familiar with the switches and we are not. If we could just have the same lighting as there was yesterday? And if you would be very kind and move between the source of light and the well. We'd be most grateful.'

Brother Dominic waited for so long, staring in front of him, that Alleyn began to wonder if he had taken some vow of silence. However, he suddenly said 'I will' in a loud voice.

'That's very kind of you. And—I hope I'm not asking for something that is not permitted—would you have your hood over your head?'

'What for would I be doing that?' asked Brother Dominic in a sudden access of communication.

'It's just to lend a touch of verisimilitude,' Alleyn began, and to his astonishment Brother Dominic instantly replied, ' "To an otherwise bald and unconvincing narrative"?'

'Bless you, Brother Dominic. You'll do it?'

'I will,' Brother Dominic repeated, and stalked off.

'These holy fathers!' Valdarno tolerantly observed. 'The one talks to distraction and the other has half a tongue. What is it you wish to demonstrate?'

'Only, in some sort, how the shadow appeared to us.'

'Ah, the shadow. You insist on the shadow?'

'Humour me.'

'My dear colleague, why else am I here? I am all attention.'

So they leant over the railing, stared into the depths and became aware of the now familiar burble of subterranean water.

'Almost,' Alleyn said, 'you can persuade yourself that you

see a glint of it in the well—almost but not quite. Yesterday I really thought I did.'

'Some trick of the light.'

'I suppose so. And pat on his cue, there goes Brother Dominic.'

A concealed lamp had been switched on. The lid of the sarcophagus, the wall behind it and the railings round the well all sprang into existence. Their view from immediately above was one of bizarre shadows and ambiguous shapes, o. exaggerated perspectives and detail. It might have been an illustration from some Victorian thriller: a story of Mystery and Imagination.

As if to underline this suggestion of the macabre a new shadow moved into the picture: that of a hooded form. It fell across the sarcophagus, mounted the wall, grew gigantic and vanished.

'Distorted,' Alleyn said, 'grotesque, even, but quite sharply defined, wasn't it? Unmistakably a monk. One could even see that the hands were concealed in the sleeves. Brother Dominic obliging, in fact. The shadow Miss Jason and I saw yesterday was equally well-defined. One saw that the left shoulder was markedly higher than the right, that the figure was a woman's and even that she carried some tray-like object slung round her neck. It was, I am persuaded, Signor Questore, the shadow of Violetta and her postcards.'

'Well, my friend, I do not argue with you. I will take it as a working hypothesis that Violetta escaped the vigilance of the good fathers and came down here. Why? Perhaps with the intention of pursuing her quarrel with Mailer. Perhaps and perhaps. Perhaps,' the Questore continued with a sardonic inflection, 'she frightened him and that is why he ran away. Or even—as you have hinted—but come—shall we continue?'

Alleyn leant over the well-rails and called out. 'Thank you, Brother Dominic. That was excellent. We are coming down.'

He had a resonant voice and it roused a concourse of echoes: '—down—ow—ow—ow—n—n.'

They descended the circular iron stairway, walked along the narrow passage and found Brother Dominic, motionless beside the wellhead. The scene was lit as it had been yesterday afternoon.

Alleyn stood by the well-head and looked up. The opening above his head showed as a brilliant square of light and far above that, the opening into the basilica. As he watched, Father Denys's head appeared at the top level, peering into the depths. If Father Denys, like Violetta, was given to spitting, Alleyn thought, he would spit straight in my eye.

'Are you all right, beneath?' asked Father Denys, and his voice seemed to come from nowhere in particular.

'We are,' boomed Brother Dominic without moving. The head was withdrawn.

'Before we turn on the fluorescent light,' Alleyn said, 'shall we check on the movements of the woman in the shawl? Brother Dominic, I take it that just now you walked from the foot of the iron stair where you turned on the usual lighting, down the passage and across the light itself to where you now stand?'

'I did,' said Brother Dominic.

'And so must she, one would think?'

'Of course,' said Valdarno.

'It wasn't quite the same, though. Violetta's shadow—we are accepting Violetta as a working hypothesis—came from the right as Brother Dominic's did and, like this, crossed to the left. But there was a sequel. It reappeared, darting into view, lying across the sarcophagus and up the wall. It paused. It turned this way and that and then shot off to the right. The suggestion, a vivid one, was of a furtive person looking for a hiding-place. Miss Jason thought so, too.'

'Did Mailer comment?'

'He pooh-poohed the idea of it being Violetta and changed the subject.' Alleyn looked about him. 'If we extend the "working hypothesis" which, by the way, Signor Questore, is a nice alternative to the hateful word "conjecture", we must allow that there are plenty of places where she *could* hide. Look what a black shadow the sarcophagus throws, for instance.'

Alleyn had a torch and now used it. He flashed it along the well-rails, which turned out to be makeshift contruction of roughly-finished wood.

'You would like the working lights, Signore?' said one of the men.

But the darting beam paused and sharpened its focus. Alleyn stooped and peered at the rail.

'There's a thread of some material caught here,' he said. 'Yes, may we have the lights, please?'

The man went back down the passage, his retreating footfall loud on the stone floor.

The torchlight moved away from the rails, played across the lid of the sarcophagus, caused little carved garlands to leap up in strong relief, found the edge of the lid. Stopped.

'Look here.'

Valdarno used his torch and the other two men came forward with theirs. As they closed in, the pool of light contracted and intensified.

The lid of the sarcophagus was not perfectly closed. Something black protruded and from the protrusion dangled three strands of wool.

'*Dio mio!*' whispered the Questore.

Alleyn said, 'Brother Dominic, we must remove the lid.'

'Do so.'

The two men slid it a little to one side, tilted it and with a grating noise, let it slip down at an angle. The edge of the lid hit the floor with a heavy and resounding thud, like the shutting of a monstrous door.

The torchlights fastened on Violetta's face.

Her thickened eyes stared sightlessly into theirs. Her tongue was thrust out as if to insult them.

Valdarno's torch clattered on the stone floor.

The long silence was broken by a voice: uninflected, deep, rapid.

Brother Dominic prayed aloud for the dead.

TWO

A consultation was held in the vestibule. The church was shut and the iron grille into the underworld locked, awaiting the arrival of Valdarno's Squadra Omicidi. It was strange, Alleyn found, to hear the familiar orders being laid on by somebody else in another language.

Valdarno was business-like and succinct. An ambulance and a doctor were sent for, the doctor being, as far as Alleyn could make out, the equivalent of a Home Office pathologist. The guard at all points of departure from Rome was to be instantly stepped up. Toni's premises were to be searched and the staff examined. Mailer's apartment was to be occupied in such a way that if he returned he would walk into a trap. Violetta's known associates were to be closely questioned.

Alleyn listened, approved and said nothing.

Having set up this operational scheme, the Questore turned his deceptively languishing gaze upon Alleyn.

'*Ecco!*' he said. 'Forgive me, my friend, if I have been precipitate. This was routine. Now we collaborate and you shall tell me how we proceed.'

'Far be it from me,' Alleyn rejoined in the nearest Italian equivalent to this idiom that he could at the moment concoct, 'to do anything of the sort. May we continue in English?'

'Of course,' cried the Questore in that language.

'I suppose,' Alleyn said, 'that now you have so efficiently set up the appropriate action we should return to the persons who were nearest to the crime at the time it was committed.'

'Of course. I was about to say so. And so,' Valdarno archly pointed out, 'you interview yourself, isn't it?'

'Among others. Or perhaps I may put myself in your hands. How would you set about me, Signor Questore?'

Valdarno joined his fingertips and laid them across his mouth. 'In the first place,' he said, 'it is important to ascertain the movements of this Mailer. I would ask that as far as possible you trace them. When you last saw him, for example.'

'The classic question. When the party was near the iron stairway on the middle level. We were about to go down to the Mithraic household on the lowest level when Lady Braceley said she was nervous and wanted to return to the top. She asked for her nephew to take her up but we found that he was not with us. Mailer said he had returned to photograph the statue of Apollo and that he would fetch him. Lady Braceley wouldn't wait and in the upshot Major Sweet took her up to the basilica garden—the atrium—and rejoined us later. When they left us, Mailer set off along the passage, ostensibly to retrieve Kenneth Dorne. The rest of us—the Van der Veghels, Miss Jason and I, with Barnaby Grant as guide, went down the iron stair to the Mithraeum. We had been there perhaps eight minutes when Major Sweet made himself known—I put it like that because at this point he spoke. He may have actually returned un-noticed before he spoke. The place is full of shadows. It was some five or six minutes later that Kenneth Dorne appeared, asking for his aunt.'

'So Mailer had not met this Dorne after all?'

'Apparently not, but there is some evidence——'

'Ah! I had forgotten. But on the face of it no one had seen Mailer after he walked down the passage?'

'On the face of it—nobody.'

'We must question these people.'

'I agree with you,' said Alleyn.

For some seconds the Questore fixed his mournful gaze upon Alleyn.

'It must be done with tact,' he said. 'They are persons o some consequence. There could be undesirable developments. All but two,' he added, 'are British citizens.'

Alleyn waited.

'In fact,' said Valdarno, 'it appears to me, my Super-intendent, that there is no longer any cause for you to preserve your anonymity.'

'I haven't thought that one out but—no, I suppose you're right.'

One of the Agenti came in.

'The Squadra Omicidi, Signor Questore, the ambulance, Vice-Questore and the doctor.'

'Very well. Bring them.'

When the man had gone Valdarno said, 'I have, of course, sent for the officer who would normally conduct this inquiry, Il Vice-Questore Bergarmi. It would not be fitting for me to engage myself in my subordinate's duties. But in view of extraordinary circumstances and international implications I shall not entirely dissociate myself. Besides,' he added with a totally unexpected flash of candour, 'I am enjoying myself prodigiously.'

For Alleyn the confrontation at close quarters with a strangled woman had not triggered off an upsurge of pleasure. However, he said something vague about fieldwork as an antidote to the desk.

Valdarno developed his theme.

'My suggestion,' he said, 'is this and you shall tell me if I am faulty. I propose to invite these people to my office where they will be received with *ceremoniale*. There will be no hint of

154

compulsion but on the contrary a glass of wine. I present you in your professional role. I explain a little but not too much. I implore their help and I then push them over to you.'

'Thank you. It will, don't you feel, be a little difficult to sustain the interview at this level? I mean, on his own admission to me, Kenneth Dorne has been introduced to soft and then to hard drugs by Mailer. And so, after last night, I believe, has Lady Braceley. And I'm perfectly certain Mailer exercised some sort of pull over Barnaby Grant. Nothing short of blackmail, it seems to me, would have induced Grant to take on the role of prime attraction in yesterday's conducted tour.'

'In which case he, at least, will be glad to help in bringing about the arrest of Mailer.'

'Not if it means publicity of a very damaging kind.'

'But my dear colleague, will you not assure them that the matter at issue is murder and nothing else? Nothing, as you say, personal.'

'I think,' Alleyn said dryly, 'that they are not so simple as to swallow that one.'

The Questore hitched his shoulders and spread his hands. 'They can be assured,' he threw out, 'of our discretion.'

Alleyn said: 'What's Mailer's nationality—has he taken out Italian citizenship?'

'That can be ascertained. You are thinking, of course, of extradition.'

'Am I?' Alleyn muttered absently. '*Am* I?'

The doctor, the ambulance men, the Questore's subordinate, Vice-Questore Bergarmi and the Roman version of a homicide squad now arrived with their appropriate gear: cameras, tripods, lamps, cases, a stretcher and a canvas sheet; routine props in the international crime show.

The men were solemnly presented. Alleyn supposed Bergarmi to be the opposite number in rank of a detective-inspector.

They were given their instructions. Everyone was immensely

deferential to Il Questore Valdarno and, since it was clearly indicated, to Alleyn. The grille was unlocked and the new arrivals went below.

'We shall not accompany them,' Valdarno said. 'It is not necessary. It would be inappropriate. In due course they will report themselves. After all, one does not need a medical officer to tell one when a woman has been strangled.'

Alleyn thought: I've got to tread delicately here. This is going to be tricky.

He said, 'When your photographer has taken his pictures I would be very glad to have another look round, if I might. Particularly at the top railing round the well. Before that fragment of material, whatever it is, is removed. May I?'

'But of course. You find some significance in this fragment? The rail has a rough surface, many, many persons have brushed past it and grasped it. I saw that you examined the area closely after the lights were on. What did you see? What was this material?'

'Some kind of black stuff. It's the position that I find interesting. The rail is about five by two inches. It is indeed rough on the inside surface and it is on the inside surface near the lower edge that this scrap of material has been caught.'

After a considerable pause Valdarno said, 'This is perhaps a little curious but, I would suggest, not of great moment. Some person has leant over the rail, lolling his arms down, peering into the depths and——' He stopped, frowned and then said, 'by all means go down, my friend, and examine the area as you require. You have my full authority.'

'How very kind,' Alleyn said and took immediate advantage of the offer.

He went below and found Valdarno's 'people' very active in the familiar routine under Bergarmi. Violetta had been photographed *in situ* and was now transferred to the stretcher where the surgeon hung over her terrible face. The lid of

156

the sarcophagus was being treated by a finger-print officer. Alleyn didn't for a moment suppose that they would find anything.

Bergarmi received his principal's card with elaborate courtesy and little enthusiasm.

Alleyn had his own and very particular little camera. While Bergarmi and his staff were fully extended in other directions, he took three quick shots of the inner-side rails. He then returned to the basilica.

He told Valdarno what he had done and said that he would now take advantage of his kind offer and visit Mailer's apartment. Valdarno instructed one of his drivers to take him there and, having shaken hands elaborately for the second time in an hour, they parted.

Mailer's apartment was in a side street behind the Pantheon. It was reached through a little run-down courtyard and up the first flight of a narrow outdoor stairway. Valdarno's man on duty let Alleyn in and, after a look at the all-powerful card, left him to his own devices.

The rooms, there were three of them, struck Alleyn as being on their way up. One or two new and lusciously upholstered armchairs, a fine desk, a sumptuous divan, and on Mr Mailer's bed, a heavily embroidered and rather repellent velvet cover, all pointed to affluence. A dilapidated kitchenette, murky bathroom and blistered walls suggested that it was of recent origin.

The bookshelves contained a comprehensive line in high-camp pornography, some of it extremely expensive, and a selection of mere pornography, all of it cheap and excessively nasty.

Signor Valdarno's man was whiling away his vigil with a sample of the latter kind.

Alleyn asked him if the contents of the desk had been examined. He said Vice-Questore Bergarmi had intimated that he would attend to it later on if Mailer did not return.

'He has not returned,' Alleyn said. 'I will look at it. You, perhaps, would prefer to telephone Il Questore Valdarno before I do so.'

This did the trick. The man returned to his book and Alleyn tackled the desk. The only lock that gave him any trouble was that of a concealed cupboard at the back of the knee-hole and it was in this cupboard, finally, that he struck oil: a neatly kept ledger: a sort of diary-cum-reference book. Here, at intervals, opposite a date, was a tick with one, or sometimes two letters beside it.

Alleyn consulted his own notebook and found that these entries tallied with those connected with suspected shipments of heroin from Izmir to Naples and thence, via Corsica, to Marseilles.

He came to a date a little over a year ago and found: '*Ang. in Aug.* B.G.' and four days later: 'B.G. *S. in L.*' This, he thought very rum indeed, until, in a drawer of the desk he found a manuscript entitled *Angelo in August*. He returned to the ledger.

Nothing of interest until he came to an entry for May of the previous year. 'V. der V. Confirmed. Wait.' From now on there appeared at intervals entries of large sums of money with no explanation but bearing a relationship to the dates of shipment.

He plodded on. The Agente yawned over his book. Entries for the current year. 'Perugia. K.D. L.100,000.' Several entries under K.D. After that: merely a note of the first and subsequent Il Cicerone tours.

Alleyn completed his search of the desk. He found in a locked cash box a number of letters that clearly indicated Mr Mailer's activities in the blackmailing line and one in a language that he did not know but took to be Dutch. This he copied out and then photographed, together with several entries in the diary.

It was now half past eleven. He sighed, said good morning

158

to the Agente and set out for Valdarno's office, reflecting that he had probably just completed a bare-faced piece of malfeasance but not in the least regretting it.

THREE

At noon, Mr Mailer's unhappy band of pilgrims assembled in the Questore Valdarno's sumptuous office.

Lady Braceley, Kenneth Dorne and Major Sweet all bore shattering witness to the extravagances of the previous night. The Van der Veghels looked astonished, Barnaby Grant anxious and Sophy Jason shocked. They sat in a semi-circle on imitation renaissance chairs of great splendour and little ease while Valdarno caused wine to be handed round on a lordly tray.

Lady Braceley, Kenneth and Major Sweet, turned sickly glances upon it and declined. The rest of the party sipped uncomfortably while the Questore addressed them at length.

Alleyn sat a little apart from the others who, as the Questore proceeded, eyed him with increasing consternation.

Without much elaboration, Valdarno told them of the discovery of Violetta's body and remarked upon Sebastian Mailer's continued non-appearance.

He sat behind his magnificent desk. Alleyn noticed that the centre drawer was half-open and that it contained paper. The Questore had placed his folded hands negligently across the drawer but as he warmed to his theme he forgot himself and gestured freely.

His audience shifted uneasily. Major Sweet, rousing himself, said that he'd known from the first that there was something fishy about the fellow Mailer. Nobody followed this up.

'My Lady, Ladies, Gentlemen,' the Questore concluded, 'you will, I am sure, perceive that it is important for this Mr

Mailer to be traced. I speak from the highest authority when I assure you of our great concern that none of you should be unduly inconvenienced and that your visit to Rome, we hope a pleasurable one, should not be in any way——' he paused and glanced into the drawer of his desk—'diminished,' he said, 'by this unfortunate occurrence.'

He made the slight mistake of absent-mindedly closing the drawer with his thumb. Otherwise, Alleyn thought, he had managed beautifully.

Major Sweet said, 'Very civil, I'm sure. Do what we can.' The Van der Veghels and Sophy said, 'Of course.' Lady Braceley looked vaguely about her. 'No, but *really*!' she said. 'I mean, how too off-putting and peculiar.' She opened her cigarette case but made a sad botch of helping herself. Her hands jerked, cigarettes shot about the floor.

'*Excellenza!*' the Questore ejaculated. '*Scusi!* Allow me!' He leapt to his feet.

'No! No! Please! Kenneth! Too stupid of me. No!'

Kenneth gathered the cigarettes, pushed them back into the case and with some difficulty lit the one that shook between her lips. They all looked away from Lady Braceley and Kenneth.

Grant said loudly, 'You haven't actually told us so, but I suppose I am right in thinking you suspect Mailer of this murder?'

Kenneth Dorne gave out a noise somewhere between a laugh and a snort.

The Questore made one of his more ornate gestures. 'One must not be precipitate,' he said. 'Let us say, Mr Grant, that we feel he may——'

'"*Help the police in their investigation*",' Kenneth said, 'that's got a familiar ring about it! "Inspector or Superintendent Flookamapush says he's anxious to trace Mr Sebastian Mailer who the police believe may help——"'

He broke off, staring at Alleyn. 'My *God*!' he said and got to his feet. 'I was right! My *God*. I remember, now. I knew I'd seen that fabulous face before. My God, you *are* a policeman!'

He turned to the others. 'He's a bloody policeman,' he said. 'He's the detective they're always writing up in the papers. "Handsome" something—— What is it?—yes—by God— "Handsome Alleyn".' He pointed to Alleyn. 'He's no tourist, he's a spy. Last night. At Toni's. Spying. That's what he was doing.'

Alleyn watched all the heads turn in his direction and all the shutters come down. I'm back in business, he thought.

He stood up.

'Mr Dorne,' he said, 'has beaten us to the post by one second. I think the Questore was about to explain.'

The Questore did explain, with one or two significant evasions and a couple of downright lies that Alleyn would have avoided.

He said that the highly distinguished Superintendent was on holiday but had made a courtesy call at police headquarters in Rome, that he had expressed a wish to remain incognito which the Questore had of course respected. It was by pure accident, he lied, that Alleyn had joined in the Cicerone tour but when Mailer disappeared he had felt it his duty to report the circumstance. For which the Questore and his subordinates were greatly obliged to him.

Here he paused. Of his audience, Sophy and the Van der Veghels looked perfectly satisfied. The others exhibited distrust and scepticism in varying degrees.

The Questore continued. In view of the death of this unfortunate woman, and because Mr Mailer was a British subject, he had asked Superintendent Alleyn to assist, which he had most graciously consented to do. The Questore felt sure that the Superintendent's fellow-countrymen would greatly prefer the few inquiries to be under his guidance. In any case, he ended, the proceedings would probably be very short and there would be no radical interference in their holidays.

He bowed to the Van der Veghels and added that he hoped they, also, would find themselves in agreement with this plan.

'But, of course,' the Baron said. 'It is a satisfactory and intelligent suggestion. A crime has been committed. It is our duty to assist. At the same time I am glad of your assurance that we shall not be detained for very long. After all,' and he bowed to Alleyn, 'we are also on vacation.'

With many mellifluous assurances the Questore begged them to withdraw to a room which had been placed at Alleyn's disposal.

It was less sumptuous than the first office but more than sufficient for the purpose. There was a desk for Alleyn and extra chairs were brought in for the seven travellers. He noticed that Barnaby Grant was quick to place himself next to Sophy Jason, that Major Sweet was fractionally less bleary-eyed than he had been, that Lady Braceley had better luck with a new cigarette and in controlling the tremor that was nevertheless still in evidence. Kenneth, fidgety and resentful, looked out of the corner of his eye at Alleyn and clearly was not much mollified by the official pronouncement.

Alleyn's chief concern was to avoid sounding like a re-play of the Valdarno disc.

'This is both a tragic and an absurd situation,' he said, 'and I don't really know what you'll be making of it. Cutting it down to size it amounts to this. An unfortunate woman has been murdered and a rather strange individual of presumed British nationality has disappeared. We seem to be the last people to have seen him and the police, obviously, want to get statements from all of us. Signor Valdarno is much too grand a personage to handle the case: he's the equivalent in rank of our Chief Constable or perhaps Assistant Commissioner. His man in charge doesn't speak English and because I'm a cop he's asked me to sort it out. I hope that's all right with all of you. I could hardly refuse, could I?'

'You might have told us about your job,' Major Sweet said resentfully.

'By why? You haven't told us about yours.'

The Major reddened.

'Look,' Alleyn said. 'Let's get it over shall we? The sooner the better, surely.'

'Certainly,' Sophy Jason said. 'By all means, let's.'

Grant said, 'Oh, by all means,' in a wooden voice, and Lady Braceley and Kenneth made plaintive sounds of acceptance.

'Ach, yes!' cried the Baroness. 'No more delays, isn't it? Already our plans for today look silly. Instead of fountinks at the Villa d'Este here is a stuffed room. Come! On!'

Thus encouraged, Alleyn set about his task. His situation was an odd one, removed as he was from immediate reliance upon the CID and from the sense of being an integral part of its structure.

This was an 'away match' and presented its own problems, not the least of which was to define his area of investigation. Originally this had simply been that which covered Mailer's presumed activities in the international drug racket and possible association with the key figure—the fabulous Otto Ziegfeldt.

Now, with the discovery of Violetta, staring and frightful, in a stone coffin that had held who could guess what classic bones and flesh, the case had spilled into a wider and more ambiguous affair. The handling of it became very tricky indeed.

He began: 'I think we'd better settle the question of when each of us last saw Sebastian Mailer. For my part, it was when we were on the middle level and just after Major

Sweet and Lady Braceley had left to go up to the atrium. Mr Grant, Miss Jason and the Baron and Baroness were with me and we all went down to the Mithraic dwelling together. Major Sweet and Mr Dorne joined us there separately, some five, ten, or fifteen minutes later. May I begin by asking you, Lady Braceley, if you saw anything of Mailer or of Violetta after you left us?'

Not only, Alleyn thought, was she in the grip of a formidable hangover but she was completely nonplussed at finding herself in a situation that could not be adjusted to a nineteen-twentyish formula for triteness.

She turned her lacklustre gaze from one man to another, ran her tongue round her lips and said, 'No. No, of course I didn't. No.'

'And you, Major? On your way down? Did you see either of them?'

'I did not.'

'You stayed for a minute or two with Lady Braceley and then came down to the Mithraeum?'

'Yes.'

'And met nobody on the way?'

'Nobody.'

Alleyn said casually, 'There must at that time have been, besides yourself, three persons at large between the top level —the basilica and the bottom one—the Mithraeum. Mailer himself, Violetta and Mr Kenneth Dorne. You neither saw nor heard any of them?'

'Certainly not.'

'Mr Dorne, when exactly did you leave us?'

'I haven't the faintest idea.'

'Perhaps,' Alleyn said with undiminished good humour, 'we can help you. You were with us in the middle level cloisters when Mailer made his joke about Apollo being a latter-day Lazarus.'

'How do you know?'

'Because you giggled at it.'

'Marvellous,' said Kenneth.

'It was not a nice joke,' the Baroness said. 'We did not find it amusink, did we, Gerrit?'

'No, my dear.'

'It was a silly one.'

'So.'

'You think it funnier perhaps,' Kenneth said, 'to dodge behind terra-cotta busts and bounce out at old—at highly-strung people. It takes all sorts to raise a laugh.'

'You were not there, Mr Dorne,' said the Baron. 'You had left the party. We had crossed the nave of the early church and you did not come with us. How did you know I bounced?'

'I heard of it,' Kenneth said loftily, 'from my aunt.'

Alleyn plodded on. 'We understood from Mailer that you had gone back to photograph the Apollo. Is that right?'

'Certainly.'

'And you did photograph it?'

Kenneth slid his feet about and after a pretty long pause said, 'As it happened, no. I'd run out of film.' He pulled out his packet of cigarettes and found it was empty.

'No, you hadn't,' shouted Major Sweet. 'You hadn't done any such thing. You took a photograph of Mithras when we were all poodlefaking round Grant and his book.'

Grant, most unexpectedly, burst out laughing.

'There's such a thing,' Kenneth said breathlessly, 'as putting in a new film, Major Sweet.'

'Well, yes,' said Alleyn. 'Of course there is. Tell me, did Mailer rejoin you while you were not photographing Apollo?'

This time the pause was an uncomfortably long one. Major Sweet appeared to take the opportunity to have a nap. He shut his eyes, lowered his chin and presently opened his mouth.

At last: '*No*,' Kenneth said loudly. 'No. He didn't turn up.'

'"Turn up"? You were expecting him, then?'

'No, I wasn't. Why the hell do you suppose I was? I wasn't expecting him and I didn't see him.' The cigarette packet dropped from his fingers. '*What's that?*' he demanded.

Alleyn had taken a folded handkerchief from his pocket. He opened it to display a crumpled piece of glossy blue paper.

'Do you recognize it?' he asked.

'No!'

Alleyn reached out a long arm, retrieved the cigarette packet from the floor and dropped it on the desk.

He said, 'I was given two boxes wrapped in similar paper to this at Toni's Pad last night.'

'I'm afraid,' Kenneth said whitely, 'my only comment to that is: "So, dear Mr Superintendent Alleyn, what?"'

'In one of them there were eight tablets of heroin. Each, I would guess, containing one-sixth of a grain. In the other, an equal amount of cocaine in powder form. Mr Mailer's very own merchandise, I was informed.'

The Van der Veghels broke into scandalized ejaculations, first in their own language and then in English.

'You didn't throw this paper behind the statue of Apollo, Mr Dorne?'

'No. *Christ!*' Kenneth screamed out, 'what the hell is all this? What idiot stuff are you trying to sell me? All right, so this was an H. and C. wrapping. And how many people go through Saint what's-his-name's every day? What about the old woman? For all you know she may have peddled it. To anyone. Why, for God's sake, pick on me?'

'Kenneth—darling—no. Please! No!'

'Partly,' Alleyn said, 'because up to that time you had exhibited withdrawal symptoms but on your arrival in the Mithraeum appeared to be relieved of them.'

'No!'

166

'We needn't labour the point. If necessary, we can take fingerprints.' He pointed to the paper, and to the empty cigarette packet. 'And in any case, last night you were perfectly frank about your experiments with drugs. You told me that Mailer introduced you to them. Why are you kicking up such a dust now?'

'I didn't know who you were.'

'I'm not going to run you in here, in Rome, for making a mess of yourself with drugs, you silly chap. I simply want to know if, for whatever reason, you met Mailer by the statue of Apollo in the middle level at S. Tommaso.'

'Kenneth—*no!*'

'Auntie, do you mind! I've told him—no, no, *no.*'

'Very well. We'll go on. You returned to photograph Apollo, found you had used up the film in your camera, continued on down to the bottom level and joined us in the Mithraeum. At what stage did you put a new film in your camera?'

'I don't remember.'

'Where is the old film?'

'In my pocket, for God's sake. In my room.'

'You didn't encounter Major Sweet either, although he must have been on his way down, just ahead of you?'

'No.'

'You passed the Apollo, Major, on your way down?'

'I suppose so. Can't say I remember. Must have, of course.'

'Not necessarily. The cloisters run right round the old church at the middle level. If you'd turned right instead of left when you reached that level you would have come by a shorter route, and without passing Apollo, to the passage leading to the iron stairway.'

'I could have but I didn't.'

'Odd!' Alleyn said. 'And neither of you had sight, sound or smell of Mailer and Violetta?'

Silence.

'With the exception of Lady Braceley we all came together in the Mithraeum and were there for, I suppose, at least fifteen minutes while the Baroness and Baron and Mr Dorne took photographs and Mr Grant read to us. Then we found our several ways back to the top. You left first, Mr Dorne, by the main entrance.'

'You're so right. And I went up by the shortest route and I met nobody and heard nothing and I joined my aunt in the garden.'

'Quite so. I went back with the Baron and Baroness. We left the Mithraeum by a doorway behind the figure of the god, turned right twice and followed the cloister, if that's what it should be called, passing the well and the sarcophagus and arriving finally at the passage to the iron stairway.' He turned to the Van der Veghels. 'You agree?'

'Certainly,' said the Baroness. 'That was the way. Stoppink sometimes to examine——'

She broke off and turned in agitation to her husband, laying her hands on his arm. She spoke to him in their own language, her voice trembling.

He stooped over her, solicitous and concerned, gathered her hands in his and said gently: 'In English, my dear, should we not? Let me explain.' He turned to Alleyn. 'My wife is disturbed and unhappy,' he said. 'She has remembered, as no doubt you will remember, Mr Alleyn—or, no! You had already turned into the passage, I think. But my wife took a photograph of the sarcophagus.'

'It is so dreadful to think,' the Baroness lamented. 'Imagink! This wretched woman—her body—it may have been—no, Gerrit, it is dreadful.'

'On the contrary, Baroness,' Alleyn said. 'It may be of great assistance to the investigation. Of course, one understands that the implications are distasteful——'

'*Distasteful!*'

'Well—macabre—dreadful, if you like. But your photograph may at least prove that the sarcophagus had not been interfered with at that juncture.'

'It had not. You yourself must have seen——'

'In that lighting it looked perfectly all right but a flashlamp might bring out some abnormality, you know.'

'What was it like,' Grant said, 'when you examined it, as I gather you did, with Valdarno?'

'There was—a slight displacement,' Alleyn said. 'If the Baroness's photograph shows none it will establish that the murder was committed after we left the Mithraeum.'

'And after we had all left the building?' Grant asked.

'Not quite that, perhaps, but it might come to that. May we just define the rest of the party's movements. Yours, for instance.'

'I had offered to stay in the Mithraeum in case anybody wanted information about the rest of the insula. Miss Jason remained with me for, I suppose, ten minutes or so and we then made our way up by the shortest route: the main exit from the Mithraeum, through the antechamber and then down the short passage to the stairway. We didn't pass the well and sarcophagus, of course, and we met nobody.'

'Hear anybody? Voices?'

'No. I don't think so.'

'Wait a bit,' Sophy said.

'Yes, Miss Jason?'

'I don't suppose it matters but——' she appealed to Grant. 'Do you remember? Just as we were leaving the Mithraeum there was a sound of voices. All mixed up and booming because of the echo.'

'Was there? I've forgotten.'

'Men's or women's voices?' Alleyn asked.

'They were so distorted it's hard to say. A man's I think

and perhaps a woman's: perhaps yours and Baroness Van der Veghel's on your way up the stairs. Or Baron Van der Veghel's. Or all three.'

'Might be,' Alleyn said. 'Which way did you go back, Major Sweet?'

'Ah, 'um. I pottered round a bit. Had another look at the well and if you ask me whether the lid of the sarcophagus was out of position I can only say if it was I didn't notice it. I—ah—I went up into the nave of the old church. Matter of fact, while I was there I heard you and—ah—the Van der Veghels in the cloisters. Taking photographs.'

'That is quite so,' said the Baroness. 'I took the head of Mercury.'

'You were still at it when I went on up the stone stairs. Took my time. Didn't see the woman. Or Mailer. My opinion, he wasn't there, anywhere in the premises. Sure of it.'

'Why?' Alleyn asked.

'To be perfectly honest because if the fellow had been there I'd have found him. I thought it damned peculiar him not turning up like that, leaving us cold after taking a whacking great fee off us. So I thought: if the blighter's hanging about somewhere I'm going to dig him out. And I didn't.'

'I really can't believe,' said Grant, 'that you could have made anything remotely resembling a thorough search, Major Sweet. In that short time? In that light? And with all those side passages and excavations? No!'

'That is so,' said the Baron. 'That is undoubtedly so.'

'I resent that, sir,' said the Major and blew out his cheeks.

The Baron paid no attention to him. 'Mr Alleyn,' he said. 'Surely it is not impossible that this Mailer was hiding down there, perhaps already with the body of the woman he had murdered, and that he waited until we had gone before putting it—where it was found. Mr Alleyn—what do you say? Is it possible?'

'I think it's possible, Baron, yes. But when, in that case, did he make his escape?'

'Perhaps he's still there,' Kenneth suggested, and gave his little whinnying laugh.

'I have thought of that,' the Baron said, disregarding Kenneth. 'I have thought that perhaps he waited until the good fathers made their search. That he hid himself somewhere near the top and while they looked elsewhere, contrived to elude them and again hid himself in the basilica until we had driven away and then made his escape. I do not know. Perhaps it is an absurd suggestion but—he is gone, after all.'

'I think,' Lady Braceley said, 'it's a very clever suggestion.' And she actually summoned up the wreck of an arch glance for the Baron, who bowed and looked horrified.

'To sum up,' Alleyn said, 'if that's not a laughable phrase in the context. None of us saw Mailer or Violetta after Mailer left us, ostensibly to join Mr. Dorne at the statue of Apollo in the cloisters of the old church at the middle level of S. Tommaso.'

Sophy had given a little ejaculation.

'Yes, Miss Jason? You've thought of something?'

'Only just. It may be—it probably is—nothing. But it was during the group-photograph episode.'

'Yes?'

'There was a noise somewhere outside the Mithraeum. Not far away, I'd have thought, but all mixed up and distorted by echoes. A woman's voice, I think, and then it was —well, kind of cut off. And then—later—a kind of thud. At the time I supposed somebody—somewhere—had shut a very heavy door.'

'I remember!' the Baron ejaculated. 'I remember perfectly! It was when I took my picture of the group.'

'You do?' Sophy said. 'A kind of bang—thumping noise?'

'Exactly.'

'Like a door?'

'A very heavy door.'

'Yes,' Alleyn agreed, 'it did sound rather like that, didn't it?'

'But,' Sophy said, turning white, 'there aren't any heavy doors down there that I can remember.' She appealed to Grant. 'Are there?'

'No. No doors,' he said.

'So I wonder if it was something else—something being dropped, for instance. Not from a great height. Just a little way. But something very heavy.'

'Like a stone lid?' Alleyn suggested.

Sophy nodded.

7. Afternoon

WHEN ALLEYN ASKED the travellers not to leave Rome for
the present there was a great outcry from Lady Braceley and
Major Sweet. The Major talked noisily about his rights as a
British subject. Lady Braceley lamented and referred to
persons in high places to whom she commanded immediate
access.

She was silenced at last by her nephew, who muttered and
cajoled. She shed tears which she dexterously manipulated
with the folded edge of her handkerchief.

The Major seemed to be sensibly influenced by the information that additional expenses would be met. He subsided into
a sullen and wary acquiescence.

Grant, Sophy and the Van der Veghels were temperate in
their reactions. What, as the Baroness rhetorically and vaguely
asked, could one do against Fate? Her husband, at a more
realistic level, said that while it was inconvenient, it was at
the same time obligatory upon them to remain *in situ* if
circumstances seemed to require their presence.

Grant said impatiently that he had intended to stay in
Rome anyway and Sophy said her holiday extended over the
next four weeks. While she had made vague plans for Perugia
and Florence she was perfectly ready to postpone them.

They broke up at half past one. The travellers, with the
exception of Grant and Sophy, availed themselves of the large
car provided by Valdarno.

Alleyn had a brief talk with the Questore and with appropriate regrets declined an invitation for luncheon. He had, he said, to write a report.

When he finally emerged from the building he found Grant and Sophy waiting for him.

'I want to talk to you,' Grant said.

'By all means. Will you have lunch with me?' Alleyn made a bow to Sophy. 'Both of you? Do.'

'Not me,' Sophy said. 'I'm only a hanger-on.'

'You're nothing of the sort,' Grant contradicted.

'Well, whatever I am, I've got a date for lunch. So—thank you, Mr Alleyn—but I must be off.'

And before they could do anything to stop her she had in fact darted across the street and stopped a taxi.

'A lady of incisive action,' Alleyn remarked.

'She is indeed.'

'Here's another cab. Shall we go?'

They lunched at Alleyn's hotel. He caught himself wondering if to Grant the occasion seemed like a rendering in another key of his no doubt habitual acceptance of expense-account hospitality.

Alleyn was a good host. He made neither too much nor too little of the business of ordering, and when that was done, talked about the difficulties of adjusting oneself to Rome and the dangers of a surfeit of sightseeing. He asked Grant if he'd had to do a great deal of research for *Simon in Latium*.

'Of course,' Alleyn said, 'it's bloody cheek to say so, but it always seems to me that a novelist who has set his book in a foreign environment is, in some sort, like an investigating officer. I mean, in my job one is for ever having to "get up" information, to take in all sorts of details—technical, occupational, indigenous, whatever you like—in surroundings that are quite outside one's experience. It's a matter of mugging up.'

'It certainly was in the case of *Simon in Latium*.'

'You must have stayed in Rome for some time, surely?'

'Two months,' Grant said, shortly. He laid down his knife and fork. 'As a matter of fact it's about that—in a way—that I want to talk to you.'

'Do you? Fair enough. Now?'

Grant thought for a moment or two. 'It's a poor compliment to a superb luncheon but—now, if you please.'

So he told Alleyn how Sebastian Mailer found his manuscript and about the sequel.

'I think I know *now* how he'd worked the whole job. When he found the MS he got his idea. He picked the lock of my case and read the book. He spent three days concocting his *Angelo in August*. He didn't make it blatantly like *Simon*. Just introduced my major theme as a minor one. Enough to make me talk about it in front of his revolting chums.

'He took me on a night-crawl, fetching up at the place you went to last night—Toni's. I don't remember much about the later part of the experience but enough to make me wish I'd forgotten the lot. Apparently I talked about the "resemblance" at the restaurant we went to—Il Eremo it's called—and to some American chum of his who would be delighted to blow it to the Press.

'I went back to England. The book came out and three weeks ago I returned to Rome, as he knew I would. I ran into him and he took me into a ghastly little parlour in the Van der Veghels' hotel and blackmailed me. He was quite shameless. He practically said, in so many words, that he'd re-hashed his story so that now it was blatantly like mine and that he had witnesses from—that night—to say I'd talked about the resemblance when I was drunk. One of them, he said, was the Roman correspondent for the *News of the World* and would make a big splash with the story. Oh yes!' Grant said when Alleyn opened his mouth. 'Oh yes. I know. Why didn't I tell

him to go to hell? You may not remember—why should you?
—what happened over my first book.'

'I remember.'

'And so would a great many other people. Nobody except
my publishers and a few friends believed that bloody business
was a coincidence. The case would be hauled into the light
again. All the filthy show re-hashed and me established as a
shameless plagiarist. I may be a louse but I couldn't face it.'

'What did he ask?'

'That's the point. Not so much, in a way. Just that I took
on these unspeakable tours.'

'It wouldn't have stopped there, you know. He was easing
you in. Why did you decide to tell me all this?'

'It's just got too much. I told Sophy about it and she suggested I tell you. After the meeting was over and we waited
outside. It's an extraordinary thing,' Grant said, 'I met that
girl yesterday. It's by no means a quick take, she's not that
sort. And yet . . . Well,' Grant said, giving it up, 'there you
are. You tell us your main interest in him is as a drug-runner.
He turns out to be a murderer. I daresay it's only of academic
interest that he happens to be a blackmailer as well.'

'Oh, everything is grist that comes to our grubby little
mill,' Alleyn said. 'I'm in a damn tricky sort of position
myself, you know. I've learnt this morning that the Roman
police have found out Mailer's definitely a British subject.
That, in a vague way, keeps me in the picture but with a shift
of emphasis: my masters sent me here on the drug-running
lay and I find myself landed with the presumptive murder of
an Italian.'

'So your presence in yesterday's ongoings was not acci-
dental?'

'No. Not.'

'I may as well tell you, Alleyn, I'm not as keen as mustard
for you to catch Mailer.'

'I suppose not. You're afraid, aren't you, that if he's brought to trial he'll blow the story of your alleged plagiarism?'

'All right. Yes. I am. I don't expect you to understand. The police,' Grant said savagely, 'are not exactly famous for their sympathy with the arts.'

'On the other hand they are acquainted with a tendency on the part of the general public, artistic or otherwise, to separate what is laughingly called justice from the concept of enlightened self-interest.'

'I imagine,' Grant said after a sufficient pause, 'that my face could scarcely be redder.'

'Don't give it another thought. As for your fear of a phoney exposure, I think I can promise you it is absolutely groundless.'

'You can? You really can do that?'

'I believe so. I'd take long odds on it.'

'I suppose the whole thing, from the police point of view, is entirely beside the point.'

'You may put it like that,' Alleyn said. 'How about a liqueur with our coffee?'

TWO

The next two days went by without further incident. Mr Mailer's guests followed, Alleyn presumed, their own inclinations. He himself wrote up a detailed report on the case and sent a précis of it to his masters. He had three indeterminate conversations with Valdarno and put a call through to London asking for detailed reports on Lady Braceley and Kenneth Dorne and a check through the Army lists on Major Hamilton Sweet.

He also asked for the appropriate branch to make inquiries through the Dutch authorities about the Van der Veghels.

On the third day Rome was engulfed in a heat wave. Pavements, walls and the sky itself quivered under its onslaught and the high saints extended their stone arms above the city in a shimmer that resembled movement. Alleyn lunched in the hotel and spent a good deal of time wondering how Fox was prospering in London.

The Latin siesta is a civilized habit. At its best it puts the sweltering heat of the day behind insect-proof barriers, gives people a rest from excitedly haranguing each other and causes a lull in the nervous activity of the streets.

For Alleyn the siesta was not a blessing. Trained to do with less sleep than most persons require and, when necessary, to catch what he could get in cat-naps and short periods of oblivion, he found the three odd hours of disengagement an irritant rather than a tranquillizer.

He stripped, slept soundly for an hour, took a shower and, freshly dressed, went out into the street.

Rome was under a haze and the Spanish Steps were deserted. No ambiguous youths displayed on their accepted beat. Flowers blazed under protective canvas or drooped where the sun had found them. All the shops down in the Via Condotti were shut and so was the travel agency where Alleyn had booked his tour.

He walked down the steps: not quite the only person abroad in the heat of the day. Ahead of him at intervals were a belated shop-girl, a workman, an old woman and—having apprently come from the hotel—Giovanni Vecchi!

Alleyn took cover behind an awning. Giovanni went on down the steps and into the Via Condotti. Alleyn followed cautiously. Giovanni stopped.

Alleyn's instant sidestep into the entrance of a closed shop was a reflex action. He watched Giovanni between two handbags in the corner window.

Giovanni glanced quickly up and down the street, and then

at his watch. A taxi appeared, stopped at a house almost opposite the shop and discharged its fare. Giovanni hailed it and came back to meet it.

Alleyn moved further into the doorway and turned his back. He heard Giovanni say 'Il Eremo' and name the street.

The door slammed, the taxi rattled off and Alleyn, looking in vain for another, set off at a gruelling pace for Navona.

Arriving there some ten minutes later, he made his way down an alley smelling of cooking oil and garlic.

There it was: the little trattoria with kerbside *caffè* where a year ago Mailer and Grant had dined together. The door into the restaurant was shut and the blinds were drawn. Chairs had been tipped forward over the outside tables. The place at first sight seemed to be quite deserted.

As Alleyn drew cautiously nearer, however, he saw that two men were seated at a table in a shadowed corner under the awning and that one of them was Giovanni. They had their backs towards him but there was no mistaking Giovanni's companion.

It was Major Sweet.

Alleyn had arrived at a yard belonging to a junk shop of the humbler sort. Bad pictures, false renaissance chairs, one or two restored pieces ruined by a deluge of cheap varnish. A large dilapidated screen.

He moved into the shelter of the screen and surveyed Major Sweet and Giovanni through the hinged gap between two leaves.

Major Sweet, from the rear, looked quite unlike himself: there was something about his back and the forward tilt of his head that suggested extreme alertness. A slight movement and his cheek, the end of his moustache and his right eye came into view. The eye was cocked backwards: the eye of a watchful man.

Giovanni leant towards the Major and talked. No Italian

can talk without hands and Giovanni's were active but, as it were, within a restricted field. The Major folded his arms and seemed to wait.

Could he, Alleyn wondered, be arranging with Giovanni for a further instalment of the other night's excesses? Somehow the two of them didn't look quite like that. They looked, he thought, as if they drove some other kind of bargain and he hoped he wasn't being too fanciful about them.

He saw that by delicate manœuvring he could cross the yard, edge up to a bin with a polyglot collection of papers under a tall cupboard, and thus bring himself much nearer to the *caffè*.

He did so, slid a disreputable but large map out of the bin and held it in front of him in case they suddenly came his way. Lucky, he thought, that he'd changed his shoes and trousers.

They spoke in English. Their voices dropped and rose and he caught only fragments of what they said, as if a volume control were being turned up and down by some irresponsible hand.

'. . . waste of time talking . . . you better understand, Vecchi . . . danger. Ziegfeldt . . .'

'. . . are you mad? How many times I tell you . . . instructions . . .'

'. . . search . . . police . . .'

'. . . OK, Signore. So they search and find nothing . . . I have made . . . "arrangements" . . .'

'. . . *arrangements*. Try that on Alleyn and see what . . . Different . . . Take it from me . . . I *can* do it. And I will. Unless . . .'

'. . . drunk . . .'

'. . . nothing to do with it. Not so drunk I didn't know . . . It's a fair offer. Make it right for me or . . .'

'You dare not.'

'Don't you believe it. Look here . . . if I report . . . Zieg-feldt . . .'

'*Taci!*'

'Shut up.'

A savage-sounding but muted exchange followed. Finally Giovanni gave a sharp ejaculation. Chair legs grated on the pavement. A palm was slapped down on the table. Alleyn, greatly stimulated, squatted behind the ruin of a velvet chair and heard them go past. Their footsteps died away and he came out of cover.

Somewhere behind a shuttered window a man yawned vocally and prodigiously. Further along the street a door opened. A youth in singlet and trousers lounged out, scratching his armpits. A woman inside the trattoria called with an operatic flourish, 'Mar—cel—lo.'

The siesta was over.

It was a long time since Alleyn had 'kept observation' on anybody and like Il Questore Valdarno, he didn't altogether object to an unexpected return to field work.

It was not an easy job. The streets were still sparsely populated and offered little cover. He watched and waited until his men had walked about two hundred yards, saw them part company and decided to follow the Major who had turned into a side alley in that part of Old Rome devoted to the sale of 'antiques'.

Here in the dealers' occupational litter it was easier going and by the time they had emerged from the region Alleyn was close behind the Major, who was headed, he realized, in the direction of his small hotel where they had deposited him in the early hours of the morning.

All that for nothing, thought Alleyn.

The Major entered the hotel. Alleyn followed as far as the glass door, watched him go to the reception-desk, collect a key and move away, presumably to a lift.

Alleyn went in, entered a telephone booth opposite the lift and rang up Valdarno as he had arranged to do at this hour. He gave the Questore a succinct account of the afternoon's work.

'This Major, hah? This Sweet? Not quite as one supposed, hah?' said the Questore.

'So it would seem.'

'What is your interpretation?'

'I got a very fragmentary impression, you know. But it points, don't you think, to Major Sweet's connection with Ziegfeldt and in a greater or less degree, with the Mailer enterprise?'

'Undoubtedly. As for the premises—this Toni's—Bergarmi conducted a search yesterday afternoon.'

'And found——?'

'Nothing. There was evidence of hurried proceedings but no more.'

'The stuff they sold me was in a very small office near the main entrance.'

'It is empty of everything but a cash-box, ledger and telephone directory. There is no lead at all so far as Mailer is concerned. We are satisfied he has not left Rome. As you know, I set a watch of the most exhaustive, immediately after you telephoned.'

If Alleyn felt less sanguine than the Questore under this heading he did not say so.

'I think,' Valdarno was saying, 'we tug in this Giovanni Vecchi. I think we have little talks with him. You say he spoke of "arrangements". What arrangements do you suppose?'

'Hard to say,' Alleyn cautiously replied. 'I seemed to smell bribery. Of a particular kind.'

There was a longish silence. He thought that perhaps it would be tactful not to mention Major Sweet's remark about himself.

'And your next move, my dear colleague?'

'Perhaps while your people have their little talk with Giovanni Vecchi, I have one with Major Sweet. And after that, Signor Questore, I'm afraid I'm going to suggest that perhaps—a close watch on the Major?'

'Where are you?'

'At his hotel. The Benvenuto.'

'That will be done. There is,' Valdarno confessed, 'some confusion. On the one hand we have the trade in illicit drugs which is your concern. On the other the murder of Violetta which is also ours. And Mailer who is the key figure in both. One asks oneself: is there a further interlockment? With the travellers? Apart, of course, from their reluctance to become involved in any publicity arising out of our proceedings. Otherwise, between the murder and these seven travellers there is no connection?'

'I wouldn't say that,' Alleyn said. 'Oh, my dear Signor Questore, I wouldn't say that, you know. Not by a long chalk.'

When he had explained this point-of-view he hung up the receiver and took counsel with himself.

At last, by no means sure that he was doing the right thing, he went to the reception desk and sent up his name to Major Sweet.

THREE

It was hard to believe that this was the same man who, half an hour ago, had muttered away with Giovanni. The Major was right back on the form that Alleyn had suspected from the first to be synthetic. There he sat in his impeccable squarish light-weight suit, wearing an RA tie, a signet ring, brown brogues polished like chestnuts and the evidence of a mighty hangover in his bloodshot eyes. The hangover, at least, was not assumed. Perhaps none of it was assumed. Perhaps the

Major was all he seemed to be and all of it gone to the bad.

'Glad you looked in, Alleyn,' he said. 'I hoped to have a word with you.'

'Really?'

'Only to say that if I can be of use I'll be delighted. Realize you're in a difficult position. Treading on foreign protocol corns, what? Don't suppose there's much I can do but such as I am—here I am. Services ought to stick together, what?'

'You're a gunner, I see.'

'*Was*, old man. *Was*. Retired list now but still good for a spell of duty, I hope.' He gave a sly comradely laugh. 'In spite of the other night. Mustn't judge me by that, you know. Bad show. Rather fun once in a while, though, what?'

'You're not a regular patron of Mr Mailer's then?'

A fractional pause, before Major Sweet said, 'Of *Mailer's*? Oh, see what you mean. Or do I? Can't stomach the feller, actually. Picked him for a wrong 'un straight off. Still, I must say that show was well-run even if I did look on the wine when it was red, but let that go.'

'I wasn't talking about alcohol. I meant hard drugs. Heroin. Cocaine.'

'I say, look here! You're not telling me they've been pushing that rot-gut at Toni's Pad! I mean regularly.'

'And you're not telling me you didn't know.'

The Major took an appreciably longer pause before he said with quiet dignity, 'That was uncalled for.'

'I would have thought it was obvious enough.'

'Not to me, sir. Hold on, though. Wait a bit. You're referring to that ghastly youth: Dorne. Sorry I spoke. Good lord, yes, I knew what *he* was up to, of course. You brought it all out next morning. Very neatly done if I may say so, though as a matter of fact I dozed off a bit. Didn't get the hang of all that was said.'

'This isn't your first visit to Rome, is it?'

184

'Oh no. No. I was here on active service in 1943. And once or twice since. Never got hold of the lingo.'

'How long have you known Giovanni Vecchi?'

The beetroot ran out of the Major's carefully shaven jaw leaving the plum behind, but only in this respect could he be said to change countenance. 'Giovanni how much?' he said. 'Oh. You mean the courier fellow.'

'Yes. The courier fellow. He's in the drug business with Mailer.'

'Good lord, you don't say so!'

'I do, you know. They're tied up,' Alleyn said, mentally taking a deep breath, 'with Otto Ziegfeldt.'

'Who's he?' asked the Major in a perfectly toneless voice. 'Some dago?'

'He's the biggest of the drug barons.'

'You don't tell me.'

'I don't think I need to, do I?'

'What you need to do,' said the Major and his voice jumped half an octave, 'is explain yourself. I'm getting sick of this.'

'Ziegfeldt imports morphine from Turkey. The usual route, by diverse means, is from Izmir via Sicily to Marseilles and thence, through France or entirely by sea, to the USA. During the past year, however, an alternative route has developed: to Naples by a Lebanese shipping line and thence by Italian coastal traders to Marseilles, where it is converted to heroin. Ziegfeldt established an agent in Naples whose job was to arrange and supervise the trans-shipments. We believe this man to have been Sebastian Mailer.'

Alleyn waited for a moment. They sat in the deserted smoking-room of the hotel. It smelt of furniture polish and curtains and was entirely without character. Major Sweet rested his elbow on the arm of his uncomfortable chair and his cheek on his hand. He might have been given over to some aimless meditation.

'It appears,' Alleyn said, 'that at one time Mailer was married to the woman Violetta. Probably she acted for him in some minor capacity. Subsequently he deserted her.'

'Now,' said the Major into the palm of his hand, 'you're talking. Threatened to expose him.'

'Very likely.'

'Killed her.'

'Highly probable.'

'There you are, then.'

'Ziegfeldt doesn't at all care for agents who help themselves to goods in transit and then set up on their own account.'

'Dare say not.'

'He has them, as a general practice, bumped off. By another agent. He sets a spy upon them. Sometimes the spy is too greedy. He extorts a pay-off from—say—Giovanni? On consideration that he will not betray Giovanni and Mailer to his master. And then, unless he is very clever indeed, he is found out by his master and he too gets bumped off.'

A little bead of sweat trickled down Sweet's forehead and got hung up in his eyebrow.

'The gunners were not in Italy in 1943. They arrived in '44,' said Alleyn. 'Where do you buy your ties?'

'—slip of the tongue. 'Forty-four.'

'All right,' Alleyn said and stood up. 'How many times can a man double-cross,' he asked of nobody in particular, 'before he loses count? What's your price?'

Sweet raised his head and stared at him.

'I wouldn't try to bolt, either. You know your own business best, of course, but Otto Ziegfeldt has a long arm. So, for a matter of fact, have Interpol and even the London Police Force.'

Sweet dabbed his mouth and forehead with a neatly folded handkerchief. 'You're making a mistake,' he said. 'You're on the wrong track.'

186

'I heard you talking to Giovanni Vecchi in the Eremo *caffè* at a quarter to four this afternoon.'

A very singular noise came from somewhere inside the massive throat.

For the first time Sweet looked fixedly at Alleyn. He mouthed rather than said: 'I don't know what you're talking about.'

'I have the advantage of you, there. I do know what you and Vecchi were talking about. Come,' Alleyn said. 'You'll do yourself no good by keeping this up. Understand me. I'm here in Rome to find out what I can about Otto Ziegfeldt's operations. I'm not here to run in his lesser agents unless by doing so I can carry my job a step further.' He thought for a moment and then said, 'And of course, unless such an agent commits some action that in itself warrants his immediate arrest. I think I know what you've been up to. I think you've been sent by Ziegfeldt to spy upon Mailer and Giovanni Vecchi and report on their side-activities in Italy. I think you've double-crossed Ziegfeldt and played along with Mailer and Giovanni and now Mailer's disappeared you're afraid he may put you away with Ziegfeldt. I think you threatened to betray Giovanni to Ziegfeldt unless he pays you off in a big way. And I think you plan to clear up and get out while the going's good. You haven't a hope. You're in a pretty ugly situation, one way and another, aren't you? The safest thing for you, after all, might be for the Roman police to lock you up. The Roman streets won't be too healthy for you.'

'What do you want?'

'A complete list of Ziegfeldt's agents and a full account of his *modus operandi* between Izmir and the USA. Step by step. With particular respect to Mailer.'

'I can't. I don't know. I—I'm not—I'm not as deeply committed——'

'Or trusted? Perhaps not. But you're fairly far in or you wouldn't have been given your present job.'

'I can't do it, Alleyn.'

'Giovanni is being questioned.'

'Give me time.'

'No.'

'I want a drink.'

'You may have a drink. Shall we go to your room?'

'All right,' said Sweet. 'All right, God damn you, all right.'

FOUR

When Alleyn got back to his hotel he found a note from Lady Braceley under his door and a message that 'Fox' had rung from London and would ring again at six.

The time was now 5.15.

Lady Braceley wrote a large, mad hand that spilled all over the paper.

'Must see you,' said the note. 'Terribly urgent. Desperate. Please, *please* come to this apartment as soon as possible. If you see K, *say nothing*. S.B.'

'This,' Alleyn said to himself, 'is going to be the bottom. Bullying a phoney Major is a pastoral symphony compared to the tune Lady B's going to call.'

He tore up the note and went to the apartment.

She received him, predictably, on a chaise-longue, wearing a gold lamé trouser suit. A hard-featured maid let him in and withdrew, presumably into the bedroom.

Lady Braceley swung her feet to the floor and held out her hands.

'Oh God!' she said. 'You've come. Oh bless you, bless you, bless you.'

'Not at all,' Alleyn said, and glanced at the bedroom door.

'It's all right. Swiss. Doesn't speak a word of English.'

'What is it, Lady Braceley? Why do you want to see me?'

'It's in deadly confidence. *Deadly*. If Kenneth knew I was telling you, I don't know what he'd say to me. But I just can't take this sort of thing. It kills me. He won't come in. He knows I always rest until six and then he always rings first. We're safe.'

'Perhaps you'll explain——'

'Of course. It's just that I'm so nervous and upset. I don't know *what* you're going to say.'

'Nor,' Alleyn said lightly, 'do I. Until I hear what it's all about.'

'It's about him. Kenneth. And me. It's—oh, he's been so naughty and stupid, I can't *think* what possessed him. And now—if you *knew* where he's landed us.'

'What has he done?'

'I don't follow it all. Well, first of all he behaved very badly in Perugia. He got into a wild set and ran out of money, it appears, and—oh, I don't know—sold something he hadn't paid for. And that wretched murderer Mailer got him out of it. Or said he had. And then—when we were in that ghastly church, Mailer spoke to me about it and said the police—the *police*—were making a fuss and unless he could "satisfy" them it would all come out and Kenneth would be—imagine it!—arrested. He wanted £500 paid into some bank somewhere. All I had to do was to write an open cheque and he would—what's the word—negotiate the whole thing and we could forget it.'

'Did you write this cheque?'

'Not there and then. He said he would hold the police off for two days and call for the cheque at midday today. And then, of course, there was this thing about him disappearing and all the murder horror. And then Giovanni—you know?—rather sweet, or so I thought. Giovanni said he knew all about it and he would arrange everything only now it would be more expensive. And he came in here after lunch today and said the situation was more difficult than he had understood from Mailer and he would want £800 in lire or it might be easier if I let him have some jewellery instead. And I've got rather a famous tiara thing my second husband gave me only it's in the bank here. And quite a lot of rings. He seemed to know all about my jewellery.'

'Did you give him anything?'

'Yes. I did. I gave him my diamond and emerald sunburst. It's insured for £900, I think. I've never really liked it frightfully. But still——'

'Lady Braceley, why are you telling me all this?'

'Because,' she said, 'I'm frightened. I'm just frightened. I'm out of my depth. Kenneth behaves so oddly and, clearly, he's got himself into the most hideous mess. And although I'm awfully fond of him I don't think it's fair to land me in it, too. And I can't cope. I feel desperately ill. That place—I don't know whether you—— Anyway they gave me something to turn me on and it wasn't anything like they tell you it'll be. It was too awful. Mr Alleyn, please, *please* be kind and help me.'

She wept and chattered and dabbed at him with her awful claws. In a moment, he thought, she'll take off into the full hysteria bit.

'You're ill,' he said. 'Is there anything I can get you?'

'Over there. In the drinks place. Tablets. And brandy.'

He found them and poured out a moderate amount of brandy. She made a botch of shaking out three tablets. He had to help her. 'Are you sure you should take three?' he asked.

She nodded, crouched over her hand, gulped and swallowed the brandy.

'Tranquillizers,' she said. 'Prescription.'

For a minute or so she sat with her eyes closed, shivering. 'I'm sorry. Do have a drink,' she offered in a travesty of her social voice.

He paid no attention to this. When she had opened her

eyes and found her handkerchief he said, 'I'll do what I can. I think it's unlikely that your nephew is in danger of arrest. I'll find out about it. In the meantime you mustn't think of giving anything else to Giovanni. He is blackmailing you and he will certainly not carry out any negotiations with the police. But I don't think he will come. It's highly possible that he himself is under arrest. I'll leave you now but before I go tell me one thing. Your nephew did meet Mailer that afternoon by the statue of Apollo, didn't he?'

'I think so.'

'To collect his drugs?'

'I think so.'

'For any other purpose, do you know? Did he tell you?'

'I—think—he'd seen Mailer talking to me and he'd seen I was upset. And—I think he wanted to find out if—if——'

'If you'd agreed to pay up?'

She nodded.

'When your nephew appears,' Alleyn said grimly, 'will you tell him I want to see him? I will be in my room, 149, for the next hour. And I think, Lady Braceley, you should go to bed. Shall I call your maid?'

'She'll come.'

She was gazing at him now with an intensity that appalled him. She suddenly burst into an incoherent babble of thanks and since there seemed no hope of stemming the flood, he left her, still talking, and returned to his room.

FIVE

Inspector Fox came through, loud and clear, at six o'clock. The department had been expeditious in collecting information about the travellers. The Dutch Embassy and the London representative of Messrs Adriaan and Welker had confirmed the Van der Veghels' account of themselves: an ancient family, a strict Lutheran background conforming with the evangelical policy of the firm.

'Very strict in their attitudes,' Fox said. 'Puritanical, you might say. The lady I talked to in their London office is one of the modern sort. Groovy. She said that the Baron's a very different type from his father who was what they call a "sport". In both senses. A bit of a lad. Edwardian playboy type and notorious in his day. She said there are some very funny stories they tell in the firm about the Baron coming face to face with himself and cutting himself dead. She said they live very quietly. In Geneva mostly. The Baroness writes some kind of religious tales for kids but she never accompanies him to The Hague and is thought to be delicate.'

Fox enlarged cosily upon his theme. Believed to be distantly related to her husband, the Baroness, it was understood, belonged to an expatriate branch of the family. The nature of the Baron's work for the firm obliged them to live abroad. A highly respected and unblemished record.

Lady Braceley: 'Nothing in our way, really,' said Fox, 'unless you count a 1937 Ascot week-end scandal. She was an unwilling witness. Recently, just the usual stuff about elderly ladies in the jet set. Do you want the list of husbands?'

'She'd love to tell me herself but—all right. In case.'

He took them down.

'The nephew's different,' said Fox. 'He's a naughty boy. Sacked from his school for pot-parties and sex. Three convictions for speeding. Got off on a charge of manslaughter but only just. Accident resulting from high jinks at what was called a "gay pad".'

'Press on, Br'er Fox.'

'This Sweet, Hamilton. Major. There's no Major Hamilton Sweet in the Royal Artillery or any other Army lists for the given period. So we looked up recent cases of False Pretences and Fraud, Army Officers, masquerading as. Less popular than it used to be.'

'See British possessions, armed forces, for the use of. Dwindling.'

'That's right. Well, anyway we looked. And came up with James Stanley Hamilton who answers to your description. Three fraudulent company affairs and two Revenue charges involving drugs. Known to have left the country. Wanted.'

'That, as they say in the late-night imported serials, figures. Thank you, Br'er Fox.'

'You mentioned Mr Barnaby Grant and Miss Sophy Jason. Nothing apart from what you know. You seem to be in a funny sort of *milieu*, Mr Alleyn,' said Fox who spoke French, '*n'est-ce pas*?'

'It gets funnier every second. *Mille remerciements, Frère Renard*, and why the hell aren't you speaking Italian? Good night to you.'

Bergarmi rang up to say the Questore had told him to report. They had pulled in Giovanni Vecchi but had not persuaded him to talk. Bergarmi thought Giovanni might be hiding Mailer and almost certainly knew where he was, but had no hard facts to support what seemed to be merely a hunch. They would continue to hold Vecchi.

Alleyn again reflected upon the apparently wide divergences between Italian and British police procedure. He asked Bergarmi if he had made any inquiries as to Kenneth Dorne's activities in Perugia.

Bergarmi had done so and found that a complaint had been made to the police by a jeweller about a cigarette case but the man had been repaid and the charge withdrawn. There had been no further developments.

'I thought as much,' Alleyn said.

He then told Bergarmi of his interview with Sweet. 'I've got a list of Ziegfeldt's top agents from him,' he said. 'I think it's genuine. He's been playing the double-agent between Ziegfeldt and Mailer and now he's got very cold feet.'

Bergarmi said he would have the Major watched. An arrest at this juncture would probably prove unfruitful, but under obvious supervision he might crack and do something revealing: clearly Bergarmi now regarded the Major as his most fruitful source of information. He added that with the material Alleyn had obtained, no doubt his mission in Rome had been accomplished. There was no mistaking the satisfaction in Bergarmi's voice.

Alleyn said that you might put it like that, he supposed, and they rang off.

As he intended to dine in the hotel, he changed into a dinner-jacket.

At half past seven Kenneth Dorne came to see him. His manner slithered about between resentment, shamefacedness and sheer funk.

Alleyn ran through Kenneth's record as supplied by Fox and asked him if it was substantially correct. Kenneth said he supposed so. 'Anyway,' he said, 'you've made up your mind so there's no point in saying it's not.'

'None whatever.'

'Very well, then. What's the object in my coming here?'

'Briefly, this: I want to know what happened between you and Mailer, by the Apollo, the other day. No,' Alleyn said and lifted a hand, 'don't lie again. You'll do yourself a lot of damage if you persist. You met him by arrangement to collect your supply of heroin and cocaine. But you also wanted to find out whether he'd been successful in blackmailing Lady Braceley on your behalf. Perhaps that's a harsh way of putting it but it's substantially what happened. You had got yourself into trouble in Perugia, Mailer had purported to get you out of it. Knowing your talent for sponging on your aunt, he came again with completely false stories of police activity and the necessity for bribery on a large scale. He told you, no doubt, that Lady Braceley had promised to comply. Do you deny any of this?'

'No comment,' said Kenneth.

'My sole concern is to get a statement from you about your parting with Mailer and where he went—in what direction—when he left you. Your wits,' Alleyn said, 'are not so befuddled with narcotics that you don't understand me. This man has not only made a fool of you and robbed your aunt. He has murdered an old woman. I suppose you know the penalty for comforting and abetting a murderer.'

'Is this Roman law?' Kenneth sneered in a shaking voice.

'You're a British subject. So is Mailer. You don't want him caught, do you? You're afraid of exposure.'

'No!'

'Then tell me where he went when he left you.'

At first Alleyn thought Kenneth was going to break down, then that he was going to refuse, but he did neither of these things. He gazed dolefully at Alleyn for several seconds and appeared to gain some kind of initiative. He folded his white hands over his mouth, bit softly at his fingers and put his head on one side.

At last he talked and, having begun, seemed to find a release in doing so.

He said that when Mailer had fixed him up with his supply of heroin and cocaine he had 'had himself a pop.' He carried his own syringe, and Mailer, guessing he would be avid for it, had provided him with an ampoule of water and helped him. He adjusted the tourniquet, using Kenneth's scarf for the purpose.

'Seb,' Kenneth said, 'is fabulous—you know—it's not easy till you get the knack. Finding the right spot. So he cooked up and fixed me, there and then, and I felt fantastic. He said I'd better carry on with the party.'

They had walked together round the end of the old church

and arrived at the iron stairway. Mailer had gone down the stairway into the insula with Kenneth but instead of entering the Mithraeum had continued along the cloister in the direction of the well.

Kenneth, saturated, Alleyn gathered, in a rising flood of well-being, had paused at the entry into the Mithraeum and idly watched Mailer.

Having got so far in his narrative he ran the tip of his tongue round his lips and, eyeing Alleyn with what actually seemed to be a kind of relish, said:

'Surprise, surprise.'

'What do you mean?'

'I saw it. Again. The same as what the Jason dolly saw. You know. The shadow.'

'Violetta's.'

'Across the thing. You know. The sarcophagus.'

'Then you saw her?'

'No, I didn't. I suppose he was between. I don't know. I was high. There's a kind of buttress thing juts out. Anyway I was high.'

'So high, perhaps, that you imagined the whole thing.'

'*No*,' Kenneth said loudly. '*No*.'

'And then?'

'I went into that marvellous place. The temple or whatever. There you were. All of you. On about the god. And the great grinning Baroness lining us up for a team-photograph. And all the time,' Kenneth said excitedly, 'all the time just round the corner, Seb was strangling the postcard woman. Wouldn't it send you!' He burst out laughing.

Alleyn looked at him. 'You can't always have been as bad as this,' he said. 'Or are you simply a born, stupid, unalterable monster? How big a hand has Mailer taken with his H. and C. and his thoughtful ever-ready ampoule of distilled water in the making of the product?'

Kenneth's smile still hung about his mouth even as he began to whimper.

'Shut up,' Alleyn said mildly. 'Don't do that. Pull yourself together if you can.'

'I'm a spoilt boy. I know that. I never had a chance. I was spoilt.'

'How old are you?'

'Twenty-three. Someone like you could have helped me. Truly.'

'Did you get any idea of why Mailer didn't go into the Mithraeum with you? Was he expecting to meet the woman?'

'No. No, I'm sure he wasn't,' Kenneth said eagerly, gazing at Alleyn. 'I'm telling the truth,' he added with a dreadful imitation of a chidden little boy. 'I'm trying to be good. And I'll tell you something else. To show.'

'Go on.'

'He told me why he wouldn't come in.'

'Why?'

'He had a date. With someone else.'

'Who?'

'He didn't say. I'd tell you if I knew. He didn't say. But he had a date. Down there in that place. He told me.'

The telephone rang.

When Alleyn answered it he received an oddly familiar sensation: an open silence broken by the distant and hollow closure of a door, a suggestion of space and emptiness. He was not altogether surprised when a rich voice asked: 'Would this be Mr Alleyn?'

'It would, Father.'

'You mentioned this morning where you were to be found. Are you alone, now?'

'No.'

'No. Well, we'll say no more under that heading. I've called upon you, Mr Alleyn, in preference to anybody else, on

197

account of a matter that has arisen. It may be no great matter and it may be all to the contrary.'

'Yes?'

'If it's not putting too much upon you I'd be very greatly obliged if you'd be kind enough to look in at the basilica.'

'Of course. Is it——?'

'Well now, it may be. It may be and then again it may not, and to tell you the truth I'm loath to call down a great concourse of the pollis upon me and then it turning out to be a rat.'

'A rat, Father Denys?'

'Or rats. The latter is more like it. Over the head of the strength.'

'The strength, did you say?'

'I did that. The strength of the aroma.'

'I'll be with you,' Alleyn said, 'in fifteen minutes.'

His professional homicide kit was in the bottom of his wardrobe. He took it with him.

8. Return of Sebastian Mailer

S. TOMMASO IN PALLARIA looked different after sunset. Its façade was dark against a darkening sky and its windows only faintly illuminated from within. Its entrance where Violetta had cursed Sebastian Mailer was quite given over to shadows and its doors were shut.

Alleyn was wondering how he would get in, when Father Denys moved out of the shadows.

'Good evening and God bless you,' he said.

He opened a little pass-door in the great entry and led the way in. The smell of incense and hot candles seemed more noticeable in the dark. Galaxies of small flaming spearheads burned motionless before the saints. A ruby lamp glowed above the high altar. It was a place fully occupied within itself. A positive place.

Brother Dominic came out of the sacristy and they walked into the vestibule with its shrouded stalls. The lights were on in there and it felt stuffy.

'It's like enough a fool's errand I've brought you on and you maybe not eaten yet,' said Father Denys. 'I may tell you it's not been done without the authority of my Superior.'

'I'm entirely at your service, Father.'

'Thank you, my son. We've had this sort of trouble before, d'ye see, over the head of the excavations and all. Rat trouble. Though Brother Dominic's been after them in a very big way and it was our belief they were exterminated. And wouldn't we look the fools if we'd stirred up Signor Bergarmi and his body of men and they fully occupied with their task?'

'Shall we have a look where the trouble seems to be?'

'A look is it? A smell, more likely. But come along, come along.'

As he made that downward journey for the third time, it seemed to Alleyn that in its quiet way it was one of the strangest he had ever taken. A monk, a lay-brother and himself, descending, if one cared to be fanciful, through a vertical section of the past.

When they reached the cloisters on the second level, Brother Dominic, who had not yet uttered, turned on the fluorescent lights and back into their immovable liveliness sprang the Apollo and the Mercury.

Down the iron spiral: two pairs of sandals and one pair of leather soles with the ever-mounting sound of flowing water. The bottom level and a right turn. This was where Kenneth Dorne had parted company with Sebastian Mailer. On their left was the little anteroom into the Mithraeum. Ahead—the lights came on—ahead, the sarcophagus and the railed well.

They walked towards them.

The lid had not been replaced. It stood on its side, leaning against the empty stone coffin where Violetta had been urgently housed.

Father Denys put his hand on Alleyn's arm.

'Now,' he said and they stopped.

'Yes,' Alleyn said.

It declared itself: sweetish, intolerable, unmistakable.

He went on alone, leant over the top rail where he had found a fragment of cloth, and looked into the well, using the torch they had given him.

It showed walls in a sharp perspective and at the bottom an indefinable darkness.

'The other day,' he said, 'when I looked down, there was a

sort of glint. I took it to be a chance flicker of light on the moving stream.'

'It could be that.'

'What is there—down below?'

'The remains of a stone grille. As old,' Father Denys said, 'as the place itself. Which is seventeen hundred years. We've lowered a light and it revealed nothing that you could call of any consequence but it was too far beneath to be of any great help.'

'The grille is above the surface of the stream?'

'It is. A few inches at the downstream end of the well. And it's the remains only. A fragment you may say.'

'Could something have been carried down by the stream and got caught up in it?'

'It's never been known in the history of this place. The water is pure. Every so often we let down a wee tin and haul up a sample for the testing. There's never been the hint of contamination in it.'

'Can one get down there?'

'Well, now——'

'I think I can see footholds and—yes——'

Brother Dominic spoke. 'You can,' he said.

'Aren't there iron pegs?'

'There are.'

'And they rotten no doubt,' Father Denys urged, 'and falling out like old teeth at the first handling.'

'Have you a rope, Father?'

'Sure, we have them for the excavations. You're not thinking——'

'I'll go down if you'll give me a hand.'

'Dominic, let you fetch a rope.'

'And a head-lamp and overalls,' Brother Dominic enumerated with a glance at Alleyn's impeccable suit. 'We have them all got. I'll fetch them, Father.'

'Do so.'

'It's unwholesome here,' Father Denys said when Brother Dominic had gone. 'Let us move away for the time being.'

They entered the Mithraeum. Father Denys had switched on the lighting used in visiting hours. The altar glowed. At the far end, the god, lit from beneath, stared out of blank eyes at nothing.

They sat on one of the stone benches where in the second century his initiates had sat, wan with their ordeal, their blanched faces painted by the altar fires.

Alleyn thought he would like to ask Father Denys what he made of the Mithraic Cult but when he turned to speak to him found that he was withdrawn into himself. His hands were pressed together and his lips moved.

Alleyn waited for a minute and then, hearing the returning slap of sandals in the cloister, went quickly out by the doorway behind the god.

This was the passage by which he and the Van der Veghels had left the Mithraeum. It was very dark indeed and the Baroness had exclaimed at it.

Two right turns brought him back into sight of the well and there was Brother Dominic with ropes, an old-fashioned head-lamp of the sort miners use, a suit of workmen's overalls and a peculiar woolly cap.

'I'm obliged to you, Brother Dominic,' said Alleyn.

'Let you put them on.'

Alleyn did so. Brother Dominic fussed about him. He fixed the head-lamp and with great efficiency made fast one end of the rope round Alleyn's chest and under his shoulders.

Alleyn transferred a minuscule camera from his homicide kit to the pocket of his overalls.

After looking about for a minute, Brother Dominic asked Alleyn to help him place the lid of the sarcophagus at right angles across the coffin. It was massive but Brother Dominic was a strong man and made little of it. He passed the slack of the rope twice round the lid, crossing it in the manner of sailors when they wear a rope in lowering a heavy load.

'We could take your weight neat between us,' he said, 'but this will be the better way. Where's Father?'

'In the Mithraeum. Saying his prayers, I think.'

'He would be that.'

'Here he is.'

Father Denys returned looking anxious.

'I hope we are right about this,' he said. 'Are you sure it's safe, now, Dominic?'

'I am, Father.'

'Mr Alleyn, would you not let me place a—a handkerchief over your—eh?'

He hovered anxiously and finally did tie his own large cotton handkerchief over Alleyn's nose and mouth.

The two Dominicans tucked back their sleeves, wetted their palms and took up the rope, Brother Dominic on Alleyn's side of the sarcophagus lid and Father Denys on the far side, close to the turn.

'That's splendid,' Alleyn said. 'I hope I won't have to trouble you. Here I go.'

'God bless you,' they said in their practical way.

He had another look at the wall. The iron pegs went down at fairly regular intervals on either side of one corner. The well itself was six feet by three.

Alleyn ducked under the bottom rail, straddled the corner with his back to the well, knelt, took his weight on his forearms, wriggled backwards and groped downwards with his right foot.

'Easy now, easy,' said both the Dominicans. He looked up at Brother Dominic's sandalled feet, at his habit and into his long-lipped Irish face. 'I have you held,' said Brother Dominic and gave a little strain on the rope to show that it was so.

Alleyn's right foot found a peg and rested on it. He tested

it, letting himself down little by little. He felt a gritting sensation and a slight movement under his foot but the peg took his weight.

'Seems OK,' he said through Father Denys's handkerchief.

He didn't look up again. His hands, one after the other, relinquished the edge and closed, right and then left, round pegs. One of them tilted, jarred and ground its way out of its centuries-old housing. It was loose in his hand and he let it fall. So long, it seemed, before he heard it hit the water. Now he had only one handhold and his feet but the rope sustained him.

He continued down. His face was close to the angle made by the walls and he must be careful lest he knock his head-lamp against stone. It cast a circle of light that made sharp and intimate the pitted surface of the rock. Details of colour, irregularities and growths of some minute lichen passed upwards through the light as he himself so carefully sank.

Already the region above seemed remote and the voices of the Dominicans disembodied. His world was now filled with the sound of running water. He would have smelt water, he thought, if it had not been for that other growing and deadly smell. How far had he gone? Why hadn't he asked Brother Dominic for the actual depth of the well? Thirty feet? More? Would the iron pegs have rusted and rotted in the damper air?

The peg under his left foot gave way. He shouted a warning and his voice reverberated and mingled with Brother Dominic's reply. Then his right foot slipped. He hung by his hands and by the rope. 'Lower away,' he called, released his hold, dangled and dropped in short jerks fending himself clear of the two walls. The voice of the stream was all about him.

A sudden icy cold shock to his feet came as a surprise. They were carried aside. At the same moment he saw and grabbed two pegs at shoulder level. 'Hold it! Hold it! I'm there.'

He was lowered another inch before the rope took up. He scrabbled with his feet against the pressure of the stream. The backs of his legs hit against something hard and firm. He explored with his feet, lifted them clear of the water and found in a moment with a kind of astonishment that he was standing on bars that pressed into his feet.

The grille.

A broken grille, the monks had said.

The surface of the stream must be almost level with the bottom of the well and about an inch below the grille which projected from its wall.

Supporting himself in the angle of the walls, Alleyn contrived to turn himself about so that he now faced outwards. His head-lamp showed the two opposite walls.

He leant back into the angle, braced himself and shouted, 'Slack off a little.'

'Slack off, it is,' said the disembodied voice.

He leant forward precariously as the rope gave, shouted 'Hold it!' and lowered his head so that his lamp illuminated the swift-flowing black waters, the fragment of grille that he stood upon and his drenched feet, planted apart and close to its broken fangs.

And between his feet? A third foot ensnared upside down in the broken fangs: a foot in a black leather shoe.

TWO

His return to the surface was a bit of a nightmare. Superintendents of the CID, while they like to keep well above average in physical fitness and have behind them a gruelling and comprehensive training to this end, are not in the habit of half-scrambling and half-dangling on the end of a rope in a well.

Alleyn's palms burnt, his joints were banged against rock walls, and once he got a knock on the back of his head that lit up stars and made him dizzy. Sometimes he climbed up by such iron pegs as remained intact. Sometimes he walked horizontally up the wall while the monks hauled in. They do these things better, he reflected, in crime films.

When he had finally been landed, the three of them sat on the floor and breathed hard: as odd a little group, it occurred to Alleyn, as might be imagined.

'You were superb,' he said. 'Thank you.'

'Ah, sure, it was nothing at all,' Father Denys panted. 'Aren't we used to this type of thing in the excavating? It's yourself should have the praise.'

They shared that peculiar sense of fellowship and gratification which is the reward of such exercises.

'Well,' Alleyn said. 'I'm afraid you'll have to ring the Questura, Father. Our man's down there and he's dead.'

'The man Mailer?' Father Denys said when they had crossed themselves. 'God have mercy on his soul.'

'Amen,' said Brother Dominic.

'What's the way of it, Mr Alleyn?'

'As I see it, he probably fell through the well head-first, and straight into the stream, missing the broken grille, which by the way, only extends a few inches from the wall. The stream swept him under the grille, but one foot, the right, was trapped between two of the broken fangs. And there he is, held in the current.'

'How are you sure it's himself?'

'By the shoe and the trouser-leg and because——' Alleyn hesitated.

'What are you trying to tell us?'

'It was just possible to see his face.'

'There's a terrible thing for you! And so drowned?'

'That,' Alleyn said, 'will no doubt appear in due course.'

206

'Are you telling us there's been—what are you telling us?—a double murder?'

'It depends upon what you mean by that, Father.'

'I mean does someone have that sin upon his soul to have killed Violetta and Sebastian Mailer, the both of them?'

'Or did Mailer kill Violetta and was then himself killed?'

'Either way, there's a terrible thing!' Father Denys repeated. 'God forgive us all. A fearful, fearful thing.'

'And I do think we should ring the Vice-Questore.'

'Bergarmi, is it? Yes, yes, yes. We'll do so.'

On the return journey, now so very familiar, they passed by the well-head on the middle level. Alleyn stopped and looked at the railings. As in the basilica, they were made of more finished wood than those in the insula. Four stout rails, well polished, about ten inches apart.

'Have you ever had any trouble in the past? Any accidents?' Alleyn asked.

Never, they said. Children were not allowed unaccompanied anywhere in the building and people obeyed the notice not to climb the railings.

'Just a moment, Father.' Alleyn walked over to the well.

'Somebody's ignored the notice,' he said and pointed to two adjacent marks across the top of the lowest rail. 'Somebody who likes brown polish on the under-instep of his shoes. Wait a moment, Father, will you?'

He squatted painfully by the rails and used his torch. The smears of brown polish were smudged across with equidistant tracks almost as if somebody had tried to erase them with an india-rubber.

'If you don't mind,' he said, 'I've got a fancy to take a shot of this.' And did so with his particular little camera.

'Will you look at that, now!' exclaimed Father Denys.

'It won't amount to a row of beans, as likely as not. Shall we go on?'

Back in the vestibule he rang up the Questura and got through to Bergarmi.

He had to go warily. As he expected, the Vice-Questore immediately said that the Dominicans should have reported the trouble to him.

Alleyn made the most of Father Denys's reluctance to bother the police with what might well turn out to be the trivial matter of a couple of dead rats.

Bergarmi gave this a sardonic reception, muttering '*Topi, topi*,' as if he used an incredulous slang equivalent of 'Rats!' This Alleyn felt to be a little unfair, but he pressed on with his report.

'You'll have a difficult job getting the body out,' he said, 'but of course you have all the resources and the expertise.'

'You have communicated this matter, Superintendent Alleyn, to Il Questore Valdarno?'

'No. I thought best to report at once to you.'

This went down much better. 'In which respect,' Bergarmi conceded, 'you have acted with propriety. We shall deal with this matter immediately. The whole complexion of the affair alters. I myself will inform Il Questore. In the meantime I will speak, if you please, with the Padre.'

While Father Denys talked volubly with Bergarmi, Alleyn washed his hands in a cubby-hole, found them to be rather more knocked about than he had realized, changed back into his own clothes and took stock of the situation.

The complexion had indeed changed. What, he sourly asked himself, was the position of a British investigator in Rome when a British subject of criminal propensities had almost certainly been murdered, possibly by another Briton, not impossibly by a Dutchman, not quite inconceivably by an Italian, on property administered by an Irish order of Dominican monks?

This is one, he thought, to be played entirely by ear and I very much wish I was shot of it.

He had an egg-shaped lump on the back of his head. H
was bruised, sore, and even a bit shaky, which made him
angry with himself.

I could do with black coffee, he thought.

Father Denys came back, caught sight of Alleyn's hands and
immediately produced a first-aid box. He insisted on putting
dressings over the raw patches.

'You'd be the better for a touch of the cratur,' he said, 'and
we've nothing of the kind to offer. There's a *caffè* over the way.
Go there, now, and take a drop of something. The pollis will
be a while yet for that fellow Bergarmi is all for getting on to
the Questore before he stirs himself. Are you all right, now?'

'I'm fine but I think it's a marvellous suggestion.'

'Away with you.'

The *caffè* was a short distance down the street: a very
modest affair with a scatter of workaday patrons who looked
curiously at him. He had coffee and brandy and forced himself
to eat a couple of large buns that turned out to be delicious.

Well, he thought, it was on the cards. From the beginning
it was on the cards and I'm glad I said as much to Valdarno.

He began a careful re-think. Suppose, he thought, as a
starting point, we accept that the noise we heard while the
Baroness was setting up that ludicrous group-photograph was,
in fact, the sound of the sarcophagus lid thumping down on
its edge, and I must say it sounded exactly like it. This would
mean presumably that Violetta had just been killed and was
about to be safely stowed.

By Mailer? If by Mailer, then he himself survived to be
killed, again presumably—no, almost certainly—before we all
reassembled.

The only members of the party who were alone were Sweet
and young Dorne who found their way up independently, and
Lady B. who was parked in the atrium.

The Van der Veghels were with me. Sophy Jason was with

Barnaby Grant. *We* met nobody on our way up and *they* say as much for themselves.

Query. If Mailer killed Violetta while we were all having our photographs taken, why did he—not a robust man—go through the elaborate and physically exhausting job of putting the body in the sarcophagus and replacing the lid instead of doing what was subsequently done to him—dispatching it down the well?

I have no answer.

On the other hand, suppose one person killed both of them. Why? I am dumb, but suppose it was so? Why, for pity's sake, make a sarcophagus job of Violetta and a well job of Mailer? Just for the hell of it?

But. But, suppose, on the third hand, Mailer killed Violetta and hadn't time to do anything further about it before he himself was knocked off and pushed down the well? How will this fadge? Rather better, I fancy. And why does his killer take the trouble to box Violetta up? That's an easier one. Much easier.

I suppose there's a fourth hand. We approach Indian god status. Suppose Violetta killed Mailer and heaved him overboard and was then—no, that I refuse to entertain.

How long were we all boxed up together under the blank eyes of Mithras? Sweet arrived first, and, about five minutes later, young Dorne. Then there was the business of the photographs. The discussion, the groping and the grouping. Sophy and I being funnymen and Grant cursing us. He had just said 'Serve you bloody well right' to Sophy, who was having trouble with the Major, when the lid, if it was the lid, thudded.

After that came the failure of the flashlight, the interminable wait while the Baroness set herself up again. At least ten minutes, I would think. Then Dorne took his photo of Mithras. Then the Baroness loosed off, this time successfully. Then she took two more shots, not without further re-arrangements and palaver. Another four minutes? All of that. And finally the Baron changed places with the Baroness and blazed away on his own account. Then Grant read his piece. Another five minutes. And then the party broke up.

After that, Dorne and Sweet are again odd men out. So it looks as if we were all together in that bloody basement for about twenty-five minutes, give or take the odd five. So everybody's got an alibi for the salient time. Everybody? No. No, not quite. Not . . . Sit still, my soul. Hold on to your hats, boys——

A great rumpus of sirens broke out in the distance, drew rapidly nearer and exploded into the little street. The police. The Squadra Omicidi in strength. Three large cars and a van, eight Agenti and four practical-looking characters in overalls.

Alleyn paid his bill and returned to the church, stiffer now about the shoulders and ribs and painful as to the head, but in other respects his own man again.

A large amount of equipment was being unloaded: two pairs of waders, ropes, pulleys, an extension ladder, a winch, a stretcher. Il Vice-Questore Bergarmi watched the operation with an air of tetchy disdain. He greeted Alleyn ceremoniously and with a fine salute.

Patrons from the little *caffè*, some groups of youths and a car or two quickly collected and were bossed about by two of the Agenti who were otherwise unoccupied.

Brother Dominic came out, surveyed the assembly, and opened the main doors.

'Il Questore Valdarno, Signor Alleyn,' said Bergarmi fairly stiffly, 'sends his compliments. He wishes me to express his hopes that you will continue to interest yourself in our investigations.'

'I am very much obliged to him,' Alleyn replied, groping about in his Italian for the correct phrases, 'and will be glad to do so without, I trust, making a nuisance of myself.'

'*Mente affalto*,' Bergarmi replied. Which was as much, Alleyn thought, as to say 'Don't let that worry you,' or even, 'Forget it.' Somehow it sounded a good deal less cordial.

It was after ten o'clock when Bergarmi's men landed Sebastian Mailer's body in the insula.

It lay on a stretcher not far from the sarcophagus, an inconsequential sequel to a flabby, fat man. It wore a ghastly resemblance to Violetta. This was because Mr Mailer, also, had been strangled.

His body had been knocked about; both before and after death, said the medical man—presumably a police surgeon—called in to make an immediate examination. His face had been scored by fangs of the broken grille. There was a heavy livid mark across the neck quite apart from the typical stigmata of manual strangulation.

Alleyn watched the routine procedure and spoke when he was spoken to. There was a certain hauteur in the attitude of the investigating officers.

'We shall, of course, perform an autopsy,' said the doctor. 'He was a man of full habit. No doubt we shall find he was killed not so very long after he had eaten. *Ecco!* We find certain manifestations. You may cover the cadaver.' They did so. 'And remove it,' added the doctor. 'Unless, of course—' he bowed to Alleyn who had moved forward—'the Signor Superintendent wishes——?'

Alleyn said, 'Thank you. I am sure, gentlemen, you have already taken every possible photograph required for the investigation, but unfortunately, as we all know, under such difficult conditions there can be accidents. When I found the body I did get a shot of it *in situ*.' He produced his very special minuscule camera. 'It seems to have survived a rather rough passage,' he said. 'If by any chance you would like a print, I shall of course be delighted to give you one.'

He knew at once by a certain momentary stillness that no

212

photographs had been taken down below by the recovery team. He hurried on. 'Perhaps I may be allowed to finish my film and then—a further favour, Signor Bergarmi—perhaps your laboratories would be kind enough to develop it.'

'Of course, Signore. Our pleasure.'

'You are very good,' Alleyn said and instantly whipped back the sheet and took four photographs of Mailer, deceased, with special attention to the right foot. He then removed the cassette and handed it with a bow to Bergarmi.

The body was re-shrouded and taken away.

Bergarmi said irritably that this was a bad evening for such an event. Student demonstrations had broken out in Navona and its surrounding district and threatened to become serious. The Agenti were fully occupied. A mammoth demonstration was planned for the morrow and the police expected it to be the worst yet. He must get this job through as quickly as possible.

He suggested that nothing further could be done at the moment but that in view of the grossly altered circumstances his chief would be glad if Alleyn would wait on him in the morning at 9.30. It seemed advisable to call the seven travellers together again. Bergarmi's officers would attend to this. A car was at Alleyn's disposal. No doubt he would like to go home.

They shook hands.

When Alleyn left, he passed Father Denys, who came as near to tipping him a wink as lay within the dignity of his office.

THREE

Sophy Jason and Barnaby Grant met for breakfast on the roof-garden. The morning sparkled freshly and was not yet too hot for comfort. From the direction of Navona there came vague sounds of singing, a discordant band and the rumour of a crowd. A detachment of police marched down their street. The waiter was full of confused chatter about riots. It seemed unreal to Sophy and Barnaby.

They talked of the blameless pleasures of the previous evening when they had walked about Roman streets until they tired and had then taken a carriage-drive fraught with the inescapable romanticism of such exercise. Finally, after a glass of wine in Navona, they had strolled home.

When they said good night Grant had kissed Sophy for the first time.

She had taken this thoughtfully with a nod as if to say 'Well, yes, I suppose so,' had blushed unexpectedly and left him in a hurry. If they could have read each other's thoughts they would have been surprised to find that they were so nearly identical. Each, in fact, speculated upon immediate as opposed to past emotions under like circumstances and each, with a kind of apprehensive delight, recognized an essential difference.

Sophy had arrived first for breakfast and had sat down determined to sort herself out in a big way but instead had idly dreamed until Grant's arrival set up a commotion under her ribs. This was quickly replaced by a renewed sense of companionship unfolding like a flower in the morning air. 'How happy I am,' each of them thought. 'I am delighted.'

In this frame of mind they discussed the coming day and speculated about the outcome of the Violetta affair and the probability of Mr Mailer being a murderer.

'I suppose it's awful,' Sophy said, 'not to be madly horrified, but truth to tell I'm not much more appalled than I would be if I'd read it in the papers.'

'I'll go one worse than you. In a way I'm rather obliged to him.'

'Honestly! What can you mean?'

'You're still hanging about in Rome instead of flouncing off to Assisi or Florence or wherever.'

'That,' Sophy said, 'is probably a remark in execrable taste although I must say I relished it.'

'Sophy,' said Grant, 'you're a sweetie. Blow me down flat if you're not.'

He reached out his hand and at that moment the waiter came out on the roof-garden.

Now it was Grant who experienced a jolt under the diaphragm. Here he had sat, and so, precisely here, had the waiter appeared, on that morning over a year ago when Sebastian Mailer was announced.

'What's the matter?' Sophy asked.

'Nothing. Why?'

'You looked—odd.'

'Did I? What is it?' he asked the waiter.

It was the Baron Van der Veghel hoping Mr Grant was free.

'Ask him to join us, please.'

Sophy stood up.

'Don't you dare,' Grant said, 'Sit down.'

'Yes, but—— Well, anyway, you shut up.'

'Siddown.'

'I'll be damned if I do,' said Sophy, and did.

The Baron arrived: large, concerned and doubtful. He begged their forgiveness for so early a call and supposed that, like him, they had received a great shock. This led to some momentary confusion until, gazing at them with those wide-open eyes of his, he said, 'But surely you must know?' and finding they did not, flatly told them.

'The man Mailer,' he said, 'has been murdered. He has been found at the bottom of the well.'

At that moment all the clocks in Rome began to strike nine and Sophy was appalled to hear a voice in her head saying: *'Ding, dong, bell. Mailer's in the well.'*

'No doubt,' the Baron said, 'you will receive a message. As we did. This, of course, changes everything. My wife is so much

215

upset. We have found where is a Protestant church and I have taken her there for some comfort. My wife is a most sensitive subject. She senses,' the Baron explained, 'that there has been a great evil amongst us. That there is still this evil. As I do. How can one escape such a feeling?'

'Not very readily,' Grant conceded, 'particularly now when I suppose we are all much more heavily involved.'

The Baron glanced anxiously at Sophy. 'Perhaps,' he said, 'we should——'

'Well, of course we're involved, Baron,' she said.

Clearly, the Baron held that ladies were to be protected. He goes through life, she thought, tenderly building protective walls round that huge, comical sex-pot of his and he's got plenty of concern left over for extra-mural sympathy. Who says the age of chivalry is dead? He's rather a dear, is the Baron.

But beneath her amusement, flowing under it and chilling it, ran a trickle of consciousness: I'm involved in a murder, thought Sophy.

She had lost track of the Baron's further remarks but gathered that he had felt the need for discussion with another man. Having left the Baroness to pursue whatever Spartan devotions accorded with her need, he had settled upon Grant as a confidant.

Deeply perturbed though she was, Sophy couldn't help feeling an indulgent amusement at the behaviour of the two men. It was so exclusively masculine.

They had moved away to the far side of the garden. Grant, with his hands in his pockets, stared between his feet and then lifted his head and contemplated the horizon. The Baron folded his arms, frowned portentously, and raised his eyebrows almost to the roots of his hair. They both pursed their lips, muttered, nodded. There were long pauses.

How different, Sophy thought, from the behaviour of women. We would exclaim, gaze at each other, gabble, ejaculate, tell each other how we felt, and talk about instinctive revulsion and how we'd always known, right along, that there was *something*.

And she suddenly thought it would be satisfactory to have such a talk with the Baroness, though not on any account with Lady Braceley.

They turned back to her, rather like doctors after a consultation.

'We have been saying, Miss Jason,' said the Baron, 'that as far as we ourselves are concerned there can be only slight formalities. Since we were in company from the time he left us, both in the Mithraeum and when we returned (you with Mr Grant and my wife and I with Mr Alleyn) until we all met in the church portion, we cannot be thought of either as witnesses or as—as——'

'Suspects?' Sophy said.

'So. You are right to be frank, my dear young lady,' said the Baron, looking at Sophy with solemn and perhaps rather shocked approval.

Grant said, 'Well, of course she is. Let's all be frank about it, for heaven's sake. Mailer was a bad lot and somebody has killed him. I don't suppose any of us condones the taking of life under any circumstances whatever, and it is, of course, horrible to think of the explosion of hatred, or alternatively the calculated manœuvring, that led to his death. But one can scarcely be expected to mourn for him.' He looked very hard at Sophy. 'I don't,' he said. 'And I won't pretend I do. It's a bad man out of the way.'

The Baron waited for a moment and said very quietly, 'You speak, Mr Grant, with conviction. Why do you say so positively that this was a bad man?'

Grant had gone very white but he answered without hesitation.

'I have first-hand knowledge,' he said. 'He was a black-

217

mailer. He blackmailed me. Alleyn knows this and so does Sophy. And if me, why not others?'

'Why not?' Van der Veghel said. 'Why not, indeed!' He hit himself on the chest and Sophy wondered why the gesture was not ridiculous. 'I too,' he said. 'I who speak to you. I too.' He waited for a moment. 'It has been a great relief to me to say this,' he said. 'A great relief. I shall not regret it, I think.'

'Well,' Grant said, 'it's lucky we are provided with alibis. I suppose a lot of people would say we have spoken like fools.'

'It is appropriate sometimes to be a fool. The belief of former times that there is God's wisdom in the utterances of fools was founded in truth,' the Baron proclaimed. 'No. I do not regret.'

A silence fell between them and into it there was insinuated the sound of a distant crowd—shrilling of whistles. A police car shot down the street with its siren blasting.

'And now, my dear Baron,' said Grant, 'having to some extent bared our respective bosoms, perhaps we had better, with Sophy's permission, consider our joint situation.'

'With the greatest pleasure,' said the Baron politely.

FOUR

Alleyn found a change in the atmosphere of Il Questore Valdarno's splendid office and in the attitude of Valdarno himself.

It was not that he was exactly less cordial but rather that he was more formally so. He was very formal indeed and overpoweringly polite. He was also worried and preoccupied and was constantly interrupted by telephone calls. Apparently the demonstrations were hotting up in Navona.

Valdarno made it perfectly clear that the discovery of Mailer's body altered the whole complexion of the case: that while he had no intention of excluding Alleyn from the investigation and hoped he would find some interest in the proceedings, they would now be absolutely in the hands of the Roman Questura, which, he added, with an unconvincing air of voicing an afterthought, was under the direct control of the Minister of the Interior.

Valdarno was very urbane. Alleyn had his own line of urbanity and retired behind it, and between them, he thought, they got exactly nowhere.

Valdarno thanked Alleyn with ceremony for having gone down the well and for being so kind as to photograph the body *in situ*. He contrived to suggest that this proceeding had, on the whole, been unnecessary if infinitely obliging.

The travellers, he said, were summoned to appear at 10.30. Conversation languished but revived with the arrival of Bergarmi who had the results of the post-mortems. Violetta had been hit on the back of the head and manually strangled. Mailer had probably been knocked out before being strangled and dropped down the well, though the bruise on his jaw might have been caused by a blow against the rails or the wall on his way down. The fragment of material Alleyn had found on the inner side of the top rail matched the black alpaca of his jacket and there was a corresponding tear in the sleeve.

At this point Valdarno, with stately punctilio, said to Bergarmi that they must acknowledge at once that Signor Alleyn had advanced the theory of Mailer's possible disappearance down the well and that he himself had not accepted it.

They both bowed, huffily, to Alleyn.

'It is of the first importance,' Valdarno continued, 'to establish whether the sound which was heard by these persons when they were in the Mithraeum was in fact the sound made by the lid of the sarcophagus falling upon its edge to the floor where, it is conjectured, it remained, propped against the casket while the body of the woman was disposed of. Your opinion, Signore, is that it was so?'

'Yes,' Alleyn said. 'You will remember that when we removed the lid it made a considerable noise. Two minutes or more before that, we heard a confused sound that might have been that of a woman's voice. It was greatly distorted by echo and stopped abruptly.'

'Screaming?'

'No.'

'One would expect the woman Violetta to scream.'

'Perhaps not, do you think, if she was there unlawfully? When she abused Mailer on the earlier occasion she didn't scream: she whispered. I got the impression of one of those harridan-voices that have worn out and can no longer scream.'

Valdarno surveyed Bergarmi. 'You realize what all this implies, no doubt?'

'Certainly, Signor Questore.'

'Well?'

'That if this was the woman Violetta and if the sound was the sound of the sarcophagus lid and if the person Mailer killed the woman Violetta and was himself killed soon after-wards——' here Bergarmi took a breath—'then, Signor Questore, the field of suspects is confined to such persons as were unaccompanied after the party left the Mithraeum. These were the Major Sweet, the Baronessa Braceley, the nephew Dorne.'

'Very well.'

'And that in fact the field of suspects remains the same,' Bergarmi said, fighting his way out, 'whether the woman Violetta was killed by the person Mailer or by the killer of the person Mailer.'

Valdarno turned to Alleyn and spread his hands.

'*Ecco!*' he said. 'You agree?'

'A masterly survey,' Alleyn said. 'There is—if I may?—just one question I would like to ask.'

'Ah?'

'Do we know where Giovanni Vecchi was?'

'Vecchi?'

'Yes,' Alleyn said apologetically. 'He was by the cars when we came out of the basilica but he might have been inside while we were in the nether regions. He wouldn't attract notice, would he? I mean he's a regular courier and must often hang about the premises while his customers are below. Part of the scenery, as it were.'

Valdarno gazed in his melancholy way at nothing in particular. 'What,' he asked Bergarmi, 'has the man Vecchi said?'

'Signor Questore—nothing.'

'Still nothing?'

'He is obstinate.'

'Has he been informed of Mailer's death?'

'Last night, Signor Questore.'

'His reaction?'

Bergarmi's shoulders rose to his ears, his eyebrows to the roots of his hair and his pupils into his head.

'Again nothing. A little pale, perhaps. I believe him to be nervous.'

'He must be examined as to his movements at the time of the crimes. The priests must be questioned.'

'Of course, Signor Questore,' said Bergarmi, who had not looked at Alleyn.

'Send for him.'

'Certainly, Signor Questore. At once.'

Valdarno waved a hand at his telephone and Bergarmi hurried to it.

An Agente came in and saluted.

'The tourists, Signore Questore,' he said.

'Very well. All of them?'

'Not yet, Signor Questore. The English *nobildonna* and her nephew. The English writer. The Signorina. The Olandese and his wife.'

'Admit them,' said Valdarno, with all the grandeur of a Shakespearian monarch.

And in they came: that now familiar and so oddly assorted company.

Alleyn stood up and so did Valdarno, who bowed with the utmost formality. He said, merely: 'Ladies and Gentlemen,' and motioned them to their seats.

Lady Braceley, who was dressed, with an over-developed sense of occasion, in black, ignored this invitation. She advanced upon Valdarno and held out her hand at the kissing level. He took it and kissed his thumb.

'*Baronessa*,' he said.

'Too shattering,' she lamented. 'I can't believe it. That's all. I simply can *not* believe it.'

'Unfortunately it is true. Please! Be seated.'

The Agente hastened to push a chair into the back of her knees.

She sat abruptly, gazed at Valdarno and shook her head slowly from side to side. The others regarded her with dismay. The Van der Veghels exchanged brief, incredulous glances. Kenneth made a discontented noise.

Bergarmi finished his orders on the telephone and seated himself at a little distance from the administrative desk.

'We shall not wait for the assembly to complete itself,' said Valdarno. He explained, loftily, that under the normal and correct form of procedure the interview would be in charge of his Vice-Questore but that as this would necessitate an interpreter he proposed to conduct it himself.

Alleyn thought that little time was saved by this departure

as Il Questore continually interrupted the proceedings with translations into Italian from which Bergarmi took notes.

The ground that had been so laboriously traversed before was traversed again and nothing new came out except a rising impatience and anxiety on the part of the subjects. When Kenneth tried to raise an objection he was reminded, icily, that with the discovery of Mailer's body they were all much more deeply involved.

Both Kenneth and his aunt looked terrified and said nothing.

Il Questore ploughed majestically on. He had arrived at the point of the departure from the Mithraeum, when Grant, who had become increasingly and obviously restive, suddenly interrupted him.

'Look here,' he said, 'I'm very sorry but I simply cannot see the point of all this reiteration. Surely by now it's abundantly clear that whether the noise we heard was or was not this bloody lid, it would have been quite impossible for the Baron, the Baroness, Alleyn, Miss Jason or me to have killed this man. I imagine that you don't entertain the idea of a conspiracy and if you don't, you have irrefutable proof that none of us was ever, throughout the whole trip, alone.'

'This may be so, Signor Grant. Nevertheless, statements must be taken——'

'All right, my dear man, all right. And they have been taken. And what are we left with, for pity's sake?'

He looked at Alleyn, who raised an eyebrow at him and very slightly shook his head.

'We're left,' Grant said, raising his voice, 'as far as the touring party is concerned with a field of three. Lady Braceley in the atrium. I'm sorry, Lady Braceley, but there you were and I'm sure nobody supposes you left it. Dorne——'

'No!' Kenneth whispered. 'No! Don't you dare. Don't dare!'

'——Dorne on his way up—and alone.'

'——and who else—who else? Go on. *Who else?*'

'——and Major Sweet, who seems to be taking an unconscionable time getting to this meeting——'

'There,' Kenneth chattered. 'There! You see? What I always said. I said——'

'And heaven knows what intruder from outside,' Grant ended. 'As far as I can see, you've no absolute proof that some complete outsider didn't lie in wait down there for Mailer, kill him and make a getaway. That's all. I've spoken out of order and I don't regret it.'

Valdarno had begun, 'Mr Grant, I must insist——' when his telephone rang. He gestured angrily at Bergarmi, who lifted the receiver.

A spate of Italian broke out at the other end. Bergarmi ejaculated and answered so rapidly that Alleyn could only just make out what he said. He picked up something like '—insufferable incompetence. At once. All of you. You hear me! All!'

He clapped the receiver down and turned to Valdarno.

'They have lost him,' he said. 'Buffoons! Idiots! Lunatics! He has given them the slip.'

'Vecchi?'

'Vecchi! No, Signor Questore, no. Sweet. Major Sweet.'

9. Death in the Morning

HE MADE his getaway during the riots.

After Alleyn left him on the previous afternoon he had begun to keep watch from behind his window-blind on a man in the street below. The man had changed three times, the second to last being a short, swarthy fellow wearing a green hat. Sweet could not be sure if these watchers were police agents or spies employed by Giovanni. The latter would be infinitely more dangerous.

He had eaten in his room, giving it out that he was unwell, and had managed to keep on the safe side of the whisky-bottle although, as evening came on, he had taken more than most men could stand.

Once when he was not looking into the street, he made a tiny fire of paper in an ashtray. Two larger papers he tore into fragments and put down the lavatory across the landing. But he had never carried much really incriminating stuff about with him and these were soon disposed of.

When it grew dark he did not turn on his light but still watched. The man in the green hat was at no pains to make himself inconspicuous. Often, he looked directly at the window so that, although Sweet knew this was not possible, he felt as if they stared into each other's eyes. When the man's relief came—he arrived on a motor-bicycle—they pointed out the window to each other.

The lavatory was at the back of the landing. He had stood

on the seat and looked through the window louvres. Yes, sure enough, there was another man, watching the rear of the hotel. When he got down he saw he had left marks of shoe-polish on the seat. He had always been particular about his shoes, liking the arches of their soles to be attended to. He wiped away the marks.

If they were *agenti* down there, it meant that Alleyn had told the police and they had decided he should be kept under observation. And if, as Alleyn had suggested, Giovanni was under arrest? He might still have managed to lay this on. And if he had done that, then things looked black indeed.

At eleven o'clock he was still watching and being watched. At five past eleven the telephone on the landing rang and went on ringing. He heard the man in the next room groan and go out. He was prepared for the bang on his own door and the slam of the neighbouring one. He answered the telephone. It was somebody speaking basic English for the Vice-Questore Bergarmi. The travellers were required to report next morning at the office where they had formerly been interviewed. At 10.30.

He waited for two or three seconds while he ran the tip of his tongue over his trim little moustache. His hand slithered on the receiver.

'Jolly good,' he said. 'Can do.'

'I beg your pardon, Signore? You said?'

'I'll be there.'

'Thank you.'

'Wait a bit. Hold on.'

'Signore?'

'Have you found Mailer?'

A pause. A consultation in Italian.

'Hullo? Are you there?'

'Yes, Signore, Mailer has been found.'

'Oh.'

'His body has been found. He has been murdered.'

He should have said something. He shouldn't have hung up the receiver without a word. Too late now.

He lay on his bed and tried to think. The hours went by and sometimes he dozed but he always came to with a jerk and returned to look down into the street. The brief quietude of the small hours came over Rome and then, with the first light, the gradual return of traffic. Presently there were movements within the hotel.

At eight o'clock he heard a vacuum cleaner whining in the passage. He got up, shaved, packed a small overnight bag and then sat looking at nothing and unable to think coherently.

At 9.30 the biggest student demonstrations of the year began. The point of assembly was Navona but as they increased in violence the crowds overflowed and erupted into the narrow street below. A gang of youths ran down it manhandling parked cars into a herringbone pattern. He could see bald-heads among them, urging them on.

He began to make frantic preparations. Still watching the street, he struggled into his overcoat. There was a scarf in the pocket. He wound it over his mouth. Then he found a tweed hat he hadn't worn since he arrived.

He checked that he had his passport and money in his pockets and took up the overnight bag.

There was now a great deal of noise in the street. A group of students milled round the watcher's motor-bicycle. They had opened the tank and then set fire to the petrol. Six or seven of them swarmed about the man.

A fight broke out.

He heard windows opening and voices in the other rooms exclaiming.

The landing and stairs were deserted.

When he reached the street the bicycle was in flames. The

crowd manhandled the owner. He struggled, caught sight of Sweet, and yelled.

Sweet dodged and ran. He was hustled and thrust aside and finally caught up in a general stampede down the street and into the main thoroughfare. Here he took to his heels and ran, disregarded, until he was winded.

There was a traffic block at an intersection. He saw an empty taxi in midstream, got to it, wrenched open the door and fell in. The driver shouted angrily at him. He pulled out his wallet and showed a L.10,000 note, '*Stazione!*' he said. '*Stazione!*'

The traffic moved and the cars behind set up a great hooting. The driver gestured, seemed to refuse but finally moved with the stream, still shouting incomprehensibly.

Then Sweet heard the siren.

The police-car was some way behind them but the traffic between made way for it. Sweet and the driver saw each other in the rear-vision glass. Sweet pounded with both fists on the driver's back.

'On!' he screamed. '*Go on!*'

The taxi screeched to a halt as the man crammed on his brakes. The police-car drew alongside and Sweet hurled himself through the opposite door.

For a moment he showed up in the sea of traffic: a well-dressed man in an English overcoat and tweed hat. Then he went down under an oncoming van.

TWO

'He is not expected,' Bergarmi said, 'to recover consciousness.'

Since Sweet's escape had been reported, less than half an hour had elapsed.

During that interval, while Valdarno and his Vice-Questore were still at blast-off potential, Giovanni had been brought in.

He was unshaven, pale and dishevelled, and had looked round the group of tourists as if he saw them for the first time. When his glance fell on Lady Braceley he half-closed his eyes, smirked and bowed. She had not looked at him.

He was questioned by Bergarmi with occasional inter-jections from Valdarno. This time there was no translation and only Alleyn knew what was said. The travellers leant forward in their chairs and strained and frowned as if they were physically rather than intellectually deaf. It was difficult, indeed, to think of any good reason why their presence was supposed to be desirable. Unless, Alleyn thought, we are to become bilingual again and some sort of confrontation is envisaged.

The official manner with Giovanni was formidable. Bergarmi shot out the questions. Valdarno folded his arms, scowled and occasionally threw in a demand if not a threat. Giovanni alternately sulked and expostulated. A good deal of what went on, Alleyn reflected, would be meat and drink to defending counsel in Great Britain.

The examination was twice interrupted by reports of further violence in the street and the Questore flung orders into the telephone with the precision of a souped-up computer. Alleyn could not escape the feeling that they all three greatly relished running through this virtuoso performance before their baffled and uncomprehending audience.

After a prolonged skirmish leading nowhere in particular, Giovanni suddenl. flung out his arms, made a complicated acknowledgement oₗ his own stainless integrity, and intimated that he was prepared to come clean.

This turned out to be the overstatement of the day. What he was prepared to do, and did, was to accuse Major Sweet of murdering Sebastian Mailer. He said that while he himself was innocent of all knowledge of Mailer's side activities and had merely acted in good faith as a top-class courier for Il Cicerone, it had come to his knowledge that there was some kind of hanky-panky going on between Mailer and Sweet.

'Something told me it was so,' said Giovanni. 'I have an instinct in such matters.'

'For "instinct",' Il Questore said, 'read "experience".' Bergarmi laughed rather in the manner of deferential junior counsel.

'And what steps,' Valdarno asked nastily, 'did this instinct prompt you to take?' He glanced at Alleyn.

Giovanni said he had observed, when Violetta attacked Mailer in the portico, that Sweet watched with a certain eagerness. He became even more interested in Sweet. When the party went below he strolled into the basilica and said a prayer to S. Tommaso for whom he had a devotion. Major Sweet, he said in parenthesis, was an atheist and made several abominable remarks about the holy saints.

'His remarks are unimportant. Continue.'

Giovanni was still in the basilica when Major Sweet returned with Lady Braceley, he said, and slid his eyes in her direction. Sweet's behaviour was peculiar and far from polite. He planted her in the atrium and hastened to return below. Giovanni, filled, if he was to be believed, with nameless misgiving, had gone to the top well-head in the basilica and looked down—to his astonishment upon Major Sweet who (against the holy fathers' regulations) had mounted the rails of the well-head directly underneath and seemed to strain over the top and peer into the Mi'' raic insula below. There was something extraordinarily furtive about the way he finally climbed down and darted out of sight.

'This is nothing,' said Valdarno, flicking it away with his fingers.

'Ah', said Giovanni, 'but wait.' Wait, as he had, for the

230

return of the party. First to arrive was Signor Dorne, who went immediately to his aunt in the atrium. And then, alone, the Major. White. Trembling. Agitated. A terrible expression in the eyes. He had passed Giovanni without seeing him and staggered into the porch. Giovanni had gone to him, had asked him if he was unwell. He had cursed Giovanni and asked him what the hell he meant and told him to get out. Giovanni had gone to his car and from there had seen the Major fortify himself from a pocket flask. His recovery was rapid. When the others appeared he was in full command of himself.

'At the time, Signor Questore, I was at a loss to understand—but now, now I understand. Signor Questore, I,' said Giovanni, slapping his chest and shaking his finger and making his point with the greatest virtuosity, 'had looked upon the face of a murderer.'

And it was at this point that the telephone had rung. Bergarmi answered it, received the news of Sweet's catastrophe and informed his Superior.

'He is not expected,' he said, 'to recover consciousness.'

And while we're on the subject of facial expression, Alleyn thought, if ever I've seen incredulous delight flash up in anybody's face it's now. And the face is Giovanni's.

THREE

Five minutes later came the information that Hamilton Sweet had died without speaking.

Valdarno unbent so far as to convey this news to the travellers. And again relief, decently restrained, was in the air.

Barnaby Grant probably voiced the majority's reaction when he said, 'For God's sake don't let's go through the motions. He was a disastrous specimen and now it seems he was a murderer. It's beastly but it's over. Better for them—all three of them—by a long chalk and for everybody else that it should be.'

Alleyn saw Sophy look steadily at Grant for a moment and then frowningly at her own clenched hands. The Baron made sounds of agreement, but his wife, disconcertingly, broke into protest.

'Ah no, ah no!' cried the Baroness. 'We cannot so coldly dismiss! Here is tragedy! Here is Nemesis! Behind this dénouement what horror is not lurkink?' She appealed from one to another of the hearers and finally to her husband. Her eyes filled with tears. 'No, Gerrit, no! It is dreadful to think,' she said. 'The Violetta and this Mailer and the Sweet: between them was such hatred! Such evil! So close to us! I am sick to think of it.'

'Never mind, my darling. It is gone. They are gone.'

He comforted her in their own language, gently patting one of her large hands between his own two enormous ones as if to warm it. He looked round at the others with that winged smile inviting them to indulge a childish distress. They responded awkwardly.

Valdarno said that they would all perceive, no doubt, that the affair now wore an entirely different complexion. It would be improper, until legal pronouncements had been made and the case formally wound up, for him to make a categorical pronouncement but he felt, nevertheless, that as representative of the Minister for the Interior he might assure them they would not be unduly troubled by further proceedings. They would be asked to sign a statement as to their unfortunate experience. Possibly they would be required to give formal evidence and should hold themselves in readiness to do so. And now, perhaps, they would be kind enough to wait in the next room while Vice-Questore Bergarmi prepared a statement. He greatly regretted——

232

He continued in this strain for a few more rounded periods and then they all stood up and responded as best they could to a ceremonial leave-taking.

Alleyn remained behind.

'If it would save trouble, Signor Questore,' he said, 'I'm at your service—you'll want an English transcription of this statement, for instance. And perhaps—as I was there, you know——?'

'You are very kind,' Valdarno began, and broke off to deal with yet another report of violence. Bergarmi had gone to some inner office and for a moment or two Alleyn and Giovanni were confronted. The Questore's back was turned to them as he apostrophized the telephone.

'You too,' Alleyn said, 'will no doubt sign a statement, will you not?'

'But certainly, Signore. On my conscience and before the saints. It is my duty.'

'Will it include an account of your talk with Major Sweet yesterday afternoon, at the Eremo?'

Giovanni, snakelike, retracted his head. Almost, Alleyn thought, you could hear him hiss. He half-closed his eyes and whispered disgustingly.

For the hundredth time that morning Valdarno shouted, '*E molto seccante! Presto!*' He clapped down the receiver, spread his hands for Alleyn's benefit, and caught sight of Giovanni. 'You! Vecchi! You are required to make a written statement.'

'Of course, Signor Questore,' Giovanni said. The intercom buzzed. Valdarno took another call.

An officer came in and removed Giovanni, who darted a look at Il Questore's back and as he passed Alleyn, rapidly mimed a spit into his face. The officer barked at him and pushed him out. Violetta, thought Alleyn, would not have stopped short at pantomime.

'These students!' cried Valdarno, leaving the telephone. 'What do they suppose they achieve? Now, they burn up Vespa motor-cycles. Why? Possibly they are other students' Vespas. Again, why? You were speaking of the signed statement. I would be greatly obliged if you would combine with Bergarmi.' The buzzer sounded. '*Basta!*' shouted Il Questore and answered it.

Alleyn joined Bergarmi, who received him with a strange blend of huffishness and relief. He had written out a résumé in Italian, based on his own notes of the now desperately familiar experiences of the travellers in the depths of S. Tommaso.

Alleyn found this accurate and put it into English. 'Would you like a check of the translation by a third person, Signor Vice-Questore?' he asked. Bergarmi made deprecatory noises. 'After all,' he said, 'it is no longer of the first importance, all this. Giovanni Vecchi's evidence and the fact that this'— he slapped the statement—'does nothing to contradict it and, above all, Sweet's attempt to escape, are sufficient for our purpose. The case is virtually closed.'

Alleyn pushed his translation across the table. 'There is just one thing I'd like to suggest.'

'Yes? And that is?'

'The Van der Veghels took photographs in the Mithraeum and the insula. Flashlights. Two by the Baroness and one by the Baron. Kenneth Dorne also took one. After that, when we were returning, the Baroness photographed the sarcophagus. I thought you might like to produce these photographs.'

'Ah. Thank you, The sarcophagus, yes. Yes. That might be interesting.'

'If it shows the piece of shawl?'

'Quite so. It would limit the time. To some extent that is true. It would show that the woman Violetta was murdered before you all left the Mithraeum. By Mailer, of course. There can be no doubt, by Mailer. It would not help us—not that we need this evidence—to fix a precise time for Sweet's attack upon Mailer. We have, my dear Signor Super,' said Bergarmi with evident pleasure in discovering this new mode of address, 'motive. From your own investigation of Sweet.' Alleyn made a wry face. 'Intent. As evidenced in suspicious behaviour noted by Vecchi. Opportunity. Apart from Signor Dorne and his Aunt Baroness (this latter being a ludicrous notion), he is the only one with opportunity.'

'With the greatest respect—the only one?'

'Signore?'

'Well,' Alleyn said apologetically, 'it's just that I wonder if Giovanni was speaking all of the truth all of the time,'

After a considerable pause Bergarmi said, 'I find no occasion to doubt it.' And after an even longer pause: 'He had no motive, no cause to attack Mailer.'

'He had every reason, though, to attack Sweet. But don't give it another thought.'

Alleyn's translation was typed, with copies, by a brisk bilingual clerk.

During this period Bergarmi was rather ostentatiously busy. When the transcription was ready he and Alleyn went to the lesser office where for the second and last time the travellers were assembled. At Bergarmi's request, Alleyn handed out the copies.

'I find this a correct summary of our joint statements,' Alleyn said, 'and am prepared to sign it. What about every-one else?'

Lady Braceley, who was doing her face, said with an unexpected flight of fancy: 'I'd sign my soul to the devil if he'd get me out of here.' She turned her raffish and disastrous gaze upon Alleyn. 'You're being too wonderful,' she predictably informed him.

He said, 'Lady Braceley, I wonder—simply out of curiosity, you know—whether you noticed anything at all odd in Sweet's manner when he took you up to the atrium. Did you?'

He thought she might seize the chance to tell them all how responsive she was to atmosphere and how she had sensed that something was wrong, or possibly come out with some really damaging bit of information.

All she said, however, was: 'I just thought him a bloody rude, common little man.' And after a moment's thought: 'And I'll eat my hat if he was ever in the Gunners.' She waited again for a moment and then said, 'All the same, it's quite something, isn't it, to have been trotted about by a murderer, however uncivil? My dear, we'll dine on it: Kenny and I. Won't we, darling?'

Her nephew looked up at her and gave a sort of restless acknowledgement. 'I just don't go with all this carry-on,' he complained.

'I *know*, darling. Too confusing. Three dead people in as many days, you might say. Still, it's a wonderful relief to be in the clear oneself.' She contemplated Bergarmi, smiling at him with her head on one side. 'He really *doesn't* speak English, does he? He's not making a nonsense of us?'

Bergarmi muttered to Alleyn, 'What is she saying? Does she object to signing? Why is she smiling at me?'

'She doesn't object. Perhaps she has taken a fancy to you, Signor Vice-Questore.'

'*Mamma mia!*'

Alleyn suggested that if they were all satisfied they would sign and Lady Braceley instantly did so, making no pretence of reading the statement. The Van der Veghels were extremely particular and examined each point with anxious care and frequent consultations. Barnaby Grant and Sophy Jason read the typescript with professional concentration. Then they all signed.

Bergarmi told them, through Alleyn, that they were free to go. They would be notified if their presence at the inquest was required. He bowed, thanked them and departed with the papers.

The six travellers rose, collected themselves and prepared, with evident signs of relief, to go their ways.

Sophy and Barnaby Grant left together and the Van der Veghels followed them.

Lady Braceley with her eye on Alleyn showed signs of lingering.

Kenneth had lounged over to the door and stood there, watching Alleyn with his customary furtive, sidelong air. 'So that would appear to be that,' he threw out.

'You remember,' Alleyn said, 'you took a photograph of Mithras when we were all down there?'

'That's right.'

'Have you had it developed?'

'No.'

'Is it in black-and-white or colour?'

'Black-and-white.' Kenneth mumbled. 'It's meant to be better for the architecture and statues bit.'

'Mine are being developed by the police expert, here. They'll only take a couple of hours. Would you like me to get yours done at the same time?'

'The film's not finished. Thank you very much, though.'

Lady Braceley said, 'No, but do let Mr Alleyn get it done, darling. You can't have many left. You never stopped clicking all through that extraordinary picnic on the what-not hill. And you must admit it will have a kind of grisly interest. Not that *I'll* be in the one Mr Alleyn's talking about, you know—the bowels of the earth. Do give it to him.'

'It's still in my camera.'

'And your camera's in the car. Whip down and get it.'

'Darling Auntie—it'll wait. Need we fuss?'

'Yes,' she said pettishly, 'we need. Go *on*, darling!' He slouched off.

'Don't come all the way back,' Alleyn called after him. 'I'll collect it down there. I won't be a moment.'

'Sweet of you,' Lady Braceley said, and kissed her hand. 'We'll wait.'

When they had gone, Alleyn went out to the lift landing and found the Van der Veghels busily assembling the massive photographic gear without which they seemed unable to move. He reminded the Baroness of the photographs she had taken in the Mithraic insula and offered to have the police develop the film.

'I think,' he said, 'that the police would still be very glad to see the shot you took of the sarcophagus, Baroness. I told them I'd ask you for it.'

'You may have it. I do not want it. I cannot bear to think of it. Gerrit, my darlink, please give it to him. We wish for no souvenirs of that terrible day. Ach, no! No!'

'Now, now, now,' the Baron gently chided. 'There is no need for such a fuss-pot. I have it here. One moment only and I produce it.'

But there was quite a lot to be done in the way of un-buckling and poking in their great rucksacks, and all to no avail. Suddenly the Baroness gave a little scream and clapped her hand to her forehead.

'But I am mad!' she cried. 'I forget next my own head.'
'How?'

'It was the young Dorne. Yesterday we arrange he takes it with his own development.'

'So,' said the Baron. 'What a nonsense,' and began with perfect good humour to re-assemble the contents of his rucksack.

'He hasn't done anything about it,' Alleyn said. 'If I may, I'll collect your film with his.'

238

'Good, good,' agreed the Baron.

Alleyn said aside to him, 'You're sure you don't want it?'

He shook his head, pursed his lips and frowned like a nanny.

'No, no, no,' he murmured. 'You see how it is. My wife prefers—No. Although,' he added rather wistfully, 'there *are* some pictures—our little group, for instance. But never mind.'

'I'll let you know how it comes out,' Alleyn said.

They went down in the lift together. He wondered if, long after the case of Sebastian Mailer had faded out of most people's memories he and the Van der Veghels would meet somewhere. The Baroness had cheered up. They were off on a coach trip to the water-gardens at the Villa d'Este.

He walked with them to the main entrance.

She went ahead with that singularly buoyant tread that made Alleyn think of the gait of some kind of huge and antique bird: a moa, perhaps.

'My wife,' said the Baron fondly regarding her, 'has the wise simplicity of the classic age. She is a most remarkable woman.' And dropping his voice, he added to himself rather than to Alleyn, 'And to my mind, very beautiful.'

'You are a fortunate man.'

'That, also, is my opinion.'

'Baron, will you have a drink with me? At about six o'clock? I will be able to show you your photographs. Since they would distress the Baroness I don't ask you to bring her with you.'

'Thank you,' he said. 'I shall be delighted. You are very considerate,' and, shifting his rucksack on his massive shoulders, he called: 'Mathilde, not so fast! Wait! I am coming.'

And he, also with springing gait, sped nimbly after his wife. They went down the street together, head and shoulders above the other pedestrians, elastically bobbing up and down and eagerly talking.

Kenneth Dorne sat at the wheel of a white sports-car with

his aunt beside him. It occurred to Alleyn that they might have been served up neat by an over-zealous casting department as type-material for yet another *Dolce Vita*. Kenneth had one of the ridiculous 'trendy' caps on his head, a raspberry-coloured affair with a little peak. He was very white and his forehead glistened.

'Here we are,' cried Lady Braceley, 'and here's the film. Such a fuss! Come and have drinks with us this evening. I suppose it's frightful of one, isn't it, but one can't help a feeling of relief. I mean that poisonous Giovanni terrifying one. And all lies. Kenneth knows that I told you. So, don't you think a little celebration? Or don't you?'

Kenneth stared at Alleyn with a pretty ghastly half-grin. His lips moved. Alleyn leant forward. 'What am I to do?' Kenneth mouthed.

Alleyn said aloud, 'I'm afraid I'm booked for this evening.' And to Kenneth, 'You don't look well. I should see a doctor if I were you. May I have the film?'

He handed it over. The carton was damp.

'I think you've got the Baroness's film too, haven't you?'

'Oh God, have I? Yes, of course. Where the hell—here!' He took it out of the glove-box and handed it over.

'*Can* we give you a lift?' Lady Braceley asked with the utmost concern. '*Do* let us give you a lift.'

'Thank you, no. I've a job to do here.'

The sports car shot dangerously into the traffic.

Alleyn went back into the building.

He sought out Bergarmi and got the name and working address of their photographic expert. Bergarmi rang the man up and arranged for the films to be developed immediately.

He offered to accompany Alleyn to the photographic laboratory and when they got there expanded on his own attitude.

'I have looked in,' Bergarmi said, 'to see our own photographs. A matter of routine, really. The case against Sweet is perfectly established by Giovanni Vecchi's evidence alone. He now admits that he was aware of a liaison of some sort between Sweet and Mailer and will swear that he heard Mailer threaten Sweet with exposure.'

'I see,' Alleyn said, 'exposure of what? And to whom?'

'Giovanni believes, Signore, that Mailer was aware of Sweet's criminal record in England and threatened to expose his identity to you whom he had recognized.'

'Very neat flashes of hindsight from Giovanni,' said Alleyn dryly. 'I don't believe a word of it. Do you?'

'Well, Signore, that is his guess! His evidence of fact I accept entirely. The important point is that Sweet was in danger, for whatever reason, and that the threat came from Mailer. Who, of course, had discovered that Sweet was set to spy upon him by Ziegfeldt. It is a familiar story, Signor Super, is it not? The cross and the double-cross. The simple solution so often the true one. The circumstance of Mailer being a *ricattatore* and of his extorting money from tourists has no real bearing on his murder, though Sweet may have hoped it would confuse the issue.' Bergarmi's quick glance played over Alleyn. 'You are in doubt, Signor Super, are you not?' he asked.

'Pay no attention to me,' Alleyn said. 'I'm a foreigner, Signor Vice-Questore, and I should not try to fit Giovanni into an English criminal mould. You know your types and I do not.'

'Well, Signore,' said Bergarmi, smiling all over his face, 'You have the great modesty to say so.'

The photographic expert came in. 'They are ready, Signor Vice-Questore.'

'*Ecco!*' said Bergarmi, clapping Alleyn on the shoulder. 'The pictures. Shall we examine?'

They were still submerged in their fixative solution along benches in the developing-room. The Questore's photographs: Violetta in the sarcophagus with her tongue out. Violetta on the stretcher in the mortuary. Mailer's jaw. Details. Alleyn's photographs of Mailer, of a scrap of alpaca caught in a rail, of Mailer's foot, sole uppermost, caught in the fangs of the grille, of boot polish on another rail. Of various papers found in Mailer's apartment. Regulation shots that would fetch up in the police records.

And now, unexpectedly, views of Rome. Conventional shots of familiar subjects always with the same large, faintly smiling figure somewhere in the foreground or the middle distance. The Baron looking waggish with his head on one side, throwing a penny into the Trevi Fountain. The Baron looking magisterial in the Forum, pontifical before the Vatican and martial underneath Marcus Aurelius. And finally a shot taken by a third person of the Van der Veghels' heads in profile with rather an Egyptian flavour, hers behind his. They even had the same large ears with heavy lobes, he noticed.

And then—nothing. A faint remnant of the Baron at the head of the Spanish Steps heavily obscured by white fog. After that—nothing. Blankness.

'It is a pity,' said the photographic expert, 'there has been a misfortune. Light has been admitted.'

'So I see,' Alleyn said.

'I think,' Bergarmi pointed out, 'you mentioned, did you not, that there was difficulty with the Baronessa's camera in the Mithraeum?'

'The flashlamp failed. Once. It worked the second time.'

'There is a fault, evidently, in the camera. Or in the removal of the film. Light,' the expert reiterated, 'has been admitted.'

'So,' Bergarmi said, 'we have no record of the sarcophagus. It is of secondary interest after all.'

'Yes,' Alleyn said. 'It is. After all. And as for the group by the statue of Mithras——'

'Ah, Signore,' said the expert. 'Here the news is better. We have the film marked Dorne. Here, Signore.'

Kenneth's photographs were reasonably good. They at once disproved his story of using the last of his film before meeting Mailer at the Apollo and of replacing it on his way to the Mithraeum. Here in order were snapshots taken in Perugia. Two of these showed Kenneth himself, *en travesti* in a garden surrounded by very dubious-looking friends, one of whom had taken off his clothes and seemed to be posing as a statue.

'*Molto sofisticato*,' said Bergarmi.

Next came pictures of Kenneth's aunt outside their hotel and of the travellers assembling near the Spanish Steps. Midway in the sequence was the picture of the god Mithras. Kenneth had stood far enough away from his subject to include in the foreground the Baroness, fussing with her camera, and beyond her the group. Alleyn and Sophy grinned on either side of the furiously embarrassed Grant and there was Sweet very clearly groping for Sophy's waist. They had the startled and rigid look of persons in darkness transfixed by a flashlight. The details of the wall behind them, their own gigantic shadows and the plump god with his Phrygian cap, his smile and his blankly staring eyes, all stood out in the greatest clarity. Kenneth had taken no other photographs in S. Tommaso. The rest of his film had been used up on the Palatine Hill.

Alleyn waited for the films and prints to dry.

Bergarmi pleaded pressure of work and said he would leave him to it.

As he was about to go, Alleyn said, 'You know, Signor Vice-Questore, there is one item in this case that I find extremely intriguing.

'Yes? And it is——?'

'This. Why on earth should Mailer, a flabby man, go to all the exertion and waste a great deal of time in stowing Violetta in the sarcophagus when he might so easily and quickly have tipped her down the well?'

Bergarmi gazed at him in silence for some moments.

'I have no answer,' he said. 'There is, of course, an answer but I cannot at the moment produce it. Forgive me, I am late.'

When he had gone Alleyn muttered, 'I can. Blow me down flat if I can't.'

It was ten to three when he got back to his hotel.

He wrote up his report, arranged a meeting with Interpol and took counsel with himself.

His mission, such as it was, was accomplished. He had got most of the information he had been told to get. He had run the Mailer case down to its grass roots and had forced Sweet to give him the most useful list yet obtained of key figures in the biggest of the drug rackets.

And Mailer and Sweet were dead.

Professionally speaking, their deaths were none of his business. They were strictly over to the Roman Questura, to Valdarno and Bergarmi and their boys, and very ably they were being handled. And yet . . .

He was greatly troubled.

At half past five he laid out all the photographs on his bed. He took a paper from his file. The writing on it was in his own hand. He looked at it for a long time and then folded it and put it in his pocket.

At six o'clock Kenneth Dorne rang up and asked apparently in some agitation if he could come and collect his film.

'Not now. I'm engaged,' Alleyn said, 'at least until seven.' He waited a moment and then said, 'You may ring again at eight.'

'Have—have they turned out all right? The photos?'

'Yours are perfectly clear. Why?'

'Is something wrong with hers—the Baroness's?'

'It's fogged.'

'Well, that's not my fault, is it? Look: I want to talk to you. Please.'

'At eight.'

'I see. Well I—yes—well, thank you. I'll ring again at eight.'

'Do that.'

At half past six the office called to say that the Baron Van der Veghel had arrived.

Alleyn asked them to send him up.

He opened his door and when he heard the lift whine, went into the corridor. Out came a waiter ushering the Baron, who greeted Alleyn from afar and springingly advanced with outstretched hand.

'I hope you don't mind my bringing you up here,' Alleyn said. 'I thought we wanted a reasonable amount of privacy and the rooms down below are like a five-star Bedlam at this hour. Do come in. What will you drink? They make quite a pleasant cold brandy-punch. Or would you rather stick to the classics?'

The Baron chose brandy-punch and while it was coming enlarged upon their visit to the water gardens at the Villa d'Este.

'We have been there before, of course,' he said, 'but with each visit the wonder grows. My wife said today that now she summons up, always at the same vista, a scarlet cardinal and his guests. She sees them through the mists of the fountains.'

'She has second sight,' Alleyn said lightly. Seeing the Baron was puzzled, he explained.

'Ach—no. No, we do not believe such phenomena, No, it is her imagination which is so very vivid. She is most sensitive to her surroundings but she does not see ghosts, Mr Alleyn.'

The drinks arrived. Alleyn attended to them and then said, 'Would you like to look at your photographs? I'm afraid you will be disappointed.'

He had left all the prints except Kenneth's on the bed.

When the Baron saw Violetta and Mailer, which he did at once, he said, 'Oh, no! This is too horrible! Please!'

'I'm so sorry,' Alleyn said and swept them away. 'Here are

245

your wife's photographs. The early ones, you see, are very good. It is when we come to S. Tommaso that the trouble begins.'

'I cannot understand this,' the Baron said. He stooped, peered at them and took them up, one by one. 'My wife's camera is in good condition: it has never happened before. The film was correctly rolled off before it was removed. Where are the negatives?'

'Here they are.'

He held them in turn up to the light. 'I am sorry,' he said. 'And I confess I am puzzled. Forgive me, but—the man who processed the film—you said he was a police photographer?'

'I honestly don't think for a moment that he was careless.'

'My wife,' said the Baron, 'will be relieved after all. She wanted no record of the visit to that place.'

'No.'

'But I am sorry. You wished for the photograph of the sarcophagus, I believe.'

'The police attach little importance to it. But there is, after all, a record of the group in the Mithraeum.'

He dropped Kenneth's print on the bed.

The Baron stooped over it.

The room was quiet. The windows were shut and the great composite voice of Rome not obtrusive. A flight of swallows flashed past almost too rapidly for recognition.

'Yes,' said the Baron. He straightened up and looked at Alleyn. 'It is a clear picture,' he said.

'Isn't it?'

The Baron sat down with his back to the windows. He drank a little of his cold brandy-punch. 'This is an excellent concoction,' he said. 'I am enjoying it.'

'Good. I wonder if you would do me a favour.'

'A favour? But certainly, if it is possible.'

'I have a copy of a letter. It's written in a language that I

246

don't know. I think it may be in Dutch. Will you look at it for me?'

'Of course.'

Alleyn gave it to him. 'You will see,' he said, 'that the original was written—typed, actually—on the letter-paper of your publishing firm—of Adriaan and Welker. Will you read it?'

There was a long silence and then the Baron said, 'You ask me here to drink with you. You show me—these things. Why do you behave in this way? Perhaps you have a microphone concealed in the room and a tape-recorder, as in some ridiculous crime film?'

'No. I am not acting for the police. My job here is finished. No doubt I should have taken this letter to them but they will find the original when they search Mailer's rooms. I doubt if they will take very much interest in it, but of course I have not read it and may be wrong. They know very well that he was a blackmailer. I have seen that your wife's name appears in the letter. I am behaving reprehensibly in this matter, I dare say, but I don't think you have any reason to throw your brandy-punch in my face, Baron. It was offered in what may fairly be called good faith.'

The Baron moved slightly.

The light from the window crossed his face and in a moment the white Apollo, the glancing Mercury, the faintly smiling Husband of the Villa Giulia seemed in turn to look through his mask.

'I must believe you,' he said. 'What else can I do?'

'If you like you can go away leaving me to deal with—for example—Kenneth Dorne and his photography.'

'Whatever I do,' said the Baron, 'it is clear that I put myself in your hands. I have no choice, I think.'

He got up and walked about the room, still with some trace of elasticity in his tread. At last he said, 'It seems to me there would be little point in my refusing to give you the content of this letter since you tell me, and I believe you, that the original is extant. You can get a translation easily enough. In effect it appears that someone—you will have seen the name —calling himself Silas J. Sebastian had written to my firm asking if they could give him any information about my wife. Apparently the writer had said he represented an American magazine and was organizing a series of articles on the incursions into the business world of persons of the old nobilities. From the point of view of their wives. The writer, it appears, went on to say that he had a personal interest in my wife as he believed they were distantly related. Evidently he asked for my wife's maiden name. This letter is an answer to their inquiry.'

'Yes?'

'It says——?' The Baron seemed to flinch from his intention. He shut his eyes for a moment and then examined the letter as if he saw it for the first time. Presently in an extraordinarily prim voice that seemed not to belong to him he said: 'In accordance with my standing instructions it states that the Baroness Van der Veghel is a permanent invalid and lives in retirement.'

'When did you first encounter Sebastian Mailer?'

'Eighteen months ago. In Geneva.'

'And a few weeks later he wrote his letter. He didn't trouble to find himself an entirely dissimilar pseudonym.'

'No doubt he felt sure of himself.'

'After all,' Alleyn said, 'this letter might be a standard reply to choke off boring inquiries.'

'He did not think so. He pursued the matter,' said the Baron. 'He extended his investigations.'

'To——?'

'I regret: I must decline to answer.'

'Very well. Let us accept that he found his material. Will

you tell me this much? When you met him again, in Rome, the other day, had you any idea——?'

'*None!* My God, none! Not until——'

'Until?'

'A week before the—before S. Tommaso.'

'And then the blackmailing process began?'

'Yes.'

'Were you prepared to pay?'

'Mr Alleyn, I had no choice. I flew to Geneva and obtained the money in notes of small denomination.'

'You presented a brave front,' Alleyn said, 'on that expedition. You and your wife. So much enthusiasm for the antiquities! Such *joie de vivre*!'

The Baron Van der Veghel looked steadily at Alleyn for some few moments and then he said, 'You yourself have a distinguished and brilliant wife, I think? We have admired her work very greatly. She is a superb painter.'

Alleyn said nothing.

'You must know, then, Mr Alleyn, that a preoccupation with the arts is not to be tampered with—my English is unable to explain me, I think—it is not to be cut off and turned on like taps. Beauty and, for us, antique beauty in especial—is absolute. No misfortune or anxiety can colour our feeling for it. When we see it we salute it and are greatly moved. The day before yesterday at S. Tommaso I was furnished with the money demanded of me as a price of silence. I was prepared to hand it over. The decision had been taken. I have to confess that a lightness of spirit came over me and a kind of relief. The beauty of the Etruscan works in that underworld did much to enhance this feeling.'

'And also it was advisable, wasn't it, to keep up appearances?'

'That, too,' said the Baron steadily, 'I admit. That too. But it was not difficult. There were the Etruscans to support

249

me. I may tell you that I believe our family, which is of great antiquity, arose in classical times in the lands between the Tiber and the Arno.'

'Your wife told me so. Did you hand over the money?'

'No. There was no opportunity. As you know, he had gone.'

'A further and very understandable relief.'

'Of course.'

'You were not his only victim in that party you know.'

'So I believe.'

Alleyn took his glass. 'Let me give you a drink.'

'It will not increase my indiscretion,' said the Baron. 'But thank you.'

When Alleyn had given it to him he said, 'You may not believe me when I say that it would solace me if I could tell you what it was that he had discovered. I cannot. But on my honour I wish that I could. I wish it with all my heart, Mr Alleyn.'

'Let us take it as read.'

Alleyn collected the Baroness's photographs, prints and negatives.

'You will take these, won't you?' he said. 'There is nothing in the earlier ones to distress your wife.' He gave them to him. The picture in profile of the Van der Veghels' heads was on top.

'It's a striking picture,' Alleyn said lightly. 'Isn't it?'

The Baron stared at it and then looked up at him.

'We think alike, too,' he said. 'My wife and I. You may have noticed it.'

'Yes,' said Alleyn. 'I noticed.'

'When such a bond occurs, and I think it occurs very seldom, it cannot be—I am lost for the English word.'

'Gainsaid?'

'Perhaps. It cannot be interrupted. You have it in your literature. In your *Wutherink Heights* you have it.'

It was not easy, Alleyn thought, to clothe the Van der Veghels in the mantles of Heathcliff and Cathy, but all the same, it was not altogether a ludicrous association.

The Baron finished his drink and with a well-managed air of briskness, lightly slapped his knees and stood up.

'And now I go,' he said. 'It is unlikely we meet again, unless at whatever formalities the authorities may require of us. I believe that I am your debtor, Mr Alleyn, to—to an indefinable extent. You would not wish me to say more, I think.'

'Not another syllable.'

'As I supposed. May we——?'

For the only time during their brief acquaintance Alleyn saw the Baron Van der Veghel really uncertain of himself. He looked at his enormous hand and then doubtfully at Alleyn.

'But of course,' Alleyn said and his own hand was briefly engulfed. 'I am truly grateful,' said the Baron.

Alleyn watched him go, bouncily as ever, to the lift.

By and large, he thought to himself, that was the nicest murderer I have met.

10. When in Rome

ONE

'THE CASE WAS CLINCHED,' Alleyn wrote, 'when I saw young Dorne's snapshot. No Baron.

'It'd been a possibility all along. While we were lined up in that preposterous group scarcely able to see each other he hadn't spoken. *She* talked to *him*. When she told him to stand farther back and not to speak he wasn't there. While she fussed about hunting for her second flashlamp—and of course the first dud was a put-up affair—he was off by the passage behind that smirking little god. He had his date with Mailer. He had to hand over the money. Mailer was to dispose of it—in the car I expect—and had stayed behind for that purpose.

'At the moment when we all heard Violetta's voice, Van der Veghel was in the passage. I don't believe he witnessed the murder. I think he came upon Mailer with Violetta dead at his feet. I think Mailer bolted and Van der Veghel chased him up the iron stairs to the next landing. There was a struggle. Mailer was knocked out and throttled and tipped over the well-head. The body fell like a plummet into the well below and in doing so a coat sleeve brushed the inner side of the rail and was torn.

'Van der Veghel climbed the rail at the upper well in order to look down and discover whether his victim had, in fact, made a straight fall into the depths. In doing so the rubber studs on his shoes scored through the brown boot polish that may well have been left there by the abominable Sweet on his way back from dumping Lady B. in the atrium. His brogues were polished underneath the instep, à la the batman he never had. Sweet may have caught sight of Violetta or Mailer or both and snooped.

'My contention is that Van der Veghel, when he looked down, saw that Mailer's body had gone and that Violetta's lay where Mailer had left it. He returned and he stowed it in the sarcophagus, deliberately leaving a bit of her shawl exposed.

'He wanted Violetta to be found.

'He wanted the police to know Mailer had killed her. He wanted them to believe Mailer had bolted with her death on his head.

'The whole business would, as one says, take less time to happen than it has taken to set it down. Eight minutes at the most, I'd say, and the Baroness was a great deal longer than that, setting up her group, fiddling and faddling, changing her "bulps", taking a second shot. He was back, on his nimble rubber-studded shoes, well in time to take his own shot of the group. When he removed the film from the Baroness's camera, he was careful to expose the greater part of it. He didn't know about young Dorne's shot.

'And the Baroness? I could have driven him harder here. I could have forced him to confirm what I believe to be her part in the performance. I think she knew they were being blackmailed by Mailer and I think her husband asked her to hold up the proceedings while he kept his assignation and paid over the cash. I don't believe she knows he killed Mailer and I don't believe it would make a scrap of difference to their passionate, their overwhelming union if she did.

'And finally—the material for blackmail? Troy, my darling, the chances of distantly related persons bearing a startling physical resemblance to each other are not impossible. But they *are* extremely remote. In our job we are taught that the ear gives one of the most valuable proofs of identification. The Van der Veghels's ears are, if not identical, as near as damn it, and very, very strange, great ears they are.

'Fox, with his genius for inspiring gossip, has gleaned from a London representative of Adriaan and Welker that the late Baron was what he describes as a bit of a lad with a European reputation as such. The Baroness is said to belong to an expatriate branch of the family. She doesn't accompany her husband on his visits to The Hague and is understood to be an invalid. She! The Baroness! An invalid!

'I've gone on about their strangeness, haven't I? Their resemblance, not only to each other but to the Etruscan antiquities to which they are so much attracted? I see them as larger than life: classical figures springing about behind, of all things, a nonconformist façade. And I think that very probably they are half-siblings.

'None of this would be provable in a court of law. Even the Baron's absence from young Dorne's snapshot could be accounted for. He would say that he had moved out of shot at that juncture and none of us could swear he hadn't.

'Giovanni? Giovanni had been double-crossed and milched and threatened by the unspeakable Sweet. He was and is greedy to get his own back upon Sweet alive or dead and he grabbed at the chance to concoct his tarradiddle about Sweet's agitation and suspicious behaviour. The only bit of it that holds up is his account of Sweet standing on the rails at the middle level. Apparently he did just that.

'And the upshot? The Roman police force will present a file in which the available evidence will point to Sweet. I haven't held anything back from them. I haven't shoved my own reading of the case under their noses. They are an able body of men and the affair is their affair. I've got the information I was sent to get and will be closeted with the Interpol chap tomorrow. Mailer and Sweet were both wanted in

England and if they had lived I would have applied for extradition and brought them back.

'I shall always think of the Baron as an antique person in a sudden antique rage, falling upon his enemy like lightning. His consort and his union had been threatened and that was his answer. When in Rome he did as the ancient Romans. I am afraid he does not in the least regret it and I'm afraid I really can't say that I do.

'The Embassy here has offered to send my report back in the Diplomatic Bag. I'll enclose this with it. And so, my dear love . . .'

TWO

'What will you do?' Barnaby Grant asked Sophy Jason, 'now that it's all over? Will you pick up your guide book and go on your way rejoicing?'

'Go on my way—yes, I think so.'

'To Florence?'

'To Perugia first.'

'And will you receive visitors in Perugia if they should happen to appear?'

'I'm not going into purdah in Perugia.'

'The odd thing is, Sophy, that I'm booked in at the Rosetta from next Monday.'

'Are you, now? Since when?'

'Well—since we danced together in Rome.'

Sophy said, 'It will be lovely to meet you again in Perugia.'

'You don't mind?'

'No. I shall look forward to it.'

'Don't be so brisk. Can't you throw me a nice, equivocal leer? Can't you stint like Juliet and say aye?'

She burst out laughing.

'Sophy, I think I love you.'

'Do you, Barnaby? Don't let's say anything about it until you're sure.'

'Look,' he said, 'isn't Rome lovely? The bells ring, the swallows rush about, the saints look down and the fountains play.'

'And in the Villa Giulia the Etruscans smile.'

'And the gardens smell of jasmine. Isn't Rome lovely?'

'Lovely!' she agreed. 'But all the same, strange things can happen under her skin.'

'And always have,' said Barnaby.